THE CURIOUS GARDENER SPOKE
LIKE A GENTLEMAN...

Whenever she was nearby, he wondered how he could possibly keep himself from falling head over heels in love with her. But there was no point in Oliver letting himself topple. He didn't have estates or a magnificent profile. He knew he would not be considered a good catch, but he was not despicable, either. He was a Sherrard of Lydbury. He had a good education, a small income, and good prospects for employment. Moira herself had said that he was lovable, and that the only basis for a good marriage was love. Now, if only she would fall in love with him....

A Brilliant Mismatch

Elizabeth Mansfield

JOVE BOOKS, NEW YORK

A BRILLIANT MISMATCH

A Jove Book / published by arrangement with
the author

PRINTING HISTORY
Jove edition / May 1991

ISBN: 0-515-10545-7

A JOVE BOOK®
Jove Books are published by The Berkley Publishing Group,
200 Madison Avenue, New York, New York 10016.
JOVE and the "J" design are trademarks
belonging to Jove Publications, Inc.

PRINTED IN THE UNITED STATES OF AMERICA

10   9   8   7   6   5   4   3   2

❧ ❧ PROLOGUE

MOIRA PATTINGER HAD BRIGHT RED HAIR AND A TEMPER TO match. Since everyone in the large household adored her, that fiery temper was called "spirit," but it was temper all the same. Even her father, the crusty Lord Pattinger, who had nasty things to say about almost everyone, called it spirit. (He'd once actually been heard to admit that he rather liked the spirit of his eldest girl, excusing this unusual lapse into praise by explaining that she'd inherited both her hair color and her temper from her bewitching Irish mother, who had died twenty years earlier, in 1796.) But Moira herself did not like that side of her character; she was convinced that it signified a reprehensible lack of self-control. That was why, in ordinary circumstances, she tried to keep her hotheadedness tightly reined. Tonight, however, the circumstances were not ordinary. If the gossip she'd just heard from her abigail turned out to be true, she intended to unleash that temper in all its explosive force.

"Not again!" she swore under her breath as she stormed down the hall to her youngest sister's room. "Confound it all, I'll not let them do this to me *again*!"

Her sister Barbara's bedroom was located at the end of a long corridor, the entire length of which Moira traversed—red curls bouncing and skirts swishing—in tight-lipped fury. She threw open the door without knocking. "Damnation, Babs," she snapped, getting to the point without roundaboutation,

1

"have you really had the temerity—the contemptible *cheek*—to accept an offer from *my Godfrey*?"

Barbara Pattinger, younger than Moira by six years (and much more prone to tears than temper), had been huddled on the window seat biting her nails in nervous anticipation of this confrontation. At the sight of her sister, standing tall and furiously proud in the doorway, she shuddered in alarm. "Oh, dear! Has Father t-told you already?"

"No, not Father. Greta told me. So it's true, then?"

Barbara's eyes fell in admission of the truth, and her ready tears began to flow. "You h-hate me now, I suppose. You m-must! I suppose the whole household will b-be saying all sorts of v-vile things about me by tomorrow."

"What did you expect?" Moira strode into the room and slammed the door behind her. "When you steal your own sister's betrothed from right under her nose, no one is likely to find you admirable."

The younger girl cringed at the venom in her sister's voice. "I didn't s-steal him. At least, n-not exactly . . ."

"Don't quibble! I assume that Father—as usual—bribed him to offer for you instead of me, but you could have *refused* him, couldn't you?"

"N-no, I couldn't," Barbara replied, weeping in earnest now. "I *l-love* him!"

The declaration shocked Moira into silence. She hadn't realized that love was playing a part in this conspiracy. The two sisters stared at each other, neither knowing what to say to the other. They were not close, for six years and two other sisters stood between them. Not that Barbara didn't adore her eldest sister. Moira had always been her idol. She was awed by Moira. She both envied and admired Moira's sharp wit and spectacular Irish beauty—the bright red-gold ringlets that curled round her face with lively vibrancy, the green eyes that could sparkle with humor as quickly as with anger, the strong, dimpled chin, the graceful neck, the shapely bosom, and the long, long legs. What man could resist a woman with such spirit and such beauty? And yet here Moira was, a virtual spinster at twenty-six. Father had "bought off" her suitors three times now. Barbara had to admit to herself that it wasn't fair.

Moira studied her younger sister with equal intensity. Was the silly chit truly in love with *her* Godfrey? Moira shook her head in disbelief. If truth be told, she herself had been finding Sir Godfrey Jayne a bit of a bore. He looked a veritable Adonis, but his conversation left much to be desired. He was always prosing on about his hunting prowess. Ever since he'd made his intentions plain, and Moira had decided to accept him, she'd been wondering how she would endure spending the rest of her life listening to his fox-hunting tales. Riding to hounds was his life's purpose, an activity to which he attached not only a sporting value but a moral one. "Fox hunting," he was wont to declare at the slightest opportunity, "is not only a manly amusement, but it builds the character and fosters and preserves the aristocratic spirit." Moira had been finding herself less and less in sympathy with him. If it weren't for the fact that Father had turned off her earlier suitors so often that she was becoming desperate, she would say that Babs was welcome to him. Babs, so gentle and pretty, with her soft auburn hair and kind eyes—could she really care for such a bore? "What makes you think you love him?" Moira asked carefully, breaking the silence.

Barbara brushed at her cheeks. "I *know* I love him. I dream of him all the time." She lifted her eyes to Moira's, her face taking on a glow. "He's so manly and handsome, isn't he? I love the way he moves . . . the way he sits a horse . . . the way he smiles. And he speaks so well, don't you agree? All those tales about fox hunting and his shooting expeditions . . . I could listen to him all day!"

Moira, her anger toward her sister melting away, ran her fingers through her red curls. She was suddenly feeling more troubled than enraged. "But Babs, my dear, doesn't it bother you that Godfrey came here courting *me*? You must realize that he offered for you only because Father bribed him with an enormous dowry—just as he did Jeffrey and Horatio—and not because he cares for you. Have you no pride?"

Barbara lowered her eyes. The dark lashes that brushed her cheeks still glistened with tears. "I can't h-help it, Moira. If you really c-cared for him, I would have r-refused him, but I know you don't. I've seen your face when you're in his company. He bores you to distraction."

"Yes, I admit it. But—"

"But he doesn't bore me, don't you see? I can make him happy. Because I'm the one who really loves him, I can . . . I *think* I can . . . make him forget you." She looked up at her sister with pleading earnestness. "Don't you think I can . . . someday?"

Moira expelled a deep breath of surrender. "Of course you can. He can't have cared for me so very much if he so promptly accepted Father's offer. Very well, take him. If you're sure he's what you want."

Barbara leaped up from the window seat and ran across the room to her sister. "Then you forgive me?" she asked, throwing her arms around Moira's neck. "You're not angry with me anymore? Please say you're not angry with me!"

Moira brushed the tears from her sister's soft cheek. "No, I'm not angry with you, Babs. This is not really your fault."

The two sisters embraced, Barbara weeping in relief. "Do you really mean it, Moira, love? You don't blame me?"

"No, not anymore, now that I understand your feelings." But there *was* someone to blame for this, Moira knew: the calculating Viscount Pattinger, her own *dear* father! Her face hardened. She released herself from her sister's hold, turned on her heel, and strode back to the door. "It's Father I'm furious with, not you."

Barbara followed her. "I don't blame you for being furious, Moira. Father has been grossly unfair to you, everyone knows that. But—" She bit her lip worriedly and put a gentle hand on her sister's arm. "Wh-what are you going to do?"

Moira looked at her sister over her shoulder, her eyes glittering dangerously. "Have it out with him, once and for all," she said between clenched teeth. "He's done this to me once too often."

Barbara winced. "Don't quarrel with him again, Moira. It's so awful when you do. If you don't want Godfrey back, what reason is there for setting Father in a passion?"

Moira shook off her sister's hold. "There is *every* reason, as you know perfectly well. When Father bribed Jeffrey to offer for Susan, I was too shocked to think clearly, so I did nothing. I really cared for the fellow, you know . . . or *believed* I did, until the bounder showed his true mettle by choosing to give me up for the proverbial mess of pottage. And then Father gave Horatio to Alberta on a silver platter! You know what a to-do I raised on *that* occasion. But *this* time . . . well, it's quite the outside of enough! I want to make sure he never, *never* does this to me again!"

"But Father is so . . . so stubborn, you know. How will you—"

Moira's green eyes flashed. "I shall threaten him with something dreadful."

"Oh, dear! *Threaten* him?" Barbara eyed her sister in real alarm. "What will you—?"

"I don't know," Moira snapped as she threw open the door and stormed off down the hall. "But you may be sure I'll think of something!"

CHAPTER
❧ ❧
ONE

THERE WAS SOMETHING MUCH TOO CHEERFUL IN OLIVER'S DEmeanor as he went about the business of packing to leave home. He was even whistling under his breath. *Whistling!* His brother, John Sherrard, the new Earl of Lydbury, paused in the doorway of Oliver's bedroom and glared at the young man within. "What on earth, Oliver Sherrard, can you possibly find in this situation to whistle about?" he asked in annoyance.

"Situation?" Oliver looked up at his brother with a grin that was both warm and teasing. "There is no 'situation' that I know of."

"When a fellow decides to leave his home for no reason and go off to an unknown destination for an unspecified length of time, it sounds like a 'situation' to me!" the Earl retorted.

Oliver did not answer. He merely continued to whistle and to pack. John watched dolefully as his brother—younger than he by more than a decade and consequently not as close as John would have liked—sorted through the pile of "necessaries" that were spread over his bedstead preparatory to cramming them into a rucksack that anyone could see would be much too small. "Why don't you take a proper portmanteau?" the Earl asked in sour disapproval.

The Honorable Oliver Sherrard, who had been studying the array of linens, wondering which of the dozens of neckerchiefs, shirts, singlets, smalls, and stockings would be absolutely necessary to his survival, looked up and smiled again at his dour-faced brother. "I say, John, don't stand there in the doorway like a frightened footman. Do come in." He turned back to the confusion on the bed and shook his head. "I don't want to take more than can be carried in this one rucksack," he explained.

His brother sighed helplessly as he crossed the threshold and sat down gingerly on the room's one easy chair, asking himself why he and Oliver never managed to see eye to eye on anything. There was nothing—not politics, economics, or even the proper attire for riding—on which they agreed. Not only were they utterly different in physical appearance, but they had diametrically opposed views on life, love, and the importance of wealth and titles. John was a traditionalist in these matters, firmly committed to the preservation of the monarchy, the social structure, and the family silver. He looked every inch an earl, being impressively tall, with lank, sandy hair, pale blue eyes, deeply creased cheeks, and a long chin that emphasized his perpetually worried expression. Even his bearing was both formal and fastidious, perfectly befitting the lordly dignities that had just come down to him.

Oliver, on the other hand, had nothing lordly about him. He was only of average height, with the sturdy frame, broad shoulders, and muscular arms of a farmhand. Even his features were not lordly; his brown eyes were too gentle for an aristocrat, his cheeks too wide, his complexion too ruddy, and his lips—always on the verge of smiling—too full for elegance, while his dark hair was so thick and rebelliously straight that his valet used to despair of ever taming it to stay for more than ten minutes in the style in which it was combed.

The personalities of the two brothers were as different as their appearances: John was conventional, scrupulous, and serious, while Oliver—yearning for freedom and adventure, scoffing at the rites and ceremonies of noble society, and chafing at the constraints that his station in life had placed on his dress and demeanor—was nonconforming, casual, and whimsical. His nonconformity had been kept in check while his father, the previous Earl, had lived, but now that the old patriarch had passed on to his reward, Oliver felt free at last to cast off the shackles of propriety and strike out on his own.

John, however, was far from happy that his brother was leaving. He loved the boy dearly and wanted him always nearby. Oliver's remarkably good nature had made him much beloved in the household, and the news of his imminent departure depressed not only the Earl but his wife, his little son, and the whole household staff, from the butler down to the lowliest scullery maid in the kitchen. John had argued and pleaded with the fellow, but nothing he'd said succeeded in dissuading Oliver from his determination to leave.

Oliver had set his mind on taking a year's walking tour of England. He was about to become his own man at last, he'd declared, and the prospect of this forthcoming freedom was a heady delight. He was, in his own words, "prime for a lark." And he would give no guarantee that he would return home at the end of the trip. "This is *your* home, John," he'd insisted, "and it suits you well. But it's not suited to me."

"What *is* suited to you, then?" John had demanded angrily.

Oliver had shrugged good-naturedly. "I don't know. At twenty-three years of age I suppose I should know what I want of life, but I don't have an inkling. Perhaps my travels will help me learn."

John was troubled by Oliver's devil-may-care philosophy, blaming the boy's indifference to wealth and social position on the fact that he was a second son. All second sons of propertied gentlemen grew up with the knowledge that in all probability they would never inherit their fathers' wealth or titles, and John couldn't help wondering if Oliver's casual dismissal of the values of his class was his defense against his disappointment at his blighted expectations. But John had to admit that he'd never discovered anything in Oliver's attitude to indicate that the boy felt the slightest disappointment in what fate had dealt him. The young man had always been amazingly indifferent to his situation. Didn't he care at all about his lack of prospects? *What,* John wondered, *is to become of the boy?*

Oliver, however, had no such concerns. He was, apparently, feeling nothing but happy anticipation at the prospect of leaving home. No sentimental regrets clouded his eyes; no mournful thoughts seemed to interfere with the sense of excited anticipation that animated his every movement. The Earl sighed again as he watched his brother stuff a starched shirt carelessly into the rucksack. "Why don't you let your man do that?" he asked.

Oliver did not look up. "I let my man go," he remarked casually.

John's eyebrows rose in shocked disapproval. "Good God, why? How can you possibly *exist* without a valet?"

Oliver couldn't help laughing. "I think I'll manage to exist. This may come as a shock to you, old man, but I've finally caught on to the technique of buttoning a button. I can do up my shirts all by myself these days."

John stiffened in offense. "Don't be a jackanapes. One can't call oneself a gentleman without a valet."

"Come now, John, must you be so bumptiously toplofty? I'm going on a simple walking tour, not a grand tour of Europe. Why on earth would I have need for a valet?"

John did not believe him. In his eyes, going off on a trip without one's valet was as unthinkable as going out in public without one's breeches. He felt a sudden spasm of guilt. The truth was plain: Oliver had let his valet go because he feared he could no longer afford him. John clenched his long fingers in dismay. He'd always known he would be the Earl of Lydbury one day, but he'd never been comfortable with the knowledge that his own good fortune would come at the expense of his brother. Now that his father was dead and the inheritance was his, John found himself positively embarrassed at being the cause of his brother's impoverishment. "Damnation, Oliver, it's not my fault," he muttered, rising from the chair awkwardly and turning away to stare out of the window.

Oliver frowned at his brother in puzzlement. "Fault? What are you talking about, John?"

"I'm talking about the deuced title." He lowered his head so that his forehead rested on the windowpane. "I didn't ask for it, you know. It's not my fault that I was born first."

Oliver blinked at his elder brother in surprise. He'd always felt, even in boyhood, that his brother would make a perfect Earl of Lydbury, whereas he himself was in every way unsuited to the role of peer of the realm. "Good God, John," he exclaimed, a look of amusement combining with the astonishment in his eyes, "are you imagining that I resent you?"

John's feeling of guilt deepened. "Is it only imagination?" he asked, turning and searching his brother's face for a sign of jealousy. "If I were in your shoes, I'd be positively sick with resentment."

"Balderdash! You'd be as glad for me as I am for you. Come now, old man, how can you believe that I would suddenly resent you? I've never had any expectations, so why should I suddenly feel that they've been dashed? I've grown up with the knowledge that I'm a second son. Why would you think I care now, when I've never cared a jot in all these years?"

"You *must* care. These antiquated laws of primogeniture are grossly unfair to everyone but the eldest sons. How can you *not* feel cheated? Do you know, Oliver, that I sometimes find myself actually believing that the system may be wrong? That perhaps a man's estate should be divided equally among all his offspring, even his daughters?"

"Even *girls*?" The younger man's eyes lit up with laughter. "How radical of you, your lordship," he teased. "For a moment you sounded like *me*! I hope you won't be foolish enough to make such pronouncements when you take your seat in the Lords." He crossed to the window, clapped an affectionate arm across his brother's shoulder, and propelled him back to the chair. "Stop glowering, John. You know that in your heart you believe there's sound logic behind the theory of primogeniture. If in past generations the Lydbury estate had been divided up into smaller and smaller parcels for each and every Sherrard ever to have been born, there would now be nothing left of this vast acreage for *anyone* to enjoy. So be thankful for your good luck, and stop worrying about me."

"But I do worry about you, Oliver," the new Earl said, sagging back against the chair cushion. "You never seem to give a thought to your future. I want you to know, my boy, that you have a home here and always will. You and whatever family you may someday have."

"I know that, John. You don't have to say it."

"Then why, for heaven's sake, are you leaving Lydbury like

this—with only the clothes on your back and a few changes of linen?"

"See here, John, we've been bickering about this for weeks now. Let's make an end. Take my word that my leaving has nothing to do with your inheriting the estate. I'm merely doing what I've always wanted to do—taking a walking tour all on my own. Whenever I asked to go before, Father refused to give me leave, saying that I had to finish school. First it was Eton and then Oxford. Do you realize I've been buried in books since I was eight? Good God, think of it! Occupied with nothing but studies for fifteen years!"

"Cut line, Oliver. You can't pretend to me that you've been a bookworm. I know better. You spent most of your schooling years in sports and fisticuffs."

"Perhaps so. But I was under the constraints of schoolmasters just the same. It seems to me that my whole life has been made up of saying yes-sir and no-sir and sorry-sir to Father and a whole army of tutors and dons. However, that is all over. I've graduated from university, and Father is gone. I'm my own man at last! Even you, I beg to remind you, my lord, have no authority over me."

John bit his lip. "Was I being lordly? I didn't mean to . . . I never intended to exercise authority over—"

"No, of course not," Oliver said in gentle reassurance. "I was merely pointing out that for the first time in my life there's no one with the authority to keep me from doing what I've always longed to do—see the world on my own."

"But you needn't tour the world like a damned gypsy," the new Earl objected, not a bit comforted by his brother's declaration of independence. "You can make your tour like a gentleman, can't you? Take a carriage—any of my carriages that suits your fancy—along with a tiger and a valet. I'd be happy to pay the necessary wages."

Oliver laughed but shook his head. "I'd much rather tour like a damned gypsy than a damned earl."

"Traveling like a gypsy is . . . is revolting! Good God, what if you run into someone we know! What will they think?" He rubbed his forehead nervously at the thought. "I hope, Oliver, that you will bring no shame to the Sherrard name."

"Dash it, John," the younger man said impatiently, "what is the shame in wishing to travel simply? I want to be unencumbered. Can't you understand that?"

The Earl shook his head. "I don't understand any of this. I myself would never wish to travel in so Spartan a manner, without servants, without an equipage, without any of the conveniences. I don't know why you desire to do it. If you ask me, it sounds not only uncomfortable, but dangerous."

"That's just it," Oliver explained eagerly. "The hint of danger makes it an adventure."

"The devil take adventures!" John rubbed the bridge of his aquiline nose with nervous fingers. "Adventures only lead to disaster. Stolen property, broken heads, that sort of thing. The world is full of footpads and thieves who wouldn't stop at a blow to the head or a bullet to the chest just to snatch a handful of pennies from your pocket."

Oliver grinned broadly. "If it's your intent to frighten me, brother mine, I'm afraid you'll have to make your prognostications bloodier than that. How about a heavy heel crushing my windpipe, or a long, rusty knife making a deep slit across my throat, or—"

"Oliver, *please*—!" The Earl shuddered, shutting his eyes in horror for a moment before he glared at his still grinning brother. "There's no point in going on with this, since I'm obviously making no impression on you. If you are truly determined to proceed with this wild scheme, let us become practical. What about funds? You'll have to have some blunt if you're not to spend your nights sleeping under hedgerows."

"I have sufficient funds to pay for lodging and meals, not that a night or two sleeping under the stars doesn't have its appeal. Don't forget that I have a bit of an income from Mama."

"Two hundred a year. A mere pittance."

"Sufficient for my purposes, old man," Oliver assured him as he turned back to the bed and stuffed an extra pair of smalls into his rucksack. "I'm taking thirty guineas with me. I hope that relieves your mind."

"Only a trifle. Will you promise to send to me for more should you run short?"

"I won't run short. Thirty guineas will do for my needs."

The Earl gnashed his teeth. Oliver was not taking a word of his advice. "Dash it all, Oliver, you are a Sherrard, not some wretched commoner." He rose from the chair and, striding across to the bed, turned his brother round to face him. "Must you be so deuced miserly in your plans? After all, even though the estate had to come to me, Father did not intend for you to be penniless. I shall settle a goodly sum on you, my boy. There is no need for you ever to live in a style unbefitting your station."

Oliver shook his brother's hand from his shoulder and frowned at him. "I don't want you do to that, John," he said with utmost sincerity. "I'm perfectly capable of supporting myself."

John frowned back at him. "I have the highest respect for your spirit of independence, Oliver, but you must think ahead. When this desire of yours for adventure has passed, you will have to settle down. What then? What if you should marry and have a family?"

"If I ever marry—an extremely unlikely event, seeing that no woman worth her salt would accept a second son with no prospects—I shall give some thought to finding a place in civil service. But until then, I intend to make do with what I have. Under no circumstances will it be necessary for you to support me."

John sighed in temporary surrender. "Very well, I'll say no more at this time. But when you've returned from this deuced walking tour of yours, we shall speak of these matters again." He went to the door, but before leaving he took one last look at his younger brother. "I can only hope, Oliver, that you'll manage to return with your body and your wits intact."

Oliver guffawed. "What? Do you really fear that I'll come back without my *wits*?"

His brother only shrugged. "I don't find this a laughing matter, you makebait! With only that rucksack on your back and a mere thirty guineas in your pocket, I have the most serious concern for your safety. Who knows what can befall a fellow alone on the highway?"

"Yes, yes, I know. The highway is full of danger," Oliver

said mockingly. "We've already gone over the possibilities of broken heads and slit throats."

"Laugh if you like, Oliver Sherrard, but if you *do* come home broken in body and mind, you'll have only yourself to blame." With those dire words the Earl left the room, closing the door firmly behind him.

Oliver grinned after him. "Yes, your lordship," he declared, bowing to the closed door. "For the first time in my life I'll have only myself to blame. Isn't that splendid?" And, executing a merry little dance step, he went back to his packing.

CHAPTER
TWO

SHORTLY AFTER DAWN THE NEXT DAY, OLIVER SET OUT ON HIS travels. As he strode down the path leading out of his brother's Surrey estate, he could feel his excitement mount. Even the blood in his veins bubbled in anticipation of the adventure ahead of him. He'd never before felt so happy and so completely free.

The sun, this mid-September morning of 1816, had not yet burned away the early mist. It slanted through the branches of Lydbury's tall oaks in thin, wispy rays and threw streaks of dappled light on the dew-silvered ground. Oliver eyed the view appreciatively, drawing in deep breaths of air as he walked along. The air had a bite of autumn, and the trees, touched with rust and gold, looked hazy and magical. Fallen leaves crackled under his boots. A crisp breeze ruffled his hair, and he smelled the fresh aroma of damp grass tinged with the spice of distant chimney smoke. The world had never seemed more beautiful, and it set his heart beating with the eager excitement of a freed prisoner.

He turned southeast toward Kent. He'd chosen Ramsgate as an official starting place, from which point he intended to travel along the southern coast all the way west to Land's End. If things went according to plan, he would be in Ramsgate in a fortnight. But he didn't care if he made it in a fortnight or not. He had no schedule, no appointments to keep. No one was expecting him. He had no responsibilities of any kind. His clothes were simple and sturdy: a pair of strong walking boots, chamois breeches, a heavy tweed coat, and a high-crowned beaver hat. And all he carried with him were the rucksack he'd tossed over his shoulder and the thirty guineas in his pocket. Being thus lightly encumbered, he could follow any path, indulge in any adventure that came his way. If ever a young man was truly free, it was he.

He walked all day without even stopping to eat. So exhilarated was he by the fact that he was actually living his dream that he felt neither hunger nor weariness. By evening he'd covered twenty-two miles and crossed into Kent.

As darkness fell and the air turned cold, he realized that he needed a meal and a rest, and he looked for the nearest inn. The first hostelry he came upon, called the Twin Elms (although the pair of elms that stood in the yard were as different as a pair could be, one being old and stunted, the other being youthfully slim and straight), was a shabby place with a gaudy red door and a row of dirty windows peeping out from beneath the overhanging thatch of the steeply pitched roof. As soon as Oliver opened the red door, his senses were assaulted by the sound of raucous laughter from the taproom and the smell of strong ale and rancid grease. He grinned with pleasure. This was exactly the seamy sort of place a young man in search of adventure wished to find.

Inside the taproom—a low-ceilinged, dark room filled with noisy revelers—the air was thick with smoke that seeped from a large fireplace in the corner. Oliver's eyes stung as he took an empty chair at the far end of one of the room's three long tables. The innkeeper's wife, an ill-kempt woman with a bottom so large that it waggled like a duck's when she walked, approached and gave him a loud greeting and a slap on the shoulder, as if they'd been friends for years. Oliver, although startled at the unwonted familiarity, nevertheless refrained from comment and merely ordered ale. Then he sat back in his chair and looked about him.

Most of the noise of the taproom seemed to emanate from the table next to his. A group of men at that table were shouting and laughing excitedly. The focus of their excitement seemed to be a huge fellow in their midst whom they were plying with compliments and ale. He was stocky and powerfully built, and they kept calling him Ironfist. Oliver soon realized that the group had just returned from a boxing match that Ironfist had evidently won. Oliver watched with interest as the crowd celebrated the victory with rowdy enthusiasm.

Ironfist, he noticed, was a quiet, modest fellow. The man blushed happily whenever anyone drank a toast to him or came over from another table to clap him on the back, but he said very little. When someone asked, "Did 'e manage to lay a glove on ye?" he merely shrugged. It was another man—obviously his best chum—who answered for him.

"Nah! Never got near us!" the chum declared with possessive pride. He was a small man, older and much slighter in build than the pugilist, and as puffed up with himself as if it had been he who fought the match. He couldn't stop bragging about it. "That bout . . . it weren't *nothin'* fer Ironfist, as I tole ye it would be from the first," he chortled repeatedly. "I'd go bail even Gentleman Jack Johnson hisself couldn' stand up t' that fist."

Oliver found the scene very amusing, for every time the smaller man made the boast, the other men cheered as if they were hearing the pronouncement for the first time. When the fifth repetition elicited an even louder cheer than the first, Oliver couldn't refrain from giving out a snort of laughter. This caught the attention of the braggart, who looked over at him with narrowed eyes. "Seems there's a stranger 'ere among us," he remarked. "A stranger wi' a very fine 'at. And wi' the cheek t' be givin' us a 'orselaugh." He turned in his chair so that he faced Oliver. "Seems t' me, stranger-wiv-a-'at, that ye don't b'lieve whut we been sayin'," he accused.

Oliver shook his head placatingly. "I have no reason not to believe you," he said gently.

"This 'ere's none other, 'n Ironfist Finley," the little man insisted, rising from his seat somewhat belligerently. "Ironfist Finley can lick anyone without half tryin'. Just ask anyone in this room."

"I don't doubt it at all," Oliver said agreeably, taking a sip of his ale.

"It ain't just a moniker we 'ung on 'im," the braggart went

on. "The fellow's got a iron fist fer real, or we'd be callin' 'im
Jim, which is 'is name. No once can best ol' Jim Finley, 'cause
of 'is fist. 'Ere, take a feel!"

Oliver obligingly leaned over to the next table and pressed
his fingers against the pugilist's clenched fist. It was truly hard
as stone. "Very impressive," Oliver said admiringly. "I'd not
wish to meet it with my jaw, I'll admit that."

The crowd laughed and applauded, and Oliver, relieved at
having won them over, told the innkeeper's wife to bring
another round for everyone at the table—at his expense.

"Let's see the color o' yer brass first," the woman said
rudely.

Instinctively, Oliver stiffened. How dared this alewife speak
to him in that way? He'd never before been spoken to with such
disrespect. He opened his mouth to give her an icy set-down,
but before the words left his tongue he clamped his lips
together. He'd suddenly realized that his instinct was misdi-
rected. After all, there was nothing about him to indicate to
even the shrewdest observer that he was the Honorable Oliver
Sherrard, son of the late Earl of Lydbury. In his sturdy boots,
plain chamois breeches, and serviceable, unadorned coat, there
was little (except possibly his hat) to set him apart from any
one of the farmers and laborers who were gathered in this
room. And that was what he wanted, wasn't it? If he'd wanted
to be treated like nobility, he'd have taken his brother's advice
and traveled with all the trappings—valet, carriage, clothes,
and all the rest of it.

He smiled inwardly. This rudeness, this rough camaraderie,
was just what he wanted. He'd determined to embark upon this
walking tour like any ordinary Englishman, and he was
succeeding. If the innkeeper's wife saw fit to speak to him in
the same disparaging way she addressed the usual ragtag
company that patronized the taproom of the Twin Elms Inn,
that was just as it should be.

He looked up at her with a twinkle. "Here, woman," he
said, pulling one of his guineas from his pocket, "will this
do?"

The woman stared at the gold coin in some surprise. Then a
slow smile suffused her face. "Oh, yes, sir!" she assured him,

snatching up the coin with a quick movement of her hand. "Ye kin call me Maggs," she added, testing the coin with her teeth. Then, satisfied that it was genuine, she waddled off to fetch the ale and his change.

There was nothing in the little exchange between the serving woman and Oliver to attract the attention of the others, for innkeepers were always asking to see the color of one's money. So the matter was either ignored or soon forgotten by most of the revelers at the next table. Only the little braggart found something extraordinary in the incident: his sharp eyes caught sight of something gold. The stranger in the fine beaver hat had paid with a gold coin! Since gold guineas were not commonly seen in these surroundings, he found the discovery to be interesting indeed.

The din in the taproom grew louder as the revelers drank to Oliver's health and then returned to congratulating the pugilist on his victory. Not until midnight did the celebration end. By that time, Oliver had long since bespoken a room and retired for the night. The little braggart and his protégé, Ironfist Finley, were the last to leave. Unwilling to see the end of their evening of triumph, they sat huddled together at the end of the table, refusing to go home. Maggs gave up trying to evict them. She simply ordered them to lock up after themselves and went off to bed.

The two men remained seated, staring groggily into their almost empty mugs. "Did you see the yellowboy that stranger pulled from 'is pocket?" the braggart asked after a long silence.

"Yellowboy?" Ironfist Finley mumbled sleepily. "Wha' yellowboy?"

"The yellowboy he gave Maggs t' pay fer the drinks. Didn't ye see it? I'd go bail 'e had a few more of 'em on 'im, too."

The pugilist lifted his head and blinked at his chum. "More yellowboys? Ain't likely."

"Sure it's likely. A man'd have t' be a noddle to throw away a yellowboy on drinks fer the 'ouse unless 'e had a few more in 'is pocket."

Finley shrugged indifferently. "I s'pose it might be so . . ."

The braggart's eyes glittered. "What say we relieve 'im of 'em? It wouldn't be much trouble. The whopstraw's right upstairs in the back bedroom, sleepin' it off. All we'd 'ave t' do is creep in on 'im—we'd take off our boots an' walk on our stockin'd pettitoes—an' paw through 'is breeches."

Jim Finley frowned dubiously. "I dunno, ol' chap. Don't seem right. Not t'day . . ."

"Whut's the day got t' do wi' it?"

The pugilist shrugged again but wasn't able to find words to express his feelings.

The braggart studied his chum closely and then frowned in understanding. "Don't wish t' spoil the day, eh? The day of yer bein' a champeen? Can't say as I blame ye. But bein' able t' pocket a few gold guineas'd make as good an end t' the day as any I could think of."

The reluctant fighter didn't answer. He merely shook his head.

"Look, Jim," the little braggart pressed, "I'll do it all. I'll go in alone. All ye 'ave t' do is stand outside 'is door an' be ready if I need ye."

"Ready?" Jim echoed, confused.

"Wi' yer fives. If 'e wakes, I might need yer iron fist."

With his plan made—if such a rudimentary scheme for robbery could be called a plan—the little braggart rose from the table. Finley of the iron fist, still reluctant, nevertheless got up also. The smaller man looked round carefully to make sure that no one still lingered about, and then he went out to the hallway. At the foot of the stairs, he pulled off his boots. Jim Finley loyally followed and did the same. The braggart winked at his friend as he lined up both pairs of boots near the door. Then, everything being ready, they crept silently up the stairs.

CHAPTER
ҩ҉ ҩ҉
THREE

Oliver, snug in the featherbed that Maggs had provided for him under the eaves of the Twin Elms Inn, had been deeply asleep for two hours. The little fire had gone out, and even the ashes had lost their faint red glow. The room was dark and still.

He never knew what it was that woke him. All he could recollect later was that something—a sound, a movement of air, perhaps, or even the workings of some mysterious sixth sense—brought his consciousness swimming up to the surface. His mind came instantly awake, although he didn't move or even open his eyes. Something or someone, he was positive, was in the room with him!

He lay motionless, trying to decipher the tiny clues that reached his ears from the almost silent air. There was the faintest rustle of cloth, the faintest hint of someone breathing. Where were the sounds coming from? It took a moment for him to remember that he'd hung his clothes on the back of a chair just to the right of the bedstead. As soon as he recollected it, he knew what his ears were hearing. *Someone was rifling through his pockets!*

He turned his head in the direction of the chair and opened his eyes. Holding his breath, he waited for his eyes to become accustomed to the dark. When he could make out a shadowy shape bending over the chair, he leaped from the bed with a frightening roar and fell upon the shadow. The man—for that's what the shadow proved to be—gave a choking cry and toppled over onto the floor, with Oliver on top of him. "Jim—'elp!" he managed to cry. *"Jim!"*

Oliver pummeled furiously at whatever part of the miscreant's body he could manage to reach, for the fellow beneath was flailing about wildly, and in the dark it was impossible to tell what was what. But just as he'd determined where the fellow's chin was, and he'd lifted his arm to land the fellow a proper facer, the door flew open. Oliver paused in the act of delivering the blow and lifted his head to see who'd opened it. In that moment, the creature beneath him squirmed from his grasp and leaped to his feet. Oliver, swearing under his breath, jumped up also. He could see, looming in the doorway, another man, much larger than the first. For a brief second he thought it might be the innkeeper who'd arrived to help him, but when he heard the little thief sigh in relief, he knew that the second man was an accomplice.

The thief tried to scramble to the door, but Oliver grabbed him by the arm, threw his free arm across the fellow's chest, and held tight. "No, you don't," he barked. "If you don't want my fist dislodging your teeth, you'll stay put."

The fellow wriggled like a demented eel. "Get 'im, Jim," he hissed. "Quick, now, before 'e mangles me!"

The new arrival hesitated for a moment in the doorway. The dim light of the hallway behind him threw his shadow— enormous and terrifying—across Oliver's line of vision, causing the interloper's appearance to be completely obscured and making it difficult to see what the fellow was doing. Oliver edged to his right to get a better view, but the new arrival took two steps into the room and swung. The man whom Oliver held imprisoned against him ducked just in time, and the blow struck Oliver's chin. It connected with a dreadful sound; the fist felt like a hammer. Oliver staggered backward, a searing pain shooting from his jaw to his ear. He tasted blood on his lip. His head swam. Stunned and dizzy, he would have liked to slide to the ground and let his mind sink into blackness, but he clenched his teeth, which caused a flash of additional pain, and held tightly on to consciousness. He held on tightly to his prisoner, too; the blow had not rattled his wits.

His mind was working so well, in fact, that he could guess

who'd struck him. The new assailant was Ironfist Finley, that much was quite clear. What was also clear was that with Ironfist as his adversary, he was not likely to box his way out of this altercation.

The pugilist took a boxer's stance, legs slightly bent and fists raised in readiness for the next blow. He moved cautiously to his right to let more light into the room. As he eyed Oliver warily, the imprisoned thief cursed at him. "Don't just stand there, ye blasted lummox!" he swore. "Let 'im 'ave it!"

Oliver, knowing quite well that he couldn't easily withstand another such blow, made a sudden move out the door, dragging his prisoner with him. The little fellow cursed as the bemused boxer followed. "Whut're ye waitin' fer, ye clodpole! *Wallop 'im*, damn ye!"

Ironfist obligingly swung, but Oliver dodged the blow. Backing up cautiously along the wall, Oliver dragged his little captive to the top of the stairs. There he stopped and waited while Ironfist, who'd stalked clumsily after him, positioned himself for the next blow. The top of the stairs was just where Oliver wanted him to be. At the moment Ironfist swung out his arm, Oliver whirled his prisoner round with a sudden swing and pushed him against the pugilist. Ironfist, caught at the moment when his body was half twisted to make his swing, lost his balance. The force of Oliver's thrust caused the two assailants to fall, and, one tumbling after the other, they bounced painfully down the stairs.

Oliver stood at the top, his chest heaving. He rubbed his sore chin as he looked down at them. "I'd take myself off, if I were you," he said calmly, "before I set the law on you."

The smaller man, groaning and cursing, hauled Finley to his feet and, throwing Oliver a look of utter fury, limped to the door. In the dim light of the candles in the wall sconces, Oliver could see him pick up his boots and, with Finley dazedly in tow, scurry out the front door.

Oliver watched them go and then returned to his room. Before going back to his bed, however, he propped a chair under the doorknob. It was true that he wanted adventure, but he'd had quite enough for one day.

* * *

The next morning, at daybreak, he set off again on his travels, but his mood was not nearly as joyful as it had been the day before. Dark clouds obscured the sun, the wind was cold, his face was swollen on one side, and his whole head ached. *Perhaps John was right,* he found himself thinking. *Perhaps I should have traveled like a gentleman.*

After a while, however, his spirits rose. It was adventure he'd wanted, and adventure he was getting. He lifted the collar of his coat closer round his neck as protection against the wind and began to whistle. Even with a swollen jaw, it was good to be alive.

He soon discovered that a little mongrel dog—part Scottish terrier, part Cairn, but for the most part indeterminate—was following him. He turned and petted the dog's head. "Where do you belong, little fellow?" he asked. "Go on home."

But the dog continued to trot after him on its short, furry little legs. "Go on home, I say!" Oliver ordered. "If you're looking for something to eat, you're on the wrong track. I've nothing edible in this rucksack."

The dog merely gazed up at him lovingly. It was an endearing animal, although it had obviously seen hard times. Its coat was ragged and neglected, the end of its tail was blunted, and part of one of its little pointed ears had been ripped away in some long-forgotten battle. There was a gray beard surrounding its button of a nose, and the bushy eyebrows over its wet black eyes matched the beard. Oliver was immediately drawn to the animal, but he reminded himself that he'd sworn to travel unencumbered. Therefore, he shooed the animal away again and kept on walking. The dog hesitated for a moment and then followed again. Oliver shrugged. "Do as you please, of course," he said to the animal over his shoulder, "but if you can't find your way back home, don't blame—"

At that moment a masked figure stepped out from behind the hedge at the side of the road. "Pretty frisky this mornin', ain't ye?" he said, planting himself right in Oliver's path. "We'll see 'ow frisky ye'll be a minute from now."

Both the voice and the man's small stature were instantly recognizable. "I *knew* I should have gone to the magistrate last night," Oliver muttered in self-reproach. "Get out of my way, fellow, or I'll find a magistrate right now."

"Before ye make threats, jobbernowl," the little fellow sneered, "take a look behind ye."

Oliver glanced over his shoulder. Standing right behind him, also masked but instantly recognizable by his broad shoulders, was Ironfist Finley, fists at the ready. Oliver barely had time to duck a blow; it grazed the chin that was already bruised. Realizing with a sinking heart that he was about to have another adventure, Oliver swung with all his might at the pugilist's jaw and had the immense satisfaction of seeing the fellow reel.

The little dog began to bark furiously, bounding up and down like a circus performer on a springboard.

"Get 'im, Jim," the small man cried, "or I'll 'ave t' use the cudgel."

Finley, regaining his balance, bore in again. Oliver parried the swing and managed to deliver another blow to the boxer's chin. Finley, roaring in rage and pain, swung hard at Oliver's nose. Red streaks flashed through Oliver's brain, and he was certain he heard, above the groans and shouts of his assailants and the dog's wild barking, the sound of breaking bone. Stunned, he slipped down on one knee and held up his arms to protect his head from the next blow that he was sure was about to come. When it didn't, he looked up to find that the boxer was struggling to ward off the attacks of the little dog, who was bravely leaping about in his attempt to bite Finley's hands.

Finally, in response to his chum's commands, the boxer gave the brave dog a sharp blow that knocked the little animal senseless. The sight of the poor little creature lying motionless at the side of the road infuriated Oliver. With a cry, he pulled himself erect and bore down on his assailant with murderous rage. He landed a telling right on Finley's eye and was about to follow up his advantage with a quick left to the jaw when he felt an excruciating blow at the back of his head. The world immediately went black, and he knew nothing more.

The next sensation of which he was aware was something wet licking his nose. He tried to open his eyes. His head was throbbing so painfully that even the movement of his eyelids seemed too great an effort, so he waited until he could gather strength enough to manage it. When he did, he found himself staring into the sad eyes of the mongrel dog. "What? You still here, little chap?" he asked thickly, his lips and tongue feeling so numb that they might have belonged to someone else.

The dog barked excitedly and licked his face in joyful welcome.

"Yes, little one," Oliver muttered, "I'm glad you're better, too. You were a game fighter, I give you that. You've the courage of a lion in that little mongrel heart."

A spatter of rain on his forehead made him suddenly aware of his surroundings. It was dark, so he couldn't see that he was under a bush. He lifted himself on one elbow and looked about. It took a moment to realize that he was lying underneath a canopy of tangled branches. "Good God!" he exclaimed. "They knocked me senseless and dragged me under a hedgerow!"

He pulled himself painfully to his feet and discovered, to his surprise, that the sky was dark. It was already night. He'd been lying unconscious all day!

Though the night was a dark one, and the now steady rain obscured his vision still further, he could see that the hedgerow under which he'd been ditched edged a wide, rolling field that stretched to the horizon. Before he could further examine the landscape, he realized that his feet were ice cold. This thought led to his next discovery: he was standing on the wet, muddy ground in his stockinged feet. The damned thieves had taken his *boots*! Also his coat, he realized, shivering. He soon made a couple of other painful discoveries. His rucksack was gone. And all his money. He had nothing now but the clothes on his back. "Damnation," he said glumly to the dog who was sniffing his feet curiously, "I suppose I should be thankful they left me my breeches!"

The dog rubbed his cheek on Oliver's leg sympathetically.

Oliver reached down and patted the animal fondly. "Yes, old fellow, I see what you mean. I'm not utterly bereft. I still have you." He brushed the raindrops from the dog's floppy ears. "You were as brave and loyal as . . . as Damon, who stood ready to die for his friend Pythias. That's what you are, a little Scottish Damon."

The little terrier, sensing affection, leaped into Oliver's arms.

Oliver laughed. "Determined to stay with me, are you, old fellow? In that case, I'll have to give you a name. Scottish Damon is too long. I know! I shall call you MacDamon! Mac for short."

MacDamon barked his pleasure. At that moment a gust of wind, bringing with it a shower of raindrops, cut through Oliver to the skin. He shivered again. His feet were cold and damp in their thin stockings, his shirt was soaked through, and the pain in his head was so severe that he was convinced his skull had been cracked right down the middle. *How I'd love to get my hands on those despicable miscreants,* he thought. It would not be hard to find them, for he had no doubt as to their identities, and when he did, he'd have both revenge and restitution! He'd make sure of that. But what he needed now, before he could even think of revenge and restitution, was a warm, dry place to rest.

As his eyes grew accustomed to the dark, he could see the silhouette of a low building not many yards away. From the shape he guessed it was a stable. "Come on, Mac, old fellow, let's go to our night's lodging," he said, scooping the damp little dog up in his arms.

MacDamon yipped happily and licked Oliver's face.

"What's that you say, MacDamon?" Oliver asked, tucking him under one arm. "A stable isn't a proper lodging for a Sherrard of Lydbury? Perhaps not, old chap, but it's as good a place as any to house a mongrel dog and a coatless vagabond with no money." And through the driving rain, with his newly acquired companion cheerfully wagging the stubby tail that hung out from under his arm, Oliver gingerly picked his way across the field to the only shelter he could now afford.

CHAPTER
❧ ❧
FOUR

OLIVER HAD NO WAY OF KNOWING THAT THE STABLE WHERE HE was taking refuge was part of an extensive estate known as Pattinger Downs and that the manor house itself was only a short walk from where he was. But Oliver, his head reeling from the severity of the cudgel-blow, had no real sense of his surroundings. He was not even fully aware that the rain was pelting down on the stable roof and that the wind was howling with increasing ferocity. He knew only that he had to get some sleep. He was thankful that he'd found a haven—humble though it was—so close at hand. Although it occurred to him that he might be trespassing, he put the thought aside. He would deal with it tomorrow, he told himself. Tomorrow would be time enough to face his problems.

But inside the manor house, just a few hundred yards beyond the stable, another storm was brewing, a storm as threatening as the one raging outside, for this was the night that Moira Pattinger had made up her mind to have it out with her father.

It was not that Moira really minded losing Sir Godfrey Jayne to her sister. Babs could have him! As far as Moira was concerned, Godfrey was no better than her other so-called suitors. Moira could now add him to the list of make-baits who had claimed to love her but who'd promptly given her up when their greedy noses detected the smell of gold with which her father had scented the air. She despised them all now, although two of them were her brothers-in-law and the third was about

28

to be. They were, all three, beneath contempt. She wasted no emotion on them. It was her father who enraged her. His underhanded treatment of her was beyond bearing.

She knew where she would find him. At this hour of the evening, Lord Pattinger would be in his private retreat, his sanctum sanctorum. It was a study, a cozy room in the west wing where he closeted himself to work on his accounts or to read his *Times*. There was nothing in the room but his desk and writing chair, and a favorite armchair near the fireplace for reading. When he enclosed himself in that room, everyone in the household knew that he was not to be disturbed for any reason short of actual emergency, like fire or mortal illness. It was an unbreakable household rule. But Moira didn't care about his rules. Not now. In fact, the thought of breaking in on him in his sanctum sanctorum gave her a feeling of real pleasure. Delightful, spiteful, wicked pleasure.

She stalked down the hall from her sister's bedroom toward her father's study, but just as she rounded the bend into the west wing, she heard her name called. She turned back and saw Alberta hurrying clumsily down the hall after her. "Moira, wait!" her sister said breathlessly, holding a hand against her swollen belly as she trundled down the hall, her skirt ballooning out around her. Alberta was with child, and with the baby expected only a month from now, her condition was obvious even under the most billowy garments.

"Stand still, Alberta," Moira ordered. "I'm coming." And she retraced her steps until she faced her sister.

Alberta and her Horatio had been living at the family home ever since their marriage almost two years earlier, waiting for repairs on Horatio's estate in Lincolnshire to be completed. The couple had hoped that they might be able to move out in time to have the baby in their own home, but the latest word from Becclesworth Manor was not promising. The news had been a severe disappointment to Alberta and aggravated the high-strung nervousness that was part of her normal character and that had already been intensified by the stress of her condition. The heightened nervousness was immediately apparent; as soon as Moira came up to her, Alberta clutched her arm with clawlike fingers. "Don't do it, Moira," she said in a dramatic, tremulous whisper. "Please don't."

"Do what?" Moira countered, wondering how Alberta had managed to learn about this latest crisis.

"Don't have it out with Father! You know how difficult life is in this house when he is cross."

"How on earth did you find out I'm going to 'have it out' with Father?"

"Everyone knows," Alberta said with a shudder. "Horatio heard about Sir Godfrey's change of heart from his man. My hairdresser knows too. Even my new tirewoman was whispering about it. And when I saw you stalking down toward the west wing in that killing stride of yours—"

Moira groaned. "Is there nothing in this house that's ever *private*?"

Alberta released her grip on Moira's arm and wrung her hands. "I know it's dreadful that Father's done this to you again, but you don't really want Sir Godfrey anyway, so let it be. Please, my dear, let it be."

"I can't let it be, Bertie," Moira explained, taking her sister's hand and patting it soothingly. "Try to understand. I must have a life of my own, and the only way I will ever get it is to fight for it. Susan is mistress of her own home, and soon you will be too. And Babs, who's only twenty, will probably be wed by June. You will all be gone, and I will be left, a slave to Father's will. You must see that I cannot let that happen."

Alberta's underlip began to tremble. "But if you have words with him, he'll be so angry. We'll have to sit at dinner and endure his glowers. He'll bark at the servants. And he'll say nasty things to everyone. It makes poor Horatio so uncomfortable when Father is in one of his moods—"

"I know, Bertie, I know. But I won't let him use you or Horatio badly, I promise. Every time he starts in on one of you, I'll give him so sharp a taste of my saucy tongue that he'll have to save all his barbs for me."

Alberta sighed hopelessly. "Oh, Moira, you know you can't—"

"Yes, I can. Stop worrying, Bertie. Why don't you go down

to the music room and play the piano. You know how music soothes you. Go on, for the baby's sake . . ."

Alberta was finally appeased, and Moira turned once more toward her father's study. As she strode down the hall, her fury returned in full force. It was not fair that she alone, of the six members of the family (if you counted her two brothers-in-law with her three sisters), had the courage to stand up to him. It was not pleasant having to do battle all alone. But she would not let her sisters dissuade her. A battle was necessary.

She burst into his study with the same rudeness she'd shown to her sister; she did not stop to knock. She did not even offer a good-evening. She made her warlike mood even more obvious by slamming the door behind her. "How *dared* you do this to me *again*?" she demanded furiously.

Lord Pattinger was sitting at his desk, peering through a pince-nez (which, when not perched on the bridge of his beaked nose, was always hanging round his neck on a long black ribbon) at the accounts, a task that occupied hours of his time weekly but that he would entrust to no one else. His daughter's dramatic entrance forced him to raise his eyes. He glared at her over the eyeglasses. "Is the house burning?" he asked icily.

"I asked you a question, Father," Moira said, ignoring his sarcasm.

"I asked *you* a question. Perhaps someone has died? That might make this intrusion somewhat forgivable. Or is it that you've run into some problem with the correspondence with Lord Harcourt, a letter I should have had on my desk by this time?"

"There is no fire and no one has died. And I have no problem with the letter to Lord Harcourt, which I will finish and have on your desk by tomorrow afternoon. May we now turn our attention to the matter that brought me here?" she retorted.

"How can it be that a daughter of mine has so far forgotten her breeding that she breaks into a room without knocking?" he asked in a voice that resonated with revulsion. "And *this* room in particular!"

His lordship was a tall, bony gentleman of fifty-odd years

whose aquiline nose was but one of the features that made his appearance awesome. The others were a pair of ice-blue eyes that seemed sharp and penetrating even behind his spectacles, and a head of pure white hair that had not thinned despite his years. None of these features, however, gave any impression of warmth. Moira supposed that he must have been a warmer, kinder person when her mother was alive—after all, she had borne him four daughters—but since her death almost two decades before, the man had become sardonic, calculating, and cold-hearted. No one in the household escaped either the bite of his sarcasm or the ice of his indifference. Only to Moira did he offer some small scraps of affection, and even those were given with a niggardly, ungenerous reluctance. It was commonly supposed that he was more drawn to Moira than to his other daughters because she most resembled her mother, but Moira herself—whose recollections of her mother were very vague, Lady Pattinger having died when she was six—felt that the resemblance must be faint indeed, for the signs of her father's affection were few and far between.

"I insist, my lord, that you answer me," the girl said defiantly.

"And I insist that you go out again and reenter in the proper manner," he retorted, turning his eyes back to his accounts.

"I will *not* go out again!" Moira snapped. "Treating me like a naughty child is a ploy to put me off, but this time, Father, it will not work. You have played this game with me for the last time."

"Oh? And what game is that?"

"The game of buying off my suitors."

Lord Pattinger peered at her for a moment. Then he sighed, removed his pince-nez, and rubbed his nose. "Barbara told you, I suppose. I shall wring the blasted chit's neck. I told her not to speak of the matter until I'd told you myself."

"It was *not* Babs who told me, so you needn't try to divert attention from the issue under discussion. The entire staff is whispering about Godfrey's defection. You, my lord, have managed to make me appear the jilted female to the whole household! Again!"

His lordship raised his eyebrows, his lips twisting in a sneer.

"So the scullery maids think you've been jilted, eh? Am I to trouble myself about the misconceptions of the scullery maids? You can't expect me to care—or to believe *you* care—what the servants think."

"You may well believe it! When one is jilted, it is at the very least a painful experience. To be jilted in favor of one's own sister is worse. To have it happen *three times*—in the same house right under the noses of the same staff—is the very height of humiliation! And if you don't see that, you are completely insensitive to a woman's feelings."

Lord Pattinger leaned back in his chair and, tapping his fingers on the edge of his pince-nez, studied her disdainfully. "My dear Moira, you exaggerate. You know the servants think too well of you to lose their respect. And as for the pain of being jilted, I've never been aware that you've shed a tear for any one of those bounders you thought you fancied."

"Perhaps not, but they were not bounders until you made them so."

Her father's eyebrows rose. "I? *I* made them bounders? Of what are you accusing me?"

"Don't play the innocent with me! I know you bought them off. I don't know the sordid details, but I can guess. How much did it take, Father? I've always wanted to know. Jeffrey, for instance. He was the best of them. How much did you give him to offer for Susan in place of me? Five thousand? Six?"

"You value yourself too cheaply, my dear," her father answered with an ironic half-smile. "Jeffrey would not surrender his love and his honor until I'd raised the price to ten."

Moira stared at her father, aghast. She'd known from the first that he'd bribed them, but this was the first time he'd actually admitted it. And the first time she'd heard the actual amount. She sank down in his reading chair (a liberty she'd never before taken), her fingertips pressed to her lips. "Ten thousand!" she muttered.

"Why should that upset you, my dear! It's a considerable sum."

"I suppose it is. But the sum does not seem so considerable when it's the measure of one's worth. It's quite a shock to learn what one is actually worth in pounds sterling."

"You are worth a great deal more . . . to me," her father admitted in a low voice.

Moira looked up in surprise. "Why, Father?"

"Why? That's a silly question. You're my daughter."

"Yes, but so are Susan and Bertie and Babs. Yet you didn't place a price on *their* heads to keep them from marrying."

"They *have* to be married. They are good for nothing else."

Moira stiffened. "That's a *dreadful* thing to say!"

"It is true, nevertheless," Lord Pattinger said calmly. "They are pretty girls with meager talents and small intellect. You, on the other hand, are unusually capable and clever."

"You underestimate them and overestimate me. But even if your valuation were true, I don't see why it follows that *I* should not be married. I've never heard that being capable and clever were qualities detrimental to a happy marriage."

"You would not have had a happy marriage with any of the three specimens you presented to me."

"You can't be sure of that. Jeffrey was a very decent chap until you subverted him. And he is making Susan a perfectly satisfactory husband."

"He would not have been satisfactory for you," his lordship insisted.

Moira eyed him with a troubled frown. "Can you not see the inconsistency of your position, Father? You claim that I am unusually capable, yet you do not find me capable of choosing my own mate."

"That, my dear, is utter nonsense. It isn't *I* who's done the choosing. I've just protected you from the unwise choices *you've* made so far. When the time comes that you present me with a proper candidate, I shall be happy to approve of him."

Moira eyed him speculatively. His words were properly conciliatory, but she hesitated to believe him. He had never shown the slightest interest in seeing her wed. In the last few years she'd gotten the impression that her father *wanted* her to remain a spinster. Whenever his sister, her aunt Joanna, had written to invite her to spend the Season in London, which was, of course, the best place in all of England for a girl to catch herself a proper swain, he'd consistently refused. After a half dozen of those refusals, Moira began to believe that the man was unnatural. All the other fathers she'd ever heard of were eager for their daughters to wed. But *he*, although he was quick enough to buy husbands for her sisters, had never given a sign that he wanted a man for *her*. But now, at last, he'd indicated that he would approve of a "proper candidate." Did he really mean it? Had she misunderstood him all these years? Was he really only waiting for her to find just the right suitor? "Are you sincere, Father? Do you really mean what you just said? If you do, then let me go to London to Aunt Joanna. I'm not likely to find myself a proper candidate here in Kent, but in London—"

Lord Pattinger's expression hardened. "It is out of the question. I need you here." He placed the pince-nez back on his nose. "Now, go. I have indulged you long enough. You are interrupting me." He made a dismissive gesture with his hand and turned his eyes back to his accounts.

"No!" the girl cried, crushed. So he'd *not* been sincere. She'd been right about him all along! She jumped up from the chair with such furious energy that her red curls bounced. "No, my lord, I won't let you dismiss the matter so easily. It is time we spoke the truth. We must face it squarely at last. The truth is that you don't wish me to wed *anyone*!"

"My dear girl," he said, quietly cold, "I've already said that the subject is closed." The tone of his voice was such that anyone knowing him would have been warned to get out of his way.

But Moira didn't care. Her rage made her brave. "If you were sincere, you'd have sent me off to Aunt Joanna years ago, when she first wanted to bring me out. But no, you wouldn't hear of it. You said even then that I couldn't be spared. That you needed me. But the truth is that you were afraid that in London I'd find a really proper candidate, someone you couldn't buy off. And then, with me married, you'd be forced to find someone else to act as your hostess, to run the household, to deal with your correspondence. That would not have been convenient, would it? Without me, a housekeeper and a secretary would have to be hired and paid. What an annoyance! And how unnecessary, if you could keep me here at the Downs forever! The truth is, Father, that you want me unwed for your own convenience! You want to keep me *prisoner*!"

Lord Pattinger rose slowly from his chair, his eyes icy behind the glasses. "That will be quite enough. I have always admired your spirit, my girl, but this is beyond a display of spirit. This is hysterics, and a display of hysterics I will not abide. Go to your room, and don't come out of it until you are calm and ready to apologize for this revolting outburst."

"What will you do, Father, lock me in?" Her eyes flashed fire as she wheeled about and stormed to the door. "Try it, and see how long you can keep me there! And when I free myself, do you know what I shall do?"

"Something spitefully foolish, no doubt," her father said dryly.

"Yes, indeed! Very spiteful and very foolish!" She threw open the door and cast him a last, burning glare. "I shall marry the very first stranger to cross my path! Be he pauper or prince I shall wed him! Handsome or ugly, old or young, courtier or clodpole, I don't care! Whoever he is, I shall wed him! I swear I shall! *The very first man I see!*"

CHAPTER
❧ ❧
FIVE

ALTHOUGH THE STORM WITHIN THE MANOR HOUSE LASTED A MERE quarter hour (having ended with Moira's banishment to her bedroom, where she threw herself on her bed and cried herself to sleep), the storm outside raged all night. By morning the downpour had slackened to a mere drizzle, and the gale had subdued itself to a light wind. Although the sky was still darkly gray, there was a sign of brightening on the southern horizon, giving one hope that the sun might yet make an appearance before nightfall.

Moira awoke early. She knew it was early because her abigail, Greta, had not yet appeared to stoke up the fire. Shivering, she slipped out from under her blankets and ran to the window. She thrust aside the draperies and discovered, to her chagrin, that the rain still fell. It was not a day for riding. Nevertheless, riding was what she was determined to do. As soon as Greta showed herself, she would put on her favorite brown velvet riding dress. No one would stop her, unless. . . .

She eyed the door suspiciously, wondering if her father had lived up to his threat and locked her in during the night. She ran across the cold floor in her bare feet and tried the knob. The door was, to her relief, unlocked. She had been foolish to worry. Her father was a selfish tyrant, but he would not go so far as literally to lock her in. To him, the mere giving of the order was enough. She was not to leave her room unless she apologized. That was the order, and she was expected to obey. Physical locks, he undoubtedly believed, were not necessary.

She gave a rebellious toss of her head. If her father thought that his mere order was enough to keep her in this room, he would soon learn how wrong he was. She would not permit him to keep her from going about as she pleased. And she would *not* apologize to him! Never! Not even if he tied her to a rack and tortured her for the rest of her life!

Later, dressed in her riding habit, with a cocky, high-crowned riding hat perched at a rakish angle on her head, she went down to the breakfast room. She was quite prepared for another battle. There *would* be another battle, she was sure of it. She had chosen to disobey her father's explicit order. It was like throwing down the gauntlet. The battle lines were drawn.

She paused nervously in the breakfast room doorway and peered inside. Things within looked quite ordinary. Her father and Barbara were already at the table, and Horatio was standing at the buffet, being helped to a serving of shirred eggs. Alberta was not to be seen. Moira surmised that she'd used her "condition" as an excuse for remaining abed. The only other persons in view were Pearce, the butler, and a housemaid who was stationed behind the buffet table to assist in the serving.

Lord Pattinger seemed quite himself, although Barbara looked peaked and uneasy. Evidently Barbara had already heard about last night's quarrel. Moira sighed inwardly. It was frustrating to realize that nothing that occurred in this household could be kept private. The servants had an elaborate system of news gathering and gossip spreading; there were no secrets in this house. It was therefore very likely that everyone knew about her father's order and would now be watching to see if she'd make the apology her father expected. She wouldn't be surprised if the two footmen she'd passed in the hallway had made bets on the matter. She wondered what the odds might be against her.

Calling up her reserves of courage, Moira came striding into the room with a bounce in her step. "Good morning, Father,

Horatio. *Good* morning, Babs." She exuded cheerfulness as she leaned down to plant a kiss on her sister's cheek.

The worry in Barbara's soft eyes lightened in relief at the cheerful sound of her sister's voice. "*Here* you are, dearest!" she exclaimed. "I was beginning to be afraid that . . . I mean, I thought you might not . . . not . . ." She glanced nervously over at her father and, eyes falling, lapsed into silence.

"That I might not come down?" Moira finished for her. "Well, you needn't have worried. Here I am." She sat down at her place and looked up at the butler, who was standing wooden-faced beside the buffet. "I'll only take time for some tea and a muffin, Pearce."

"Is that all, Miss Moira?" the butler asked. "May I suggest a bite of the soused herring this morning? Cook says it's quite excellent."

"No, thank you, Pearce. I have no time." She stole a sidelong glance at her father. "You see, I'm off for a ride."

Everyone in the room, sensing that this little remark was a challenge to his lordship, stiffened. Horatio, who'd already taken his seat and had just put a forkful of egg into his mouth, choked. Lord Pattinger regarded him with eyebrows raised. "Really, Horatio, do try to consume your breakfast with a modicum of good manners," he said with his accustomed sarcasm. "Surely at some time in your childhood one of your governesses must have taught you not to stuff your mouth."

Horatio, Lord Becclesworth, a small, rather scholarly, serious fellow, reddened painfully. "I . . . I'm sorry . . ."

Moira jumped immediately to his defense. "No need to be sorry, Horatio," she said, glaring at her father. "Anyone, no matter how mannerly, might sometimes be forced to cough at the table. Even Father must have choked on a morsel a few times in his life."

"Never so noticeably," his lordship retorted blandly. Then he turned the full force of his icy stare on his eldest daughter. "Did you say something a moment ago about going riding?"

"Yes, Father," she answered, lifting the teacup that Pearce

had just set before her with exaggerated casualness, "as soon as I've drunk my tea."

"But not, I hope, before you come up to my study and *exchange a few words with me,*" his lordship enunciated pointedly.

Moira gave him a look of bland innocence. "Words, Father? I don't remember that I have any particular words to say to you this morning."

"Don't you, indeed?" Lord Pattinger buttered a piece of toast with cool deliberation. "Then perhaps you'd better return to your room until you remember what the 'particular words' were."

Moira took a sip of tea and then stood up. "I'm afraid, Father dear, that I must go riding first." She put up her chin rebelliously. "I *do* remember that I have a 'particular' bit of *business* to take care of this morning."

His lordship's hand paused in the act of buttering. "Business?" he asked coldly.

"Yes. You do remember, don't you? The business of finding myself a husband."

Barbara gasped. Poor Horatio choked again. The butler and the housemaid exchanged glances. Lord Pattinger put down his toast and glared up at her. "Don't talk fustian, miss. Foolishness doesn't suit you. I shall ignore what you just said and permit you to sit down and finish your tea. You will then, of course, return to your room."

"There is no 'of course' about it," Moira snapped. "I made a pledge. I made it to myself, and I made it to you. I intend to keep it. Therefore, I must—and *shall*—go riding this morning."

Their eyes locked across the table, tense and angry. Each silently and stubbornly dared the other to take the first step, to break the impasse to which her hot words and his cold ones had brought them. No one—not Barbara, not Horatio, not Pearce, not even the housemaid—expelled a breath. The atmosphere was charged and ready for an explosion.

Then his lordship shrugged. Instead of exploding, he merely turned his eyes away from her and reached for his toast. "Go, then," he said calmly. He took a bite, chewed it carefully, and swallowed. "I have never before thought of you as a brainless wet-goose, Moira Pattinger," he added in a tone of disdainful unconcern, "but if you insist on behaving like one, I shan't bother to stop you." That said, he made a flipping gesture with his hand, waving her out of the room. She was dismissed.

CHAPTER

❧ ❧

SIX

GEORGE VARNEY, LORD PATTINGER'S ELDERLY GROOM, WHO lived in a room in the stable loft, had had a bad night. The gale winds and driving rain had kept him awake, to say nothing of the fact that he'd imagined, sometime around midnight, that he'd heard a dog barking. Since all the dogs on the estate were kept in the barns, a goodly distance from the stable, Varney was unaccustomed to the sound. He'd almost, but not quite, been tempted to throw off his blankets and go down to look, for a dog who blundered into the stable might disturb the horses. But the dank night air was not conducive to midnight rambles, so the groom hesitated to emerge from beneath his cozy coverings. After a while, not hearing anything more than the wind, he'd decided to remain in bed. Nevertheless, he didn't sleep at all well.

He rose, as usual, at half-past five to take care of his customary morning chore of feeding and watering the horses. (The stableboys, who were housed at the barns, would come in later to do the currying and cleaning up.) But when he went out with his buckets to the well, he saw that the rain was still falling and that the sky was not likely to clear before afternoon. None of the family would be riding on a day like this, he realized, so he decided that when his morning chores were done, he'd go back upstairs to catch another hour or two of sleep.

After feeding and watering the horses, he pulled down a bale of hay from the loft and put it near the stable door so that the boys would find it easily and not have to disturb him when they came in. That was the last job he set himself for the morning. He was now free to climb up the ladder to his room.

He did not notice, when he passed his lordship's shiny new phaeton—which he'd dragged into the stable the night before to protect it from rain spatters and had left standing just to the right of the stable door in case it might be needed early this morning—that a trespasser had ensconced himself on the upholstered seat of the carriage, wrapped himself with his lordship's own lap robe, and, with a little mongrel dog napping in his arms, was now curled up and deeply asleep. George Varney was too weary to notice anything. He merely walked by the carriage, yawned, scratched the back of his neck, and made his way back up to his bed.

The groom and the trespassers were still asleep when, shortly after nine, Moira Pattinger slid the heavy wooden door of the stable open just enough to slip in. Once inside, she looked round for the groom, but he was nowhere to be seen. This was most unusual. Whenever she'd showed up at the stable before, he was right at hand, but now there was not a sign of him. Where on earth was he, she wondered, on this day of all days, when her need for him was urgent?

She was about to shout for him when a thought stopped her. *Why am I in such a hurry?* she asked herself. *What on earth is so urgent? I don't even know where I ought to go!*

She sank down on the bale of hay the groom had placed there, feeling abruptly deflated. She hadn't given this matter sufficient thought. In fact, she hadn't thought it through at all! A dozen questions suddenly occurred to her for which she had not a single answer. There was only one thing she was certain of: she was going to honor her pledge. She would wed the first stranger she came upon . . . somehow. No matter how difficult it proved to be, she *had* to go through with it, if only to save face! But how was she to go about it?

She had made a vague plan in her mind: to ride her horse to the High Road, position herself at the crossroads, and try to accost the very first man who passed by. But she was now beginning to realize that it was easier said than done. What, for instance, could she do if the first man she saw passed by in a quickly moving carriage? How could she stop him? The answer was not hard to come by: a man passing by quickly in a vehicle need not be counted as a candidate. After all, *she* was the one making up the rules in this game. Though she was honor-bound to abide by her declaration that the fellow she chose would be the first one she saw, she could not possibly stop a man who was racing by in a coach-and-four. No, the conditions had to be amended to mean the first man to go by in a slow-moving vehicle, on a cantering horse, or on foot. In that event, she would simply stop him and say . . . what? Good God, what *could* she say to him—*Good morning, sir, will you be good enough to marry me?*

How was she to do it? She could, she supposed, strike up some sort of casual conversation. She could make a remark about the weather or ask for directions to Maidstone. But how could she possibly lead an innocuous conversation round to the subject of marriage? It would be awkward, to say the least.

Then, too, there was the problem of the man himself. She had sworn to her father that she did not care what the fellow would look like or what sort of character he had, but of course she did care. She had a strong dislike of certain types of men—those with large mustaches, for example. And those with long arms and stooped shoulders who looked like apes when they walked. And overbearing types who believed all females were simpleminded dolts and treated them as such. But to amend the conditions of her pledge to eliminate such candidates would not be honest.

Good God, she thought, *the first man to come along might be a monster! A murderer, a thief, a creature with hairy hands or beady eyes!* Perhaps she'd made a bad mistake. Perhaps her hasty pledge would catapult her into a worse situation than the one she was already in. . . .

But perhaps, for once in her life, she'd be lucky. "Just this once, God, please?" she whispered. She shut her eyes, praying fervently for just a little good fortune. *Let him be tall,* she prayed, *so that I don't tower over him. And let him be passably prepossessing. And passably kind. And don't let him be bald, or foppish, or very stupid, or—*

At that moment, she was startled out of her reverie by a strange sound, a sound that floated down to her from somewhere over her head. It was a *snore*! A man's snore! There was no doubt about it. And it was coming from within the phaeton just behind her! "Varney?" she asked, rising and turning slowly. "Is that you?"

The only answer was another snore.

She peered up at the carriage door but couldn't see inside it. She could guess, however, who was snoring within. Varney had apparently found her father's new carriage a comfortable place in which to take a snooze. Annoyed, she climbed up on the phaeton's step and pulled open the door. "Varney, you slugabed, get up this inst—!"

But the man who shook himself awake at the sound of her voice was not Varney. He was a frightening-looking creature with matted hair, a horribly discolored eye, a bruised, misshapen jaw, and, most dreadful of all, a face smeared with the blood from his battered, swollen nose. One look at him was enough to send even the most intrepid female flying for safety. But Moira was more than intrepid; she was courageous. Too courageous to run away. So she only screamed.

Her scream reached Varney, who sat up with a start, leaped out of his bed, and came clambering down the ladder as fast as his old legs could carry him. Meanwhile, however, little MacDamon began to bark furiously as Oliver blinked up confusedly at a pair of spectacularly green eyes. Those eyes, astonishingly lovely despite the fact that they were wide with terror, were set in a face that seemed to him too beautiful to be real. Below the eyes was an upturned little Irish nose, a full-lipped, luscious mouth, and a strong chin. And above them was a broad forehead, a mass of glinting red curls, and a fetching brown hat with a high crown and small brim that sat on the curls with a saucy tilt. To awaken from a nightmare of pain to such a face as this was utterly incongruous. "I'm dreaming," he said aloud. "I must certainly be dreaming."

"Who *are* you?" Moira gasped. "And what are you doing hiding in my father's phaeton?"

"I'm not hiding," Oliver said, sitting up gingerly and putting a hand to a head that was pounding painfully. "I'm only resting."

"*Resting?*" She tossed her head scornfully, her terror diminishing because of something in his expression, something gentle and unthreatening. "A likely tale!"

Despite his pain, Oliver peered up at her appreciatively. "*Am* I dreaming?" he asked through lips that were cracked and stiff. "You are most decidedly a creature of fantasy—something created by my overwrought imagination, I suspect—but this deuced headache seems real enough."

Varney, meanwhile, having snatched up a pitchfork, jumped up on the step on the other side of the carriage, threw open the door, and prodded the interloper with the tines. " 'Ere, you. What're you up to?"

"Nothing," Oliver said, forced to turn his attention to this new arrival. He pushed the pitchfork aside. "Nothing at all. You and your pitchfork, old fellow, have succeeded in convincing me I'm *not* dreaming. Put it away, will you? You don't need any weapons. I mean no harm."

Varney, getting his first glimpse of Oliver's face, sucked in his breath. "Blimey! It's a bleedin' maulin' you've taken! Were ye trodden on by a fleein' stallion?"

"Almost," Oliver said, grimacing ruefully. "I was trounced by an iron fist."

"You prob'ly deserved it. What're ye doin' here, chappie? Up to some mischief, I'll be bound."

MacDamon, yapping wildly, had been leaping from Varney to Moira and back again, as if warning them not to lay a hand on his master. Oliver, despite the excruciating pain it caused him, bent down, scooped up the mongrel, and tried to calm him. "Hush, Mac, hush. Don't take offense. This gentleman didn't mean to insult me."

Varney gave a snort. "Didn't I just? Speak up, man. What're you up to?"

The effort of bending had made Oliver dizzy. "I give you both my word," he said, lying back down on the seat, "that I came in here only to get out of the rain."

"That's prob'ly a hum," Varney said suspiciously, "but I

ain't no magistrate. It ain't up to me to make judgments. What do *you* want to do wi' him, Miss Moira?"

"*Do* with him?" Moira, who'd been studying the trespasser's bruised face with a horrified fascination, looked over at the groom in surprise. "I haven't the slightest idea. Must we do something? Why can't we just let him go on his way?"

The groom shrugged. "Seems to me we should do more 'n just let 'im go. We ought t' get 'is name, at least. When a stranger comes sneakin' in like—"

Moira gasped. "Did you say *stranger*?"

"That I did, ma'am. An' that's whut 'e is. I ain't seen 'im before, 'ave you?"

Moira turned pale. From the moment she'd heard the snore, the purpose for which she'd come had slipped from her mind. But the word *stranger* brought everything rushing back to her consciousness. "Oh, my *God*!" she murmured, aghast. "He *is* a stranger! The first one I've laid eyes on today!"

Both the groom and the trespasser stared at her curiously. "Yes, ma'am," Varney said, puzzled. "Ain't that whut I said?"

She winced, her heart sinking like lead in her chest. "He's the one, then . . ."

Varney wondered if she'd turned balmy. "The *one*?"

"Yes, God help me, the one." She peered at Oliver in undisguised horror for a long moment. Then she expelled a long breath. "Will you come down, please, sir?" she said in a shaken voice. "I want to take a better look at you."

She stepped down from the carriage and stood back as Oliver obligingly but painfully lifted himself out of the carriage seat. His head swam as he climbed down, the dog still in his arms. Swaying dizzily, he looked down at his damp, stockinged feet and realized in hideous embarrassment that he looked frightfully pathetic. His brother would be ashamed of him. He could almost hear John's voice: *I hope, Oliver, that you will bring no shame to the Sherrard name.*

By sheer force of will, he straightened up and tried not to reveal how awkward he felt standing before this lovely creature in his still damp shirt and stockinged feet. "Forgive me, ma'am," he muttered shamefacedly. "They took my boots, you see. And my coat . . ."

"Robbed, were ye?" Varney asked, coming round the carriage to stand beside his mistress.

"Yes," Oliver said. "Of everything I own."

"Too bad, if it's true," the groom observed.

"It's all too true. I've the lump on my head to prove it."

Varney went to look. "It's a lump all right, Miss Moira," he said. "The poor fellow's been sorely mauled. Where did this 'appen to ye, laddie?"

"Just a little way down the road."

The groom shook his head sympathetically. "What were ye doin' round these parts? Lookin' fer work?"

Oliver hesitated. He was not the sort to lie, but he'd promised his brother he'd not bring shame on the family. It would be better, he decided, to let them think what they liked than to tell them the truth. Besides, he was too dizzy and in too much pain to go into details. "Yes," he murmured. "Looking for work."

Moira gazed at him, her initial despair moderating to a cautious hopefulness. The man's face was certainly appalling, but it was possible that once his bruises healed and the swellings went down, his appearance would be less revolting. He did, after all, have gentle eyes. And despite his sore and swollen mouth, he spoke fairly well. Almost like a gentleman. In fact, when he'd called her a fantasy, she'd quite liked the compliment.

She walked slowly round him, studying him carefully from top to bottom. "Not really tall," she murmured, "but passable. Good shoulders. Very decent posture . . ."

"I beg pardon, ma'am," Oliver said, a spark of amusement flaring up in him despite his dizzying pain, "but are you measuring me for a suit of clothes?"

"Quite possibly I am," she retorted. "What is your name, may I ask?"

"Oli—" he began and then, remembering his brother, wanted to bite his tongue. "Thomas Oliver, ma'am," he corrected.

"Well, Mr. Oliver, you seem to be of sound mind and, except for your bruises, in good health."

"Yes, ma'am," he said, bewildered. With his head pounding, his mouth stiff, and his whole body so unsteady that he wondered how he remained erect, he didn't see how he could be said to be in good health, but he let it pass.

"And you are looking for work?"

"Yes, ma'am." He grinned at her, though it hurt his lips to smile. "I'm in dire need of work, as you can see. I'd do anything to earn a pair of boots."

Moira felt her tension ease. There was something decidedly appealing in this fellow's grin, despite the distortion of the rest of his face. There was no menace in that smile, but rather a sign of inner sweetness. At least the fellow was no monster. So there was nothing for it, now, but to go ahead and ask him. "Well, Mr. Oliver," she said bravely, "I have a proposition for you that will certainly earn you a pair of boots. And a new coat as well."

"Now, Miss Moira," the groom cautioned, "per'aps you shouldn't be too 'asty in takin' this fellow in yer employ. You don't even know whut 'e *is*, or whut he kin *do*. He might be a *thatchgallows*—"

"Quiet, Varney. Stay out of this." She came a step closer to her prey. "Are you interested, Mr. Oliver?"

The throbbing in Oliver's head was getting worse. He felt an urgent desire to shut his eyes and sink to the ground, but he fought it off by blinking at the girl intently. "Very interested, ma'am," he said with an effort. "I swear I'm no thatchgallows. And as for what I can do, well . . ."

"Yes, laddie, whut *can* you do?" the groom demanded.

"I've no special training, but I think I can take care of horses. I certainly can drive them. Or I can chop wood, or whitewash walls, or milk cows, if you have a dairy." He grinned woozily at the thought of all these talents he'd suddenly developed. "I can scythe the lawn, or polish the silver, or do any kind of fetching and carrying. I don't think I can cook, but I'd be willing to learn. I'll try anything, ma'am. Anything at all."

Moira took a deep breath and looked him squarely in the eye. "Then, Mr. Oliver, will you be good enough to marry me?"

CHAPTER
❦ ❦
SEVEN

WHAT'S THAT, MA'AM?

That was the question Oliver wanted to ask, but before he could get the words out, he felt himself lose balance and lurch forward like a drunken sot. He thought he would topple over, but he managed to steady himself. Dizzy and confused, he was nevertheless quite certain he hadn't heard the lady rightly. Something was decidedly amiss in his head, he decided. The cudgel-blow must have damaged his brain. He was suffering all sorts of strange symptoms. There was this quirk in his hearing, for one thing; he could have sworn the lady had said something about marriage. His sense of balance was upset, for another. And his eyesight was becoming fuzzy. Something was very wrong with him.

He put a hand to his throbbing forehead and tried to focus his eyes on the lady's face. "I'm sorry, ma'am," he asked thickly. "What did you say?"

Moira, so uncomfortably aware of Varney's popeyed gape that she barely noticed Oliver's stumble, reddened. "I asked if you would marry me."

Oliver shook his head, causing the whole stable to spin around. "I . . . must apologize, ma'am. Not . . . myself today. I keep hearing the . . . strangest . . ." His knees gave way, and he sank down on them, dropping MacDamon from his suddenly lifeless arms. The dog landed on his feet and peered up at Oliver, yapping worriedly. Oliver, however, could only sit back on his heels and let his head fall forward. He seemed not to have enough energy to lift it up.

"Good God!" Moira gasped, instinctively grabbing him under his arms to keep him from toppling over. "What *is* it, Mr. Oliver? What's wrong?"

"The lad's 'ad a terrible bad blow," Varney said, lifting Oliver's head and peering into his eyes. "Can you 'old him like that fer a minute, Miss Moira? I've a bottle o' spirits in my room."

As he ran off, MacDamon began to leap up and down, attempting to jump high enough to lick Oliver's face. Oliver barely had the strength to smile at him. "Mac, you . . . poor li'l fellow. Needn't be upset. I'll be better . . . soon. Just need a minute to . . . catch my breath . . ."

Varney returned in a trice and held a bottle to Oliver's lips. Oliver took a hefty swig. The liquor burned his gullet, though it seemed to clear his head and sharpen his eyesight. But something in his stomach rebelled at taking more of it. He coughed and pushed the bottle away.

"Better?" Varney asked.

"I think so."

Varney frowned. "The lad needs a doctor, if you was to ask me, Miss Moira."

Moira bent over him. "If we help you up, Mr. Oliver, do you think you could walk?"

"Yes, I think so. But where—?"

"I kin fix 'im in a straw pallet in one o' the empty stalls," the groom offered.

"No, he'll do better at the house. Come, Varney, give me a hand with him."

George Varney thought his mistress was behaving very strangely indeed. What had she meant when she said that strange thing about marrying? And why on earth would she wish to take this battered, impoverished stranger up to the manor house? But it was not his place to question her. He shrugged and, grasping Oliver under the arms, heaved him to his feet. Then, with Moira supporting the dazed fellow on one side and the groom on the other, they made their way slowly to the door.

MacDamon came trotting behind them, whimpering. Oliver turned his head. "My dog—!"

"Don't you worry none about yer animal," Varney assured him. "I'll take care of 'im."

Oliver shook his head. "I don't know where you're taking me . . . but if the dog doesn't go, I . . . don't go either."

Varney looked over at his mistress. "Well, ma'am?"

Moira shrugged. "Very well, let him come."

" 'Is lordship won't like a mongrel dog in the 'ouse," Varney pointed out.

Moira laughed ruefully. "There's so much in this affair that his lordship won't like, Varney, that the dog will be the very least of it!"

It took the strength of all three of them to make it to the house. The footman who opened the door was so startled by the sight of them that he actually gaped. Moira frowned at him. "Close your mouth, Henry, and help Varney get this fellow upstairs!"

The footman closed his mouth, but his face continued to express his shock. "*Upstairs*, miss?"

"Yes. The green bedroom, I think. And tell Greta to find some nightclothes for him. Do you think you can manage to undress him by yourself, or shall I send for Pearce?"

"I'm right here, Miss Moira," the butler said, hurrying across the hall. "Has there been an accident?"

"So it seems. Will you send someone to fetch Dr. Dunning?"

Oliver was only dimly aware of what was going on around him. Exhausted by the walk from the stable, he was near the end of his tether. The pounding in his head was so painful that his very brain felt rattled. In addition, the sharpening effect of the liquor he'd drunk had worn off; his vision and his thinking had become fuzzy again. He tried to think clearly, but the pain and dizziness made all his thoughts distorted, as in a nightmare. The beautiful girl who'd brought him here was being extraordinarily kind, he knew, but the reason for that kindness was not at all clear. She wanted something from him . . . something strange . . . and he felt quite uneasy about it.

Perhaps, he thought, it would be better not to become too indebted to her. "Too kind," he mumbled aloud, "but I don't need . . . a doctor . . ."

The butler, meanwhile, was eyeing the mongrel dog with loathing. "Shall I also have this . . . er . . . *animal* removed, Miss Moira?" he asked.

"Good God, what's all this?" came a voice from the corridor to their right. It was Horatio coming from the library with the *Times* under his arm.

Before Moira could answer, Barbara emerged from the corridor on their left, where she'd been engaged with her seamstress in the small sitting room until the noise from the entry hall had drawn her out. "Moira!" she gasped, staring at Oliver in horror. "Who—?"

"It's a *thief*! Varney's captured a thief!" This last came from Alberta, who was coming down the stairway. She goggled at Oliver's bloody face for a moment and then, clutching her distended belly, gave a horrified cry. "Oh, my heavens!" she wailed. "Just *look* at him! It's lucky we weren't all *murdered* in our *beds*!"

"Come, come, my love," Horatio said, running up to her side and taking her hand, "don't take on so. He's not a thief. I think there's been an accident. Let Moira explain—"

But Alberta's wails had set MacDamon to barking, and suddenly everyone began to talk at once. Pearce ordered the footman to quiet the dog; Barbara begged desperately to learn who it was her sister had dragged in from the road; Alberta continued to indulge in hysterics despite her husband's attempts to calm her; Varney tried to explain to the butler that the dog was brought in on his mistress's express order; and Moira herself made repeated attempts to convince the bemused servants to follow her instructions and get the poor stranger to bed.

In the midst of this uproar, Lord Pattinger himself appeared on the landing above them. "What the devil is the meaning of this?" he bellowed.

Everyone fell silent at once and looked up at him. The tension in the room, already palpable, grew a great deal worse. Even MacDamon felt it and stopped barking. Barbara began to

tremble. Alberta whitened as if she were about to faint. Horatio
stiffened in alarm, although he wasn't sure why; no part of this
scene had anything to do with him, but he feared he would be
blamed for something anyway. The butler, having been caught
holding the filthy mongrel dog in his arms, braced himself for
a tongue-lashing. Varney, who always dressed in livery when
he was summoned to the house but was now wearing only his
rumpled, dirty work clothes, wished he could slip away
unnoticed. Oliver, despite his dazed condition, could sense that
the atmosphere had undergone a change—that a person of
impressive power had made an appearance—and he looked up,
too, trying to focus his eyes on the tall figure who stood behind
the railing of the landing and glared down at them.

"I asked a question," came his lordship's icy voice. "What
is going on down there?"

Moira stepped forward. "It is only a welcoming party,
Father," she said bravely, ignoring the frightened beating of
her heart. "To greet my new intended."

If there can be such a thing as a silent gasp, it occurred at
that moment. Everyone drew in a silent breath. Every eye fixed
itself on Oliver's face. If the bruises, swellings, discolorations,
and smeared blood were not noted before, they were now.
Noted, too, were his filthy shirt, his matted hair, his stocking-
clad feet.

"Intended?" his lordship asked in disbelief. "*That* is your
intended?"

"Yes, Father. May I present Mr. Thomas Oliver? Mr. Oliver,
the gentleman looking down on us is my father, Lord Pattinger."

Oliver didn't grasp what was going on, but he knew an
introduction when he heard one. He looked up at the landing
and tried to smile. "How do you do, my lord?" he asked, dazed
but polite.

His lordship leaned over the railing, his ice-blue eyes fixed
on his eldest daughter's face. "Is this some sort of jest? If it is,
miss, you have a streak of vulgarity in you that I didn't know
existed."

"I'm not jesting, Father. I told you last evening I would do
it. Mr. Oliver is the man I pledged to find—the first stranger to
cross my path. I've asked him to marry me. Of course he's not,

at the moment, in any condition to accept my offer, but I hope he will do so in time. You will consider my proposal once you're feeling better, won't you, Mr. Oliver?"

Oliver squinted at the charming face so close to his own. He could make out the gleam of her red curls, the wonderful green eyes, the appealingly full lips. It was beyond a doubt the loveliest face he'd ever seen. But he was aware that his grasp of reality was becoming very weak. This was some sort of dream, he told himself, a most interesting dream. If he didn't have this deuced headache, he would be enjoying it to the hilt. But a black cloud seemed to be filtering in on the edges of his vision, threatening to obliterate this delicious view. He blinked, trying to hold on to the sight of her. "Delighted to . . . consider it, ma'am," he muttered thickly. "No one in the . . . world I'd rather . . . wed."

Then something in his legs gave way. He felt himself pitch forward. The elegant, gold-veined marble floor seemed to be rising up to meet him. But before he struck the ground, that black cloud seeped in and blotted out all the light.

CHAPTER

❦ ❦

EIGHT

OLIVER'S NEXT CONSCIOUS THOUGHT WAS THAT THE ROOM HAD suddenly become very quiet. *Where has everyone gone?* he wondered. The pain in his head, though it still throbbed, had eased considerably. A moment ago it had been excruciating; now it could only be called mild. He felt so much better! It seemed miraculous to have made so quick a recovery.

His thought processes slowly began to activate themselves. It took a moment to realize that he was not on the marble floor where he'd fallen but was lying on his back in a bed . . . a very comfortable bed. The sheets smelled sweet and clean. Carefully he opened his eyes. He was looking up at a smooth white ceiling on which little patches of firelight flickered. He lifted himself up on an elbow and looked about him. He was ensconced in a high four-poster bed hung with flowered draperies. The draperies proved to be much more cheerful than the walls of the room in which he lay, walls that were painted a rather bilious green. Like a prisoner left alone in his cell for the first time, Oliver examined everything in the room with intense interest. He discovered that he faced a door flanked by two small tables and two portraits of frowning gentlemen with wigs, that on his right was a bank of three windows with a mirrored dressing table before it, and that on his left—besides a writing table, a commode, and a winged armchair—was the source of the flickers on the ceiling: the fireplace in which a cheerful fire was burning. But the discovery that made him sit up with a start was that the armchair was occupied. In it sat a drowsing girl.

He stared at the creature in some perturbation. To the best of his recollection, he'd never seen her before. What was a strange young woman doing in his bedroom? Or—a much more reasonable question—was *he* in *her* bedroom? The question made him grin. What could be more to a young man's liking than to wake up in the bedroom of a strange young lady? When he'd set out on his trip, this sort of adventure was just what he had in the back of his mind. But if he *were* going to wake up in the bedroom of some strange female, he rather hoped it would be the redhead he'd just been dreaming of . . . the one who, in his befogged fantasy, had asked him to marry her.

Not that *this* particular female was in any way repulsive. She was a very pretty little thing, with soft brown hair braided round her head and dark lashes brushing against plump pink cheeks. But who was she?

It was then that Oliver became aware that someone or something else was in the room. There was some movement in a low-sided basket near the hearth. As he peered at it, a pointed ear rose up out of it, immediately followed by the rest of a familiar canine head. It was MacDamon. "Mac!" Oliver cried joyfully.

The animal peered over at him for a moment, as if he were trying to determine if the man he was looking at was indeed real. Then, his tail wagging madly, the dog bounded from the basket, trundled on his little legs across the room, leaped up into Oliver's arms, and, yapping crazily, licked Oliver's face in demented ecstasy.

The stir awakened the girl in the chair. "Mr. Oliver!" she exclaimed. "You're awake!"

"How do you do?" Oliver said awkwardly, trying to hold the excited MacDamon down.

The girl jumped to her feet and clapped her hands. "Awake at last! How wonderful!"

"Wonderful?" Oliver echoed, puzzled.

"Well, yes. We were beginning to fear you'd never— But

here you are, wide awake and looking quite alert! Moira will be so glad!"

Oliver peered at her in some alarm. Nothing she said quite made sense. Was he still befogged? "Are you saying that I've been asleep for some time?" he asked.

"Oh, yes. Four days and a half."

"Four *days*—?" Oliver could scarcely believe her.

"Yes, indeed. Dr. Dunning did warn us that you'd sleep for a long spell, but even *he* didn't expect it to be quite so protracted a sleep as that." The girl came up to the bed, piled up the pillows behind him, and gently urged him back against them. "Now, you mustn't try to get up, Mr. Oliver. Even your little dog mustn't be permitted to excite you."

MacDamon, as if he understood and feared she would take him away, dived with a whine under the blanket and snuggled against Oliver's side. He was not going to be parted from his master again, not if he could help it!

"I can't believe that a little dog like MacDamon can do me any harm, ma'am," Oliver said, patting his pet fondly.

"Is that the creature's name? MacDamon? How very odd. But you must be careful, Mr. Oliver, and not frolic about with the animal. Dr. Dunning says that you must have complete bed rest for a fortnight at least. You've had a severe concussion."

"Concussion? Really?"

"Yes. That's what the doctor called it. It refers to the injury to the skull caused by a blow violent enough to cause the brain to become somewhat engorged with blood."

"Good God!" Oliver exclaimed, putting his hand to the back of his head to feel the lump. It was there, but much diminished.

"Yes, having blood engorging one's brain is an appalling thought, isn't it?" the girl remarked in cheerful sympathy while she poured water into a glass from a pitcher on the nightstand. "But you are not to worry. Dr. Dunning bled the swelling right away, and he is certain you'll make a complete recovery." She handed him the glass. "He is not quite so sanguine about the injury to your nose, however. I'm afraid that even when it heals, you'll always have a little bump just below the bridge."

"Will I, indeed?" He lifted his hand to his nose and discovered that a thick bandage had been plastered over it.

"Damnation!" he muttered. "I suspected that the deuced pugilist had broken it!" *This is a fine mess;* he thought. *When next John gets a look at me; I'll have to endure a good, loud I-told-you-so!*

"Don't look so downhearted, Mr. Oliver," the girl said soothingly. "Dr. Dunning intends to remove the plaster quite soon."

Oliver nodded. Then, realizing he was dreadfully thirsty, he drank down the water she'd given him in one gulp. "I'm giving you a great deal of trouble," he said gratefully, handing her back the glass, "and I don't even know who you are."

"I'm Barbara, Moira's sister," she said. "And speaking of Moira, I must go and fetch her. She will want to know that you've awakened." She walked briskly to the door, but there she paused. "I wonder, Mr. Oliver . . ." she said, turning back. "Er . . . before I go for Moira, might I ask you something? Something of a . . . a personal nature?"

"I'd be the world's worst ingrate to refuse you anything, ma'am," he assured her. "Ask away."

She came to the side of the bed and looked down at him hesitantly. "I've been wondering if . . . if you truly intend to marry her."

Oliver blinked. There was that word again. Marry. Perhaps his hearing was still affected by the blow. Perhaps blood on the brain made one hear strange things. "Marry . . . ?" he asked cautiously.

"You see, she's only doing this out of pique. Not that I blame her, of course, but pique cannot be a good basis for wedlock, don't you agree?"

"I most certainly do, ma'am, although, you know, I'm no expert on such matters."

The girl nodded with a kind of urgent eagerness. "Oh, I'm *so* glad you agree! Then I assume you'll also agree that one wouldn't want to rush headlong into a marriage and then discover, when it is too late, that one's partner is unsuitable. And anyone with sense would understand that it couldn't possibly be suitable for the daughter of a viscount to wed a fellow who wandered into her stable looking for work. Oh, I don't mean to disparage you, Mr. Oliver, not at all. I'm certain that you have many fine qualities, but, after all, Moira *is* the daughter of a peer of the realm!"

"Is she indeed?" Oliver murmured.

Barbara rattled on urgently, as if she hadn't heard the interruption. "I've thought and thought about this, you see, and since I know that Moira will not listen to *me,* I've decided that my only recourse is to reach her through you. If she persists in her intention of going through with this ridiculous plan, perhaps *you* can be the one to dissuade her. Please, Mr. Oliver, tell her that I'm even willing to give up Godfrey if it will change her mind."

"Godfrey?"

"If she's willing to take him back, you must convince her that giving Godfrey up will not b-break my heart." She twisted her hands together, and her pretty eyes filled with tears. "Hearts don't break so easily, I'm t-told," she went on bravely. "I'm quite willing to stay here and . . . and to d-devote my life to Father in her place. Will you do your best to convince her of that?"

"I would be quite willing to try, ma'am," he answered softly, "if I knew what you were talking about."

The girl's face fell, and she gaped at him. "Mr. Oliver! What do you mean?"

"I mean, ma'am, that I don't know anything about marrying anyone. How can I marry someone whose name I don't know? Well, to be honest, I have a feeling I may have heard the name Moira before, but I'm not certain. But I am sure I've never heard of this Godfrey. The truth is, I don't have an inkling of the meaning of any of the complicated problems you've referred to. And what's worse, ma'am, I don't even know where I am!"

"Oh, dear!" Barbara exclaimed in alarm. She stared at him for a moment and then put a hand to his forehead. "This is dreadful, Mr. Oliver! I'm afraid the blow on your head has made you forget the past!"

"No, ma'am, it hasn't. I know quite well who I am, where I came from and where I was going before certain unforeseen events forced me to seek refuge in a stable. *Your* stable, I suspect. So, you see, the past is as clear as a bell in my mind. What is *not* clear is the *present*."

The bemused young lady studied him worriedly a moment more and then backed to the door. "I'd better get Moira. Just rest, Mr. Oliver. Everything will be fine. I'm sure your memory will come back in a day or two. Just rest." And with those not-so-comforting words, she whisked herself out the door.

Oliver stared bewilderedly after her. She'd looked at him as if he'd lost his mind. But he felt sane enough. Quite clear-headed, really. There was not a sign remaining of the hallucinatory impressions he'd had earlier. And there was nothing wrong with his memory, either. He remembered leaving Surrey, he remembered the night at the Twin Elms, he remembered the pair who accosted him on the road, he even remembered climbing into the phaeton in the dark stable and going to sleep. "I even remember you, Mac, old fellow," he said, lifting the dog up to take a better look at him. "Good God, MacDamon, what have they done to you? You're looking almost respectable. They've bathed you and combed you and probably even wormed you. If we don't take care, you may become too grand for a penniless vagabond like me."

The dog nuzzled him in an unmistakable declaration of undying loyalty. The door opened at that moment. Oliver looked up to see a woman's face peeping in at him, the rest of her hidden behind the door. The face was not familiar, but the brown hair and plump cheeks were very like Barbara's. This, he guessed, was the sister.

"He's awake," the woman said to someone outside.

"Come in," Oliver urged, hiding his disappointment that his visitor was, again, not the red-haired lady. "You must be Moira."

"Good heavens! Me?" the lady said, entering. "Of course I'm not Moira."

She was followed in by a slim fellow with a receding hairline, thin lips, and a pair of intelligent, friendly eyes behind thick spectacles perched on his nose.

Oliver was surprised to see that the lady was big with child.

"I'm Alberta," she said in a high-pitched, nervous voice, "and this is my husband, Lord Becclesworth."

"How do you do?" Oliver said politely. "Forgive me for not getting up."

"We quite understand," Horatio assured him with a wan smile. "Dr. Dunning gave us an explicit explanation of your condition."

The lady looked down at Oliver with a frown. "How can you have mistaken me for Moira, Mr. Oliver? We do not look at all alike."

"I beg your pardon, Lady Becclesworth. I'm afraid I'm not doing very well with identities. I'm not familiar with the family structure, you see."

"Then let me refresh your memory. I'm Moira's sister."

"You, too, ma'am?" Oliver grinned up at her. "Are there many of you? I hope not, for I'm finding myself confused enough already."

"There are four sisters, but only three in residence," Horatio explained in a kindly way. "Moira is the eldest, Susan is the next—she lives in Shrewsbury—then comes Alberta and finally there's—"

"I think I can guess," Oliver said triumphantly. "Barbara."

"Right!" Horatio gave him an approving nod.

But Alberta continued to study him worriedly, unable to understand how he and Moira had managed to come to an understanding when the fellow knew so little about the family he intended to marry into. "I'm glad to find you awake, Mr. Oliver," she said after an awkward pause. "I've been most eager to have a private chat with you."

"Have you, ma'am?"

"Oh, yes! You've been very much on our minds—Horatio's and mine—since the first moment we laid eyes on you, when you came tottering into the Great Hall all bruised and bloody. You gave us quite a turn that day, I can tell you! We thought you were a murderer!"

Her husband reddened. "Bertie, my love, that is not kind."

"That's all right, sir," Oliver said. "I know I must have been a sight that day."

"But you're looking so much better now, truly," Alberta

assured him, giving him a conciliatory smile to make up for her former slight. But her smile immediately faded, and she put a hand against her back, as if in pain, and sighed loudly.

"Is there something bothering you, my love?" her husband asked solicitously.

"Yes, I'm growing tired. Horatio, my dear, please bring me that bench from the dressing table so that I might sit down and talk to Mr. Oliver properly." She turned to Oliver and blushed. "I cannot stand on my feet for very long these days, you see. My condition . . ."

The bench was brought, and Horatio assisted his wife in lowering herself upon it. When she was made comfortable, she looked over at Oliver with knit brows. "You mustn't do it, Mr. Oliver," she said in sepulchral tones.

Oliver blinked at her. "Do what, ma'am?"

"Marry Moira. You mustn't. It would be disastrous for everyone!"

Horatio colored uncomfortably. "You can't be sure of that, my dear. You promised you wouldn't say these things."

"Well, it *would* be disastrous. The daughter of a viscount wedding a gardener. It is too ridiculous to think of!"

"But we don't even know if he *is* a gardener," Horatio muttered, embarrassed.

"That's what Varney said he is," Alberta retorted. She looked at Oliver questioningly. "Isn't that true, Mr. Oliver? Didn't you tell Varney you're a gardener?"

"Varney?" Oliver asked, playing for time.

"Our groom. Don't you remember him?"

"Oh, the old fellow in the stable," Oliver murmured, his brow clearing. "Yes, of course I remember him. He prodded me with a pitchfork."

"Then do you also remember telling him you're a gardener?"

Oliver shrugged. "I might have done so."

Alberta threw her husband a look of triumph. "There! I told you so!"

Horatio shook his head. "He also told him he was a groom. And a general factotum."

"A great deal of difference *that* makes!" she told her

husband dismissively. "They are all equally inappropriate for Moira, are they not?"

"But, my love, it is not up to us to tell Moira how to live her life!" Horatio remonstrated. "You promised you wouldn't say these things."

"I can't help it," Alberta said, looking down at her clenched hands shamefacedly. "I never seem able to keep myself from speaking my mind."

"Then let *me* say what we came to say," Horatio said. He put his hand on his wife's shoulder and faced Oliver squarely. "As you may have gathered, Mr. Oliver, it is our hope that this union between you and Moira will never come to pass. But if it does, we have a favor to ask of you. We beg that you will not do it until we have moved away from Pattinger Downs."

"Oh?" Oliver asked noncommittally.

"Our move will come soon—surely not more than three months hence," Alberta added. "We're hoping that Beccles-worth Manor will be ready for us much sooner, but we must be prepared for the worst."

Oliver remained silent, waiting for a further explanation.

Horatio did not keep him waiting long. "I see that you're wondering what *your* marriage plans have to do with *our* moving," he said earnestly. "I can only explain by saying that you will understand us when you become better acquainted with Lord Pattinger."

"My father is not an easy man to live with," Alberta admitted, pulling a handkerchief from her sleeve and sniffing into it. "When he is angry or in one of his moods, he has a way of making the lives of everyone else perfectly miserable."

"*Very* miserable," Horatio agreed.

"And if Moira weds you, I dread to think . . ." Here she began to twist the handkerchief so nervously that her fingernail tore right through the cloth.

"My wife is quite right," Horatio murmured, squeezing Alberta's shoulder comfortingly. "If Moira weds without his approval, his lordship will be utterly impossible to bear."

"He is so unkind to Horatio even at the best of times," Alberta said tearfully. "And as to his manner toward me, well, he could always reduce me to tears. And now that I'm breeding . . ."

"Breeding does tend to make a female so much more . . . sensitive, you know . . ." Horatio explained awkwardly.

"So you see, Mr. Oliver," Alberta said, her eyes moist and beseeching, "we feel we must *beg* you to postpone any wedding plans until after we leave, or life will be dreadful beyond imagining. Will you promise us—?"

A tap on the door interrupted her. She stiffened and looked up at her husband in alarm.

Oliver, however, was relieved at the interruption. "Come in," he called. The door opened. In the doorway, looking every bit as lovely as he remembered, stood the lady with the red hair. She was not an apparition or a figment of his imagination, but as real as the bandage on his nose, the pillows at his back, or the mongrel in his arms. His heart began to beat, and his spirit, for the first time since he'd left home, lifted to the sky.

But the lady was not looking at him. She was peering at her sister and brother-in-law in surprise. "Horatio! Bertie! Here already? The fellow has scarcely been awake a quarter of an hour. Who told you—?"

Both Alberta and her Horatio reddened this time. "Everyone knows," Alberta said hastily.

"Naturally," the new arrival said with a hopeless sigh. "How could I let myself think otherwise? But did you think it was necessary to come and importune him the moment he woke up?"

Alberta's eyes fell. "We just wanted to tell Mr. Oliver how glad we are that he's finally awake."

"Of course," the red-haired lady retorted. "What *other* reason could you have for accosting the poor fellow so soon?"

"We had no other reason, I assure you," Alberta declared.

Horatio, uncomfortable with his wife's fabrications, winced. "We were just leaving," he mumbled, helping Alberta to her feet. That accomplished, he put his arm about her waist and hurriedly ushered her out of the room.

The new arrival closed the door firmly behind them and finally turned her attention to Oliver. "So . . . you *are* awake," she said.

"I hope so," he answered. "I'd like to be certain you're not a dream."

She crossed the room to his bedside and smiled down at him. "You may take my word, Mr. Oliver, that I'm no dream."

"Splendid," he said with a grin. "That's splendid. In that case, ma'am, do you think you might tell me your name?"

"Don't try to pretend you haven't guessed it by now. I'm Moira."

"Moira!" he sighed. "At last!"

CHAPTER

❧ ❧

NINE

MOIRA WOULD NOT PERMIT HIM TO ASK QUESTIONS. INSTEAD, SHE insisted that he drink some soup, a kindness for which his empty stomach was extremely grateful. After that, he tried again to learn why she'd taken him in and what she wanted of him, but she merely shook her head, called in a footman to wash him and change his nightshirt, and took her leave.

After the footman had completed his tasks and withdrawn, Oliver found himself at last without company. "Except, of course, for you, MacDamon," he said to the animal who had done his loyal best to keep the footman from attacking his master with soap and water.

With no one in the room to object, Oliver took the opportunity to test his condition. He sat up, threw his legs carefully over the side of the bed, and gingerly got to his feet. He expected to feel dizzy, but his head was perfectly steady. "See, Mac?" he said to the dog who was yipping happily at his heels, "I'm not so badly off." Relieved, he walked on bare feet to the dressing table and peered at himself in the mirror. The sight of his face shocked him. There was a purplish bruise round his left eye, the right side of his chin was still discolored and swollen, his just-washed hair hung down in wet clumps over his forehead, and, worst of all, the lumpy white plaster bandage over his nose made him look like a gargoyle. He groaned aloud. *How,* he asked himself, *am I to make a favorable impression on a girl who's a veritable vision when I'm a veritable fright?*

The veritable vision appeared in the doorway at that moment. "Mr. Oliver!" she gasped. "Has no one bothered to inform you that you *must* remain in bed? You've had a severe concus—!"

"Concussion. I know." With his appalling face turned away from her, he hurried back to the bed, threw himself upon it, and pulled the covers up over him. MacDamon jumped up on the bed, too, and tried to nuzzle in, but Oliver made no opening for him.

Moira stalked up to the bedside and ordered MacDamon down. "Back to the basket, you nuisance," she said, pointing a firm finger toward the hearth. "I mean it! Go! I wish to talk to your master without interference."

The dog, recognizing firmness when he heard it, reluctantly did as she bid.

But Oliver was not so biddable. "I don't want to talk to anyone," he growled from under the blankets.

She laughed and pulled them away from his face. Tucking them neatly under his arms, she began to scold as she plumped up his pillows. "I hope you won't get up again, please, Mr. Oliver. Dr. Dunning was quite insistent about your being kept in bed."

"I felt fine on my feet," Oliver argued. "Really fine. That is, until I got a glimpse of this face."

Moira shook her head in disagreement. "You're looking better every day, I assure you. When Dr. Dunning removes that nose plaster, I shan't be surprised to discover that you're quite handsome."

"Huh!" Oliver grunted. "I wasn't handsome *before* I was mauled."

"Come now, Mr. Oliver. Surely you heard at your grandmother's knee that handsome is as handsome does."

His eyes drank in her lovely face, luminous in the firelight. "Easy for *you* to say, ma'am," he murmured.

"You mean that as a compliment, I know, but *my* grandmother used to say that *beauty buys no beef.* I set no great value on good looks."

"That's obvious, if—as I've heard—you're set on wedding me." *There,* he said to himself, *the subject is broached. Let's see if she takes it up.*

"As to that, Mr. Oliver," she said, her smile fading, "perhaps it's time for us to discuss that matter."

He pulled himself up higher and leaned back against the pillows. "I'm all ears, ma'am. Though I cannot be comfortable sitting like this while you are forced to remain standing. If you'd care to pull up that bench . . ."

She did so and perched upon it, the skirts of her figured muslin gown spreading out gracefully round her ankles. "You must find all of this very strange," she began.

"Only because I don't understand much of what people have been telling me," he said.

"I'll try to make the situation clear, Mr. Oliver, but I fear it will still be strange even when you understand the whole. The problem is my father."

"Viscount Pattinger?"

"Yes. He is a widower, and I am his eldest daughter. My mother died twenty years ago, when I was six. In these years, my father has grown to depend on me for . . . oh, for all sorts of things. The running of the household, for instance. And his correspondence. He has many acquaintances and much interest in the world of politics, and he relies on me to help him with his letters and writings." She sighed and looked down at the hands folded in her lap. "I don't do more for him than an efficient housekeeper and a good secretary could, but I fear he believes—quite mistakenly—that I'm indispensable to him." She paused for a moment, lost in her own thoughts.

"And you find his dependency onorous?" he asked, trying to surmise what her feelings were. "Are you feeling imprisoned by him?"

She looked up at him in some surprise. "How quick you are to grasp things, Mr. Oliver. That is exactly right."

"Yes, I've sometimes felt imprisoned by family obligations too," he explained.

"Oh?" She blinked at him in sudden concern. "You have a family, then? Not . . . a *wife!*"

"No, no," he answered promptly, amused at her alarm.

"Only one brother, who now has a family of his own and therefore no need of me. But when my father was alive I felt very much imprisoned by his demands on me. When I was finally able to go off on my own, the feeling of freedom was heady indeed."

"Then you do understand, Mr. Oliver. I'm very glad, because that makes it easier to explain the rest to you."

"My part in all this, you mean?"

"Yes. It is my goal to be able to leave this house, and one way to do it is to marry. But my father will not give his consent to my marrying, so I've threatened to marry without his consent. There is nothing to prevent my doing so, no matter what he may do, for I am of age, and I have some money of my own, from my mother. All I need is a bridegroom."

"Me?"

"Yes, Mr. Oliver, you."

He stared at her for a moment, nonplussed. "I beg your pardon, ma'am, but you're not making much sense. Anyone can see that you're a lady of birth, breeding, wealth and—if I may voice what is so obvious—breathtaking beauty. No one with such outstanding attributes should have to resort to taking as her bridegroom a penniless, coatless, bootless, battered-faced vagabond she found hiding from the elements in her father's stable."

"Yes, she should, if she is Moira Pattinger. My father has dissuaded every suitor I've ever had from offering for me." She lowered her eyes in shame. "Evidently my birth, wealth, and beauty were not enough to hold them."

He shook his head. "I find that almost impossible to believe," he insisted.

"Believe it, Mr. Oliver, for it's quite true. It happened three times."

"Good God, how did he dissuade them? With a gun to their heads?"

"His method was not nearly so drastic. He merely offered each of them a few thousand pounds and one of my sisters. It worked every time. Godfrey's defection to Babs was the final humiliation. That's when I swore I would wed the very next man I met. That man turned out to be you, Mr. Oliver."

"I see. So your sister Barbara was right. You *are* marrying out of pique."

"*Pique?*" She rose from her seat in outrage. "Do you think what I feel is merely *pique*? A much better word would be *fury*!"

"Well, neither pique nor fury seems to me to be a sound basis for a marriage."

"Who said it was? There is only one sound basis for marriage and that is love. But you can hardly have expected me to fall in love with the first man who came along!"

"No, of course not," Oliver agreed ruefully, rubbing his hand over his swollen chin. "Especially *this* man."

Moira's expression softened. "You needn't be so deucedly modest, Mr. Oliver," she said, sinking down on the bench again. "I'm sure that in the right circumstances, any number of females would find you lovable. But even if I didn't fall in love with you at first sight—something which I don't believe I'm capable of doing with *anyone*—I feel very fortunate that it was you I found in the stable. You are kind, intelligent, and will undoubtedly be quite prepossessing when your bruises fade. When I consider all the dreadful characters I *might* have encountered, I positively shudder. Why, I might have come upon a drunken sot or a . . . a . . ."

"A thatchgallows?" Oliver suggested.

"Yes, exactly."

"I can't argue *that* point. I may not be an Adonis, but at least I'm no gallows bird."

"So I feel quite fortunate, you see. That is, if I can convince you to accept my proposal."

"And if I don't?"

"Then I shall have to go out and find someone else. And he might very well *be* a gallows bird."

Oliver eyed her askance. "Hmmmm," he said, frowning.

"Hmmmm is not an answer, Mr. Oliver. Do you intend to help me or not?"

"It seems to me, Miss Moira Pattinger, that for a clever female you have concocted a very stupid scheme."

She stiffened in offense. "*Stupid*, Mr. Oliver?"

"Stupid, ma'am. To escape the prison made by an overbearing father, you are choosing to enter another one that might possibly be worse."

"You think of marriage as a prison, then?"

"I think of marriage to a vagabond you hardly know as a very great risk."

"A risk for whom, sir? For you or for me?"

"Oh, it is no risk for *me*, ma'am! To have a wife like you is more than I could ever have expected or even dreamed of! The risk is all on your side."

"Ah, but the more I know you, Mr. Oliver, the less danger I see. Even your last statement shows me that you are kind and generous. When you point out that the risk is all mine, you're putting me above yourself."

"But what if this kindly manner of mine is all pretense, ma'am? How can you be sure that when I have you as wife, I won't beat you daily?"

She cocked her head at him, her eyes sparkling with amusement. "I dare you to try it!" she taunted. But then she sighed and turned serious. "Very well, Thomas Oliver, I can see there's no point in teasing you on this matter any further. The truth is that I've not been fully open with you yet, but I think it's now time to take you fully into my confidence. My plan is not quite as stupid as you think. I don't mean for us to *actually* wed each other but only to make the family believe we intend to."

His brow furrowed. "I don't understand. You don't want to wed me after all?"

"Not in the end. Don't look so confused, Thomas. May I call you Thomas?"

"You may call me anything you like, so long as you explain yourself clearly."

"It's quite simple. We will declare to the family that we are betrothed. When my father is convinced that I am serious, he will make all sorts of offers and bribes to prevent it, but if you remain steadfast, he will discover in the end that the only way to prevent our nuptials will be for him to concede to my wishes and let me go to my Aunt Joanna in London, which is all I really want. Then I'll break our troth, release you from all obligation to me, and you and I will be free to go our separate ways. You will have earned new boots, a new coat, and a great deal more—for I will pay you handsomely for your part in this—and I will have won my freedom."

"I see," Oliver said thoughtfully. "The thought of your taking a wretch like me for a husband will be so repugnant to your father that, to prevent it, he will at last succumb to your wishes. Is that it?"

Moira, belatedly realizing how offensive her plan might be in his eyes, lowered hers in shame. "I don't think of you as a wretch, Thomas. On the contrary, I've told you already that I consider myself most fortunate to have come upon you as I did. But surely you didn't *truly* expect me to wed you. You yourself said it would be stupid of me."

"Yes, I did. That was my very word. It is *I* who was stupid to think that you really intended to go through with it." It was strange, but he was really beginning to *feel* like the penniless vagabond he was pretending to be, and her rejection of him cut through him like a knife. "A destitute vagrant like me cannot expect to marry the daughter of a peer of the realm," he muttered, amazed at how hurt he felt.

Moira, seeing that she'd wounded him, winced. "Please, Thomas, stop! I don't think of you as a destitute vagrant."

"No? A destitute gardener, then? Or—what was it your groom called me?—a general factotum? The exact designation doesn't matter, does it? I would not be worthy of you in any of those guises." *Or even as Oliver Sherrard,* he added to himself bitterly. *A second son, without wealth or prospects, would not be considered suitable for such a woman.*

Moira pressed her lips together, realizing that she was merely using him. She had made her plan for her own advantage, without giving any thought to what he might feel. But she was helpless to know how to change matters now. What was done could not be undone. She'd brought him home and set them both on this road. She'd gone too far. There was no going back. "I think of you as a man I can trust," she said softly, trying by gentleness to ameliorate his pain. "But not as a husband. Surely you don't blame me for that."

He passed a hand over his forehead. "No, of course not," he said with glum sincerity. "I didn't really think you would actually wed me." Then, with a sudden shake of his head, he grinned. It was a broad grin, full of self-mockery, and only slightly dimmed by the merest shadow of disappointment. He had not come on this walking tour, he reminded himself, to get himself a wife. He'd come seeking adventure, and this lovely creature was offering one to him. To let himself wish for more from her had been a momentary lapse. "It will be my pleasure, ma'am, to help you in your scheme," he said with utmost sincerity. "It's quite the easiest way I could ever have thought of to earn new boots, and earning new boots was my intention from the first."

She expelled a long breath in relief. "Oh, I *am* glad. We shall both gain by this, I promise you. But it won't be as easy for you as you think. In the first place, you'll have to be very careful not to reveal our real plan to anyone in my family."

"Why not? Surely your sisters would wish to support you in this, if they knew your true intent."

"Yes, but nothing in this house can be kept secret. Everything that happens is spread like wildfire. If we told Babs or Bertie, or even Horatio, they would surely discuss it among themselves. Then one or another of the servants would overhear, and before an hour went by, my father would know the whole. Besides, it is best that my sisters remain upset by what they believe to be my intention. The more upset they are about my proposed nuptials, the more believable the scheme will seem to my father."

"Very well, I will be sure not to reveal the plot to anyone. What else?"

"What else?"

"You said 'in the first place' I was not to reveal the scheme. What is the second place?"

"That's the most difficult thing of all, I fear. You see, Thomas, you're going to be subjected to my father's threats and bribes. Both will be huge. I can only offer you five hundred pounds for your part in this."

"That is most generous, ma'am. Five hundred pounds would take a gardener more than ten years to earn."

"Yes, but my father may very well offer you several times

that amount to jilt me. If he does, you may find the money very hard to refuse."

"You cannot think very much of me, ma'am, if you believe I would betray you in that way. Don't you believe I have any honor?"

She rose and frowned down at him. "Three gentlemen have betrayed me already, Thomas, higher born and a great deal richer than you."

"Birth and wealth are no guarantees of honor, ma'am, as you have learned to your sorrow. On the other hand, sometimes even the poor and lowly have been known to act honorably. I've given you my word that I would help you. It's the word of a poor wretch of a man, but it's all I have to give."

Their eyes met. Hers glittered with unshed tears. "It suddenly occurs to me, Thomas Oliver, that *you* are the only one with honor in this whole enterprise." She took his hand in hers and stared down at it, fighting back an impulse to take it to her cheek. "Your word," she added softly, "is quite enough for me."

CHAPTER
❧ ❧
TEN

MOIRA DECIDED THAT THEY WOULD OFFICIALLY ANNOUNCE THEIR betrothal as soon as Mr. Oliver—Thomas—was well enough to get out of bed. Dr. Dunning, after examining his patient the next day, declared that the time would not be as long in coming as he'd first thought. "The fellow is doing remarkably well," he told Moira. "Perhaps he doesn't need a full fortnight's bed rest after all. If he continues to show his present alertness, I don't see why he shouldn't be allowed to get up in eight or ten days."

Moira was delighted with the doctor's news. She immediately began to make plans to hold a ball. "To celebrate Barbara's betrothal," she told her father, but her real reason was to create a properly public occasion in which to announce her own betrothal.

"I suppose we should give Barbara a bit of celebration," Lord Pattinger said in grudging acquiescence, relieved that his eldest daughter had nothing else to trouble him about. He'd feared, when Moira had entered his study with that purposeful stride of hers, that she would bring up the subject of that damned vagabond.

His lordship had chosen to ignore the presence of a vagrant in one of his guest rooms. He'd convinced himself that Moira's announcement that she wanted to wed the bloody vagabond had been only a vulgar jest to annoy him; she certainly couldn't have meant it. It was ridiculous to suppose she would throw herself away on an impoverished itinerant laborer. She probably intended nothing more than to show a little kindness to a person in need. If Moira wanted to offer the fellow a little care and hospitality, he would not be so petty as to stop her. Nor would he give her the satisfaction of making more of her idiotic marriage jest than the matter deserved. He would simply go on as usual, soiling neither his mind nor his dignity by giving the incident another thought. Therefore he didn't feel it necessary to rebuke her by refusing to let her give a ball for her sister. "Go ahead and hold your ball," he said to Moira when she asked his permission, "so long as you don't trouble me about it."

So Moira sent out invitations to her sister Susan and to various friends and neighbors, requesting their presence at a ball to be held a fortnight hence. She knew she might be hurrying the date, but she was eager to put her plan into action. She was counting on the doctor's prognostication that Thomas would continue to improve. If he did, he would be well enough in a fortnight to stand at her side and announce their betrothal. With the making of so public an announcement, her father would not be able to ignore the matter. The fat would be in the fire. She could hardly wait to see the flames flare up!

Oliver, meanwhile, was finding a good deal of amusement in his situation. Neither the servants nor the family knew quite what to make of him, and Oliver, still boyishly mischievous, couldn't help but be entertained by their discomfort. The hours of enforced bed rest were made less tedious by his observation of the awkward attitudes of his various visitors. The servants, for example, all regarded him with a comical mixture of awe and suspicion. Alberta, Lady Becclesworth, always spoke to him in a tone of such condescension that her innate conceit was hilariously apparent. Barbara, on the other hand, bent over backward to convince him that she thought well of him despite his low station in life. But, she made clear, her respect for him did not go so far as to win her approval of his marriage to her sister. Broad-mindedness could go only so far.

Barbara was the first one to call on him after Moira and he had come to their understanding. She had hardly finished saying good morning before reiterating her earlier request to him *not* to let Moira talk him into wedlock. "Did you tell Moira that I am willing to give Godfrey back to her?" she asked urgently.

"I'm afraid, Miss Barbara," Oliver said, hiding a grin, "that your sister is no longer interested in your Godfrey. She seems to prefer me."

"*You?*" Barbara blinked in disbelief. "I hope you won't take offense, Mr. Oliver, if I say that although I know you're a man of strength and good sense, I don't believe she could truly prefer you to a someone of Sir Godfrey Jayne's stamp."

Oliver shrugged in modest self-deprecation. "Your sister says that I have more character."

"*Character?*"

He nodded. "And more honor."

"*Honor!* Well, *really*, I—!" She gaped at him, almost too shocked for words.

"And that I'm better-looking, too," he added wickedly.

"Now *that's* going too far!" the girl declared, flouncing to the door. "You have kind eyes and a very pleasant smile, I admit, Mr. Oliver, but I'll have you know that Sir Godfrey Jayne is positively *magnificent*."

"Is he indeed?"

"Yes, he is. I can see by your expression that you don't believe me, but I'll prove it to you. I'll bring him up to you as soon as he calls, and *then* you'll see for yourself!"

"I shall be most happy to meet him," Oliver said, choking down the laugh that bubbled up in his throat. "Bring him up anytime."

But the girl had already stalked off, so he was able to release his pent-up laughter with a good loud roar.

He tried to behave better with Alberta, who came to see him, alone, just after he'd finished his luncheon. She ordered the footman, who'd come to remove his tray, to set a chair for her. When she'd made herself comfortable, she looked him over carefully. "You seem a good deal better today," she said complacently.

"Yes, ma'am," Oliver agreed. "Much better. The doctor says I shall be up and about in a little more than a week."

"I hope, Mr. Oliver, that you appreciate what we are doing

for you. It isn't every day that an itinerant laboring man finds himself in the best guest bedroom of a great house, being examined by the family's own physician, being waited on by their servants, being tended, in short, as if he were an honored guest."

"Yes, ma'am," Oliver said humbly. "I am very grateful, ma'am."

"I hope so. Why, I myself have actually called on you every day—and in my condition, too—just to see how you fare. I can't remember ever having condescended like this to a gardener before." She leaned forward and peered at him closely. "You *are* a gardener, isn't that right? We did ascertain that yesterday, didn't we?"

Alberta's persistence in trying to determine just where on the rungs of the social ladder to place him tickled Oliver's always ready sense of humor and undermined his determination to behave himself. "Well, ma'am," he drawled, "I don't know if I'd call myself a gardener, exactly. I can do gardening labor, if someone directs me. I can scythe a lawn, I suspect, without much assistance, but when it comes to weeding, I might as easily pull up a lily as a nettle."

"Are you saying you're *not* a gardener, then?" she asked in frustration.

"No, ma'am, I didn't say that either. I'd be happy to be your gardener if that's what you want me to be."

She could see that she was getting nowhere. With a sigh, she placed her hands on her swelling midsection and turned the conversation to her primary concern. "Tell me, Mr. Oliver, was anything decided between you and Moira last evening? Is she really determined to marry you?"

"I'm afraid, ma'am, that you'll have to ask Miss Moira. It would be presumptuous of me to make any sort of announcement until she gives me leave."

"Then I take it she has not yet made up her mind?" the woman prodded.

"I can't say."

Alberta sighed again. "You are not very forthcoming about anything, are you, Mr. Oliver? I suppose I shall have to be satisfied with these nonanswers. My only consolation in all of this is that the longer Moira dawdles in making up her mind, the better for me."

She terminated the interview shortly thereafter. Oliver spent the next hour watching MacDamon cavort over his bedcovers. Then, just as the shadows from the tree outside his windows were beginning to lengthen in late-afternoon gloom, Horatio called on him.

Oliver braced himself for further importuning, but none came. Horatio had no intention of digging for information. Unlike his wife, he was neither condescending nor curious. He merely came in, he said, to see how Mr. Oliver was feeling. In truth, however, he came in to have some purely masculine conversation. Having determined that Oliver was a clever fellow, and having had to endure months of listening to Alberta's complaints about her condition, he was eager for a change.

"I feel quite well," Oliver told him. "I don't even think I really need to be kept in bed."

"It's best to play it safe," Horatio said, taking the chair that his wife had vacated. "Dr. Dunning knows what he's doing. In your place, I would follow his advice."

"Very well, Lord Becclesworth," Oliver agreed. "Since you seem a sensible sort, I'll take your advice and listen to the doctor." Horatio did seem a sensible sort. That's why Oliver was puzzled by him. Moira had accused him of betrayal, but Horatio did not appear to be the the sort to betray anyone, especially someone like Moira. Oliver couldn't help wondering what Lord Pattinger had done to make Horatio give up his pursuit of Moira and marry Alberta. He therefore decided to do some prodding of his own. "On the subject of sensible advice, my lord," he asked cautiously, "can you tell me what to expect from Lord Pattinger, should he ever decide to pay a call on me?"

"It's hard to anticipate Lord Pattinger's actions," Horatio said with a sigh. "His moods are almost impossible to predict. I thought, for example, that he'd have you thrown out that first day, when you collapsed in the entryway. But he has not made a single reference to your existence from that day to this."

"That *is* strange. What do you suppose he means to gain by ignoring me?"

"I have no idea. Perhaps he, like Moira, is playing a waiting game . . . to see what's in Moira's mind before he tips his hand."

Oliver nodded. "Yes, that's a reasonable theory. If you don't mind my asking, my lord—"

The visitor put up a restraining hand. "There's no need to keep my-lording me, old boy," he said in a friendly way. "Please call me Horatio. If we are to become brothers-in-law, we may as well be comfortable with each other."

"Thank you, Horatio. I'm Oli . . . er . . . Thomas."

They shook hands. "Well, Thomas, what were you about to ask me?" Horatio wanted to know.

"Moira tells me that you—in her words—betrayed her. I find that hard to credit. I hope you won't think it presumptuous of me to ask what Lord Pattinger did to make you jilt Moira. I ask only because I think the information will help me devise some sort of defense against him."

"I didn't jilt Moira . . . exactly," Horatio explained, the tips of his ears turning a little red. "We were not yet betrothed when . . . when I had my interview with Lord Pattinger."

Oliver noticed the slight sign of embarrassment. "I don't mean to pry in matters not my concern," he said apologetically. "If you'd rather not speak of these things—"

"I rather *like* speaking of them," Horatio replied. "I don't often have the opportunity to explain myself. You see, although I *had* come courting Moira, his lordship pointed out to me that Moira did not really love me, while Alberta, on the other hand, had quite lost her head. He also pointed out that he would settle a great deal of money on Alberta but would give Moira no dowry at all. You may not believe this, Thomas, but the truth is that the dowry had nothing to do with my eventual decision."

"I do believe you, Horatio. But if not the dowry, what did you base the decision on?"

"I watched both sisters carefully after that interview, and I saw that Pattinger was quite right. Moira had made an intellectual decision to wed me, but Bertie's—Alberta's—

response to me was more . . . more emotional. More heart than head, if you follow my meaning. So I finally offered for Bertie."

"But if it was Moira you were enamored of, how could you—?"

"How could I have decided on Bertie?" He smiled thinly. "Can't you see why? Can't you imagine how painful it can be when you offer someone your whole heart, and she returns that feeling with mere dutiful politeness? That was the situation with Moira. Meanwhile, Bertie offered me real affection. After a while, I realized I was happier with that than with the conscientious friendliness I was getting from Moira."

"Yes, I can see what you mean. Tell me, Horatio, did you ever regret that decision? Did you ever wonder, later, if perhaps you had let Lord Pattinger lead you astray? It is possible, isn't it, that he'd put the suggestion in your mind, and the suggestion made you misinterpret what you saw?"

"I don't think I misinterpreted anything. Lord Pattinger is a powerful persuader, but not quite so powerful as that."

Oliver studied the other man for a long moment. "Are you still happy about your decision?" he asked at last.

Horatio hesitated. "I'm quite content," he said after a moment, "or will be, when Bertie and I are in our own home."

Oliver felt a twinge of real sympathy for the fellow. "Are you saying that it's difficult to have to see Moira every day?" he asked carefully. "That the proximity troubles you?"

"No, not at all," Horatio insisted. "I don't think about Moira in that way anymore, Thomas," he revealed with an open honesty. "My feelings for her faded when I saw how harshly she judged my actions."

"You can't really blame her for that, can you?" Oliver pointed out in her defense.

"Yes, I can. She never bothered to try to understand my motives, you see. Besides, she is too headstrong and spirited for me. I see that now. Take my word, Thomas, that I made the right decision."

"Yes, I suppose you did," Oliver said thoughtfully. "Then, as it turned out, Lord Pattinger didn't really do you harm."

"No, I suppose he didn't, if one looks at it in that way." He smiled ruefully as he made an absentminded adjustment to his spectacles. "However, that does not make living in the same house with him any easier."

Oliver, appreciating the fact that Horatio was conversing with him as with an equal, did not want to see the conversation end. "Do you think Pattinger used the same arguments with Moira's other suitors?" he pursued.

"He might have. I have no way of knowing."

"Then let me ask you something else. You're convinced that Moira didn't really care for you. Do you think she didn't care for the others, either?"

Horatio, struck by something in Oliver's question, peered intently through his spectacles at the other man. "I say, old fellow, you're not letting yourself fall in love with Moira, are you?"

Oliver dropped his eyes. "I'm trying not to," he answered as openly and honestly as Horatio had done. "But she is so damnably lovely . . ."

"Yes, she is," Horatio sighed. "But if you let yourself care for her, Thomas, you'll end in the dismals. She won't return your affection."

"Why do you say that, Horatio?" Oliver asked bluntly. "Is it because I'm so far beneath her?"

"No, that's not my reason. If you're not too far beneath her for her to *wed*, you're not too far beneath her for her to *love*. But I'm not sure she's capable of loving *any* man. She is her father's daughter, after all."

"Her father's daughter? You mean because he's a cold one—"

"Like ice."

"So she's a cold one too?" Oliver shook his head. "I can't believe Moira is the least bit cold."

"Are you sure you're objective enough to judge?"

Oliver shrugged. "Do you believe she's an ice maiden?"

"I'm not sure," Horatio said, considering the question from all sides. "Her fiery temper seems to point in the opposite direction. And she shows great warmth toward her sisters, in spite of what they've done to her."

"Then what makes you think she's like her father in that way?"

"Only the fact that I've never seen her fall in love."

Oliver's brows knit in a troubled frown. "She never loved *any* of her suitors?"

"Well, Alberta thinks she really cared for Jeffrey, Susan's husband, but I was not around to witness that affair."

They fell silent, each lost in contemplation of his own estimate of Moira's character. Suddenly, however, Oliver's mind turned to another aspect of the subject. "Assuming that Moira did care for Jeffrey," he mused, "then Lord Pattinger couldn't have dissuaded him from marrying her with the same reasoning he used with you. I wonder what reason he gave Jeffrey not to offer for her."

Horatio shrugged. "It's generally believed that Jeffrey's finances were badly scorched. In fact, I have it on good authority that he was all rolled up. Gone to pigs and whistles, as they say. I think he couldn't resist the monetary benefit of wedding Susan, especially when he learned that Lord Pattinger would not settle a cent on Moira."

"He can't have been much of a man if he was dissuaded by money."

"Do you really believe that?" Horatio asked, smiling at the younger man's naivety. "To quote the classics, 'there is no fortress so strong that money cannot take it.'"

"Yes, but I've always thought of Cicero as too cynical by half," Oliver retorted without thinking.

Horatio's head came up sharply. "You knew it was Cicero, did you?"

Now it was Oliver's turn to redden. "Well, you see, I . . . I . . ."

Horatio stared at Oliver for a long moment. "I'd wager you'd have recognized the quote in its original Latin. You've been educated in the classics, haven't you? You're a strange sort of gardener, Thomas, old fellow. Very strange indeed."

Oliver looked away, shamefaced. "I never said I was a gardener."

"You never said you weren't." Horatio got to his feet and looked down at Oliver with his earnest gaze. "Never mind, old man. Whatever your secret is, I shan't probe. Nor will I repeat any part of this conversation to anyone. I'll stand your friend whoever and whatever you are. I know a straight shooter when I see one."

Oliver looked up at him with warm gratitude. "Thank you for that, Horatio," he said, offering his hand again. "As soon as I can open up, you'll be the first I come to."

"I'll be here," Horatio assured him, turning to go. But he hesitated at the door before leaving. "Whatever your true identity, Thomas, the danger in losing your heart to Moira still exists. You do understand that, don't you?"

"Yes," Oliver sighed glumly. "Yes, I do."

Horatio threw him a last, sympathetic smile. "If ever you need help, Thomas, you'll be quite safe to come to me."

Oliver nodded. "I know that." He smiled back at his new friend. "I can recognize a straight shooter too."

CHAPTER
❧ ❧
ELEVEN

OLIVER HAD PLENTY OF TIME TO THINK ABOUT HORATIO'S warning, for Dr. Dunning was adamant in his order that his patient was not to leave his bed. To make certain that he obeyed, Pearce, the butler, assigned one of the footmen—Henry—to keep an eye on him. Henry, a good-natured, cheerful fellow about Oliver's own age (but whose hairline was so rapidly receding that he looked much older), popped his head in every half hour or so to check on his charge. And in addition to Henry's supervision, Oliver was carefully watched by Moira, Barbara, and Horatio. They visited him several times each day. Even Alberta, in spite of her "condition," visited him at least once daily. The hour before teatime usually found all of them seated around his bed, chatting and laughing and making a merry noise. Stopping in at Thomas's room became a pre-teatime ritual they all enjoyed. After a few days had passed, Barbara even remarked to her sisters that Thomas's presence seemed to have changed the atmosphere of the whole household. "It's like a holiday," she said. "Like a really festive holiday."

But when Oliver was not receiving company, he found himself thinking about Moira and wondering if, despite Horatio's warning, he might possibly win her heart. He'd never before wanted to court a lady, but he'd never before met anyone like Moira Pattinger. Every time she sat down beside his bed his heart pounded, his tongue went dry, and his eyes drank her in as if they'd thirsted for the sight of her. It wasn't only the fact that she was beautiful, for he'd met beautiful girls before. Beauty without the attributes of character soon palled. But Moira had charm, charm in the grace of her movements, in the slightly hoarse quality of her voice, in the quickness of her mind, and in her throaty, ready laugh. Horatio had warned him that she might be cold of heart, but when he was with her, Oliver couldn't believe it. Whenever she was nearby, he wondered how he could possibly keep himself from falling in love with her head over heels.

But there was no point in letting himself topple if she did not. And there was little in his favor in that regard. He didn't have estates like Horatio's, or a magnificent profile like Godfrey's. He knew he would not be considered a "catch" by any of the fortune-hunting mamas on the marriage-mart. But he was not despicable, either. He was a Sherrard of Lydbury. He had a good education, a small income, and good prospects for employment in the civil service. He was capable of providing a modestly comfortable life for a wife and family. Moira herself had said he was lovable, and that the only good basis for a good marriage was love. Now, if she would only fall in love with him. . . .

But there was the rub. Horatio had warned him that Moira was not the sort to give her heart away. And she herself had already told him that she had no such feelings for him. What did he have to offer that would make her change her mind? Only a kind nature, an open heart, and a newly broken nose. For a girl like Moira, his assets seemed woefully inadequate.

So the only thing to do, he decided, was to keep himself heart-whole. If one was determined not to fall in love, one could manage it, with a little strength of character. One needn't give way to one's yearnings. One could exercise one's will in these matters. "I'm twenty-three, not a green boy," he confided to the interested MacDamon. "I don't have to wear my heart on my sleeve, do I?"

With that purpose in mind, he determined that he would continue to keep his identity secret. There was no point in revealing who he was. It would be best just to do what he promised for her, get the false betrothal over with as soon as possible, and take his leave. For him to reveal any more of himself to her than she already knew would make an unnecessary complication and further entangle him. If he was to avoid falling in love and having his heart broken, the sooner all ties with her were cut, the better.

With this determination made, he began to look for something else with which to occupy his mind. And being forced to keep to his bed all day made the choice of occupation narrow indeed. The only thing he could think of to absorb his mind was a book. "You are delightful company, Mac," he told his dog, "but I really must find something to read. Something thoroughly engrossing."

He looked round the room, but there were no bookshelves on the green walls, no books on the writing table, no books anywhere to be seen. "Doesn't anyone in this family read?" he muttered.

His only hope was that he would find a book in one of the drawers of the dressing table or on one of the shelves of the large wardrobe in the corner. Determined to investigate, he slipped his legs over the side of the bed. MacDamon, sensing that his master was doing something improper, began to bark. "Hush, you tattler," Oliver hissed, crossing the room hurriedly, his bare legs sticking out below his nightshirt. "I'm only going a few steps."

But the writing table contained only some blank writing paper and a box of pen nibs. He turned to the wardrobe, MacDamon running wildly about his feet in disapproval, but he'd taken only two steps when there was a tapping on the door. He and the dog froze in place. "Yes?" he asked guiltily.

The door opened. It was Moira, bearing a bowl of soup and some biscuits on a tray. "Thomas Oliver, you sneak!" she exclaimed at the sight of him.

He leaped back on the bed and covered himself to his neck. "I was only . . . looking for something."

With MacDamon sniffing at her heels, Moira came up to the bed and thrust the tray at him in disgust. "You're no better than a naughty child! What on earth were you looking for that Henry couldn't find for you?"

"A book. I was looking for a book. Any book." He threw

her a guilty glance from the corner of his eye and felt, to his dismay, the familiar clench in his chest. She was looking particularly lovely this afternoon in a dress of lavender muslin, with sleeves that puffed out charmingly just above the elbow, a wide purple sash tied round the high waist, and a ruffled lace collar that accented the perfect oval shape of her face. His mouth went dry and his heart began to hammer like the green boy he'd sworn he wasn't. He was disgusted with himself. "I know this is a guest room and not a study," he said gruffly, hoping that a display of ill humor would weaken the attraction he felt for her, "but don't any of your guests ever *read*?"

Moira's eyebrows lifted. She had not expected that excuse. She'd never thought of Thomas as a reading man; none of the gardeners in her father's employ seemed even to know *how* to read. "You want something to *read*, Thomas?" she asked in surprise.

"Of course," he replied thoughtlessly. "What else can one do with oneself when confined to bed?"

She peered at him strangely. "What else indeed?" She sat down beside the bed and pushed the tray toward him, trying to determine what to make of his request. "Do drink your soup before it cools. What sort of book do you think you'd like? Father has a fine library. I can bring you almost any sort of book imaginable."

Oliver shrugged. "Something engrossing, to take my mind off this deuced incarceration. A novel, I think. I'm not a great reader of novels generally, so I'll leave the choice up to you."

She remained staring at him for a moment, wondering what he meant by that. Not a great reader of novels *generally*? Then what did he usually read? History? Biography? Philosophy? She had recognized even in the stable that her vagabond had a clever mind, but it was ridiculous to suppose he was a scholar. What sort of book should she bring him? she wondered. If she chose something simple and childlike, which might be all he was capable of understanding, it might offend him. But something sophisticated and adult might be beyond him. "I don't know what would suit you, Thomas," she admitted.

While they both tried to think of something suitable,

MacDamon leaped up on the bed, hoping to share the soup. "MacDamon, *down*!" Oliver ordered.

The dog's Scottish name immediately triggered a suggestion in Moira's mind. "How about something by Sir Walter Scott? We have a copy of *Waverly,* which is a rousing tale of—"

"No, I've read that," Oliver said, swallowing a gulp of soup. "And *Guy Mannering,* too."

Moira blinked in astonishment. "But you don't read novels generally?"

He laughed. "Well, I make an exception for Scott, you know. He's not like those womanish novelists, like Walpole and Beckford and that ridiculous Mrs. Radcliffe and the rest of that ilk. He's more . . . manly."

"More manly, is he?" She cocked her head at him. "I must say, Thomas, that I didn't expect to be engaging in literary discourse with a gardener."

Belatedly, Oliver realized he'd forgotten himself again. "I don't know why everyone thinks I'm a gardener," he mumbled.

"A groom, then. I've never met a groom before who could call Mrs. Radcliffe ridiculous and Scott manly. Whatever you are, you remain a great puzzle to me, Thomas. A great puzzle."

He lowered his eyes. "I'm sorry, ma'am."

"You've nothing to be sorry for, except for maligning 'womanly' novelists. And just for that, I shall give you *Pride and Prejudice* to read. It's written by a Miss Austen, and it's quite my favorite book in the world, so you had better have something complimentary to say about it when you've finished it."

"Thank you, ma'am," he said humbly, his tone befitting a groom. "I'm sure Miss Austen's book will be adequate. At least it will be better than nothing."

CHAPTER
❦ ❦
TWELVE

MISS AUSTEN'S NOVEL PROVED TO BE MUCH MORE THAN ADE-
quate. It was so engrossing, in fact, that on a sunny afternoon
two days later, when Sir Godfrey Jayne's carriage came
lumbering up the drive of the Pattinger manor house, right
under Oliver's window, Oliver didn't even look up from the
page. Still confined to bed by the cautious Dr. Dunning, he
was sitting back against his pillows utterly absorbed in his
reading, with MacDamon contentedly snoozing under his arm.

MacDamon, however, came instantly awake at the sounds
that wafted up from below. He leaped from beneath Oliver's
arm and ran, barking, to the window. But *Pride and Prejudice*
had so completely captured Oliver's attention that even
MacDamon's frantic barking failed to win him away from his
enraptured perusal of the words.

Down below, Sir Godfrey's carriage drew up to the door.
Although Oliver didn't notice his arrival, it was noticed by
everyone else in the household, for they'd been expecting him.
(The ball in honor of his and Barbara's betrothal was to be held
a week hence, and since those of the guests who had to come
from some distance would soon begin to gather, the groom-to-
be's presence would be required.) As soon as the carriage came
to a stop, Barbara, Moira, and a half-dozen servants came
pouring out the door to greet him.

One of the members of the welcoming staff was Henry, the
footman who had been assigned to see to Oliver's needs. Henry

knew that Mr. Oliver was particularly curious to meet Sir
Godfrey, so as soon as he could get away from his duties at the
door, he took the back stairs two at a time to bring Mr. Oliver
the news.

Henry considered himself fortunate that the butler had
placed the care of Mr. Oliver in his hands, first because the
work was easy and, second, because it raised him almost to the
social level of a valet. Nevertheless, he did not treat his charge
with any particular formality. He'd learned from Varney that
Mr. Oliver was probably nothing more than a groom or a
gardener, which made him not a bit superior to a footman, even
if he had won Miss Moira's favor. Henry waited on Mr. Oliver
cheerfully enough (for he liked the fellow, and he liked the
"cushy" job), but he wasn't at all awed by him. He conversed
with Mr. Oliver with the same breezy offhandedness he
showed to the servants below stairs. So he had no qualms about
bursting into Oliver's bedroom with the brazen announcement
that "the twiddlepoop's 'ere at last!"

Oliver (having arrived at the part in his novel where the
heroine had come upon Mr. Darcy on his home grounds and
was discovering that he was not the toplofty prig she'd
imagined him to be) was not happy at being interrupted. He
looked up from his book, frowning in annoyance. "Twiddlepoop?" he asked, bewildered.

"Jackstraw. Popinjay. Y' know 'oo I mean. Ol' Godfrey."

"*Sir* Godfrey, if you please," Oliver said reprovingly. "He's
here, is he? When did he arrive?"

"Just now. I left Jamie strugglin' with 'is bags. *Six* of 'em
bags, fer a week's stay! The man's a deuced Bartholomew
Baby, all spit 'n' polish outside an' straw inside."

"Come now, Henry, be fair. The fellow can't be as bad as
that if two of the ladies of the house wanted to wed him."

The footman shrugged. "Never *could* un'erstand a lady's
taste. Anyways, don't ye think I should do somethin' wi' yer
'air, Mr. Oliver?"

"My hair? Whatever for?"

"So ye kin look presentable, acourse. I'll wager ye a shillin'
Miss Barbara'll bring ol' Godfrey 'ere to see ye in no more 'n
ten minutes."

Oliver glowered at him. "I haven't a shilling to wager, as you well know."

"Right. I was forgettin'. That reminds me, Mr. Oliver, I found out the name of the cove 'oo cudgeled ye."

"Did you, Henry?" Oliver sat up eagerly. "That's splendid! How did you do it?"

"Went to the Twin Elms las' night. Sat there just like you tole me, an' kep' my ears open. Sure enough, two coves come paradin' in, one of 'em—the little one—throwin' 'is brass aroun' like it was water, buyin' drinks fer everyone, an' showin' off the silk linin' of 'is new coat." Henry paused in his narrative to look over at his charge with undisguised curiosity. "They must've took ye fer a pretty penny, right, Mr. Oliver?"

"They took me for enough," Oliver said, rubbing his still swollen chin ruefully.

"Anyways, I 'eard someone call the big whopstraw Finley . . . Ironfist Finley. An' the little chaffer-mouth, 'e was called Louch. I didn't get any other name. Jus' Louch."

"Louch, eh? That's enough for me." He sat back against the pillows, a look of fierce determination darkening his eyes. "Thank you, Henry. I stand in your debt."

"Tweren't nothin'. Glad t' do it. So what're ye gonna do about this Louch fellow, eh?"

"I'm not sure," Oliver said, his brows knit thoughtfully, "but you can wager your last shilling that I'll think of something. He's not going to split my skull and spend my brass without paying *something* for the privilege. And as for Ironfist, there's nothing I'd like more than another chance at a mill with him. I might be able to hold my own with him in a fair fight."

Henry grinned. "Ye kin box, eh, Mr. Oliver? 'Andy wi' yer fives? I'd like to' be there t' see ye plant 'im a facer! But take care when ye deal with Louch. 'E looks t' be a 'avey-cavey sort. Ye don' want yer skull split again. Ye might not wake up at all, the next time. Anyways, do ye want me to fix yer 'air now or not?"

"Don't bother, Henry. I want to get back to my book."

But he was not to have long to read. Moira dropped in a moment later to see how he did. Then, just as he'd launched into enthusiastic praise for the book she'd sent him, there was

another knock at the door. As Henry had predicted, it was
Barbara, pulling her betrothed after her. She had not even
given the fellow time to take off his traveling clothes. "Here he
is, Thomas," she clarioned proudly. "This is Sir Godfrey
Jayne. Godfrey, this is Thomas Oliver."

The fellow who came forward was as handsome as Barbara
had claimed. The man was the ideal Corinthian, a sportsman
from his carefully cut curls to his highly polished boots. He
was a perfect physical specimen, his impressive height and the
breadth of his shoulders in perfect proportion to his slim waist
and hips. His facial features, too, were perfect, for his straight
nose, high forehead, well-shaped lips, and chiseled chin could
have been the models for a sculptor in ancient Greece. Even the
blond curls on his head were like those on a Grecian bust.
Oliver could well understand why Moira and Barbara wanted
him.

"How do you do, Mr. Oliver?" the fellow said, taking off his
gloves. "So you are Moira's famous . . . er . . . protégé?"

Moira laughed. "What a *nice* way to put it, Godfrey!"

Barbara did not like Godfrey to be laughed at. "How else
should he have put it?" she burst out defensively. "After all,
I've scarcely had time to tell him everything. I merely told him
that Thomas was your 'discovery.'"

"Then let's tell him now. You see, Godfrey, Thomas is—or
will be, I hope—my betrothed," Moira said bluntly.

Sir Godfrey looked genuinely surprised. "Indeed? Betrothed?"

"Well, it is not yet official," Moira admitted.

Oliver, feeling awkward, put out his hand. "Forgive me for
not getting up, Sir Godfrey. Doctor's orders, you know."

Godfrey reached down stiffly and shook hands. "Yes, I
heard. A boxing accident, was it?"

"Is that what Barbara told you?" Moira giggled. "That he
was hurt in a boxing accident?"

Godfrey looked puzzled. "Well, her story was a bit incoherent. Isn't that what you said, my dear?"

"I said it was a bout of fisticuffs, I believe," Barbara
explained in embarrassment, having become too fond of

Thomas Oliver to reveal the seamy story of how he'd come among them.

"Close enough." Sir Godfrey, not really interested, dismissed the matter with a flip of his fingers. "I dislike boxing, myself. Fox hunting is the only royal sport."

"I thought," Moira teased, "that *horse racing* is called the sport of kings."

"A misnomer, I assure you. There is nothing about horse racing that is equal in any way to riding to hounds."

Since no one had anything to say to that, conversation came to an awkward halt. After a long moment, Barbara tried valiantly to start it again. "Godfrey says the roads were muddy all the way from Leicestershire."

But Sir Godfrey's mind was still latched to fox hunting. "No, I insist, no one can possibly compare horse racing to the subtlety, the hardihood, the sheer vigor of fox hunting," he said, as if the pause and Barbara's remark had not happened.

"Yes, dear," Barbara said gently, taking his arm, "but I was saying that you found the road muddy."

"Oh," he said, nodding, "yes, quite. Dreadfully muddy. Deuced time of year to travel."

"When would be a better time?" Moira asked. "The roads are almost always muddy."

"Winter, I'd say. I'd prefer winter. I wouldn't have to miss the hunts in winter." He turned to Oliver to explain. "There is no fox hunting in winter, you know."

"Heavens, Godfrey," Moira said impatiently, "one would think we've uprooted you for the season! You need remain here no more than a week! How many hunts will you miss in that time?"

"Two or three," he sighed. "At least two or three."

Barbara patted his shoulder sympathetically. "I'm sorry, dear," she murmured.

He smiled bravely down at her, making it quite clear that he would endure the sacrifice for her sake. "Yes, but you mustn't blame yourself. You had no way of knowing. Besides, I shall make it up next week. I'll organize *five* hunts next week."

"Splendid," Barbara murmured in relief. "And meanwhile,

we shall have a lovely time together, won't we? There'll be the ball, of course, and all sorts of galas and—"

"Though I shall miss my hounds," he added as if she hadn't spoken. "It's hard to be away from them for a whole week."

Oliver began to see why Henry had called the fellow a popinjay. How had Henry described him—all style outside and all straw within? Henry was quite right. Sir Godfrey Jayne was certainly, as Barbara had said, a magnificent-*looking* fellow, but he had a way of speaking that was stultifying to normal conversational progression. He seemed to turn every conversational gambit into a riding-to-hounds dead end. Had Moira really wanted to wed this . . . this *twiddlepoop*?

Oliver was desperately searching about in his mind for a congenial topic with which to reanimate the conversation when Henry appeared at the door. "The doctor's 'ere," he said excitedly.

Dr. Dunning strode in with his little black bag swinging and a pleased expression on his face, but the sight of all Oliver's visitors made him stop short. "Confound it," he muttered to the footman, "why didn't ye tell me there's a crowd here? I can't remove a nose plaster when the patient's surrounded by a gaggle o' guests, an' that's a fact!"

"Did you mean to remove it today?" Oliver asked eagerly.

"This is the very afternoon I had in mind," the doctor said.

"Oh, good!" Moira exclaimed. "Do come in, Dr. Dunning. Don't let us stop you."

"Nor us," came a voice from behind the doctor. It was Alberta, being helped over the threshold by her husband. "We want to see the unmasking too."

"Yes, indeed," Horatio agreed, pulling up the bench from the dressing table and settling his wife upon it, "this is an auspicious occasion."

Oliver glared at all of them. "Auspicious or not," he said firmly, "I'm not going to permit my new nose to be brought into public view until I've had a chance to see it *alone*. I hope you all will excuse me, but this 'unmasking' is going to be private, something between my physician and me. Good afternoon, all."

"I hope you don't imagine you'll rid yourself of *me*," Moira declared, perching on the foot of the bed. "I've waited too eagerly for this moment to withdraw now."

"There's no need to be vain, Thomas," Barbara said gently. "We won't care for you any less if your nose is not beautiful." She took Godfrey's arm possessively in hers and gazed up at him. "Not everyone can be beautiful, you know."

"And don't expect me to budge an inch!" Alberta said firmly. "You can't wish me to get up again so soon, can you, Thomas? Not in my condition."

"Ye don't mean fer *me* t' go, do ye, Mr. Oliver?" Henry asked, keeping close to the doctor's side. "Arfter all, the doctor might be needin' my assistance."

"Come now, Thomas, I can't see what harm it will do to have us here," Horatio said reasonably.

Oliver threw him a pained look. "I thought you were my friend," he muttered.

Dr. Dunning, a short, stocky fellow with a ruddy complexion, a North Country accent, and a gregarious disposition, looked from one to the other of the six onlookers and shrugged. "Very well, all o' ye may stay. But there's t' be no noise while I cut. Ye don't want t' make my hand slip, an' that's a fact!"

Oliver, outvoted, had no choice but to surrender. He swung his legs over the edge of the bed, trying not to feel embarrassed by the exposure of his nightshirted body and bare legs. The doctor stood before him and snipped away at the plaster bandages, removing little chunks bit by bit and dropping them into a wastebasket held by the grinning footman. When at last the rotund physician stepped aside and revealed his patient's visage in all its bare glory, the onlookers applauded. "I *told* you he was handsome," Moira chortled.

"Very personable," Alberta agreed.

"Almost as handsome as Godfrey," Barbara exclaimed with the enthusiasm that came naturally with her sweet disposition.

"As personable as any man would wish to be," Horatio said, beaming proudly at his friend.

Oliver eyed them suspiciously. "May I please get up and take a look in the mirror?" he pleaded with the doctor.

"Not on yer life," Dr. Dunning declared, packing his

scissors back into his bag. "Let someone bring ye a hand mirror."

Henry scurried over to the dressing table and removed one from a drawer. He handed it to Oliver with a grin. "There y' are, Mr. Oliver! Take a look."

Moira smiled as Oliver hesitated. "Go ahead, look," she urged. "You won't want to cover your head with your blankets this time, I promise you."

Oliver looked. His nose, still red from the irritation of the bandages, seemed enormous to him, and definitely disfigured by the new little bump below the bridge. In addition, his chin was still slightly distorted by the swelling, and his eye was still discolored. It was not a face, he thought despairingly, that was likely to win the love of a fair maiden. "Handsome!" he groaned aloud. "I look a *sight*! Anyone with sense would take me for a gallows bird."

"Do you know what I think, Thomas?" Moira said mockingly. "I think Barbara was right. You *are* vain."

"*Definitely* vain," Horatio chortled.

"And definitely unappreciative o' my medical skills," the doctor remarked in mock offense, "an' that's a fact! I took two mangled nasal bones an' welded 'em so well together that there's hardly a mark—"

"Hardly a *mark*!" Oliver cried, only half joking. "There's a lump as big as an *apple*—!"

"Cut line, boy!" the doctor ordered. "There's naught but a tiny bump that ye won't notice at all in a day or two, an' that's a fact!" He snapped his bag shut and, throwing Moira a wink, got up to leave. "And unless I have a word o' thanks from ye, ye young paperskull, I'll make ye spend the next *two months* in bed!"

"No! Not *that*!" Oliver pleaded in exaggerated alarm, reaching up and grasping the portly physician by his arm. "I didn't mean a word of what I said. I thank you with all my heart! I *love* my nose, I swear! Is that a good enough word of appreciation? When will you be back to end this imprisonment?"

MacDamon, not realizing that Oliver was joking, bounced up and down distractedly, barking at the doctor furiously.

"If ye call yer damn beast off," Dr. Dunning said, pulling his arm from Oliver's grip and backing to the door, "I'll be back the day after t'morra. And if ye swear ye'll not be leapin' about on the bed in the meantime, I may . . . not a promise, mind . . . but I just may let ye up then. 'Til then, good day t'all o' ye."

After he'd gone, Oliver accepted the congratulations of his visitors on the rapid restoration of his good health and returned to his bed. In ones and twos they took their leave until everyone was gone but Moira. She beamed at him as she tucked in his covers. "You aren't really displeased with your looks, are you, Thomas?" she asked.

"I don't think a hooked nose is much of an asset," he said glumly.

"It's *not* hooked. You've quite a nice nose, really. The little bump only emphasizes its pleasing shape. And that, as the doctor would say, is a fact!"

"You needn't bother to console me, ma'am," he said curtly. "I'd not be in a class with Sir Godfrey, even if my nose had never been broken."

Moira cocked her head at him interestedly. "What do you think of my soon-to-be brother-in-law," she asked, "besides agreeing with Barbara that he is a beautiful specimen?"

"Do you want the truth?"

"Of course."

"Then, I think, ma'am, that you are fortunate that he renounced you for your sister."

Moira's brows lifted. "Why do you say that?"

"I think you know perfectly well why. If your Miss Austen could have heard his conversation, I think she would have enjoyed using him in one of her books." He looked up at her, eyes twinkling. "As one of her comic fools."

Moira did not give him the satisfaction of laughing. "You, Thomas Oliver, have a wicked tongue," she said, forcing herself to frown at him. She turned and sauntered to the door. "A very wicked tongue," she repeated, adding, "and a very sharp eye."

She closed the door behind her, but he could hear her gurgling laughter as she strolled off down the hall.

CHAPTER
❧ ❧
THIRTEEN

THE EARLIEST LIGHT OF THE DAY CREPT IN THROUGH THE NARROW openings between the draperies a few days later to find Oliver wide awake and cavorting with MacDamon on the covers of his bed. Oliver would have liked to be still asleep, for there was something depressing about a large household in which one is the only person stirring, but his enforced bedrest was not conducive to long slumbers. After spending all day lying on his bed, he never grew tired enough to sleep through the whole night. The fault lay in the lack of exercise. Except for the few minutes a day he spent frisking about with MacDamon, he'd not had any exercise at all since the day he was carried up to this room.

He was mistaken, of course, in thinking that he was the only one awake. Every servant in the house had long since been roused from bed, and by first light they were dressed and busily occupied with their tasks. By the time Oliver began playing with his dog, just before seven, his man Henry had been awake for two hours. He and the other members of the household staff had plenty to do before the family stirred.

Usually Henry waited until nine before making his first stop in Mr. Oliver's room, but this morning was an exception. It was barely eight when he poked his head in Oliver's door. "He's *comin'*!" he hissed at Oliver in an urgent undervoice. *"Watch out!"*

"What?" Oliver asked, arrested. "Who's—?"

But Henry had thrown open the door and taken a stiff stance beside it, ramrod straight, with shoulders thrown back, head erect, and eyes forward. "Lord Pattinger!" he announced in loud, formal tones.

Oh, Good God! Oliver swore to himself, diving under the covers. *Why now, when I'm not at all prepared?*

His lordship marched in like a potentate entering his throne room. Once over the threshold, he stopped, lifted his pince-nez to his eyes and scanned the room slowly from left to right, pausing at the bed only long enough to catch a brief glimpse of Oliver's eyes peering at him nervously over the edge of the coverlet he'd pulled up to his nose. When Lord Pattinger finished casting his eyes over the entire room, he returned his stare to the bed. Oliver, unable to avoid the confrontation, reluctantly pulled himself up to a sitting position and lowered the coverlet. "Good m-morning, your lordship," he managed. "I would very much like to stand up, but I'm not . . . dressed . . ."

"Don't bother," his lordship said brusquely, his voice deeper and stronger than his thin frame would lead one to expect.

MacDamon, sensing the presence of an enemy, began to growl. His lordship beckoned to the footman, still standing stiffly at the door. "You, Henry! Take yourself and that mongrel dog for a walk!" he ordered.

"Yes, your lordship." Henry came up to the bed and, lifting the dog in his arms, threw Oliver a look that said as clearly as words, *You're in for it now, old chum!* Then he scooted as quickly as a proper footman's demeanor permitted out the door and closed it softly behind him.

Lord Pattinger took a couple of steps closer to the bed and squinted at Oliver through his spectacles. "So," he said in a tone of mild revulsion, "*you're* the vagrant."

"Yes, but I do have a name, your lordship," Oliver retorted in quick, instinctive offense. "I'm Thomas Oliver."

"That was loftily said," his lordship noted. "I take it you don't like to be called a vagrant, eh?"

"No, my lord, I don't. Would you?"

"But there's no question of *my* being called so," Lord

Pattinger said with a thin, patronizing smile. "No one would dare."

"It is possible, my lord, that even *you* might be designated a vagrant under certain conditions," Oliver pointed out. "If for example, you were, by some accident, marooned in a strange place without identification and your usual accouterments."

"*Accouterments,* eh?" He peered at Oliver closely. "A strange word for a vagrant to use. But I disagree with your example, fellow. I think my manner and general demeanor would be sufficient identification even without 'accouterments.'"

"I don't deny that your demeanor is impressive, my lord. But I can conceive of circumstances where, if your identity were unknown and your clothes sufficiently shabby, your impressive dignity might not be noticed. I suppose, in the end, the outcome would depend on the willingness of those who found you to be impressed."

"You are saying that people see only what they wish to see, eh?" Lord Pattinger's lips turned up just enough to suggest a shadow of a smile. "A good point, fellow. Very good indeed. Do you, by your little example, mean to imply that you yourself are a vagrant only by virtue of the fact that you were found in a strange place without identification or accouterments?"

"No, my lord. I was not implying anything."

"You're a clever rascal, I can see that. And very good at avoiding giving direct answers. Not quite what one would expect of a vagrant."

"What *would* one expect from a vagrant, my lord?"

"Certainly not a word like accouterments. Most vagrants, I suspect, do not speak like educated men. You do."

"I would not make too much of that detail, my lord, if I were you. It has little significance. My mother, who was rather well educated herself, made quite a business of requiring that her sons speak the King's English at the table. If we were slovenly or rowdy in our speech, we'd get no pudding." He grinned, remembering his boyhood days at his mother's tea table, where she'd smack his fingers with her fan every time he cursed or swore. "My mother's pudding is to blame for any sign in me of propriety or proper speech."

"That is an evasive little tale," his lordship remarked, "and of a piece with the rest of your responses. It tells me nothing about you."

"There's nothing to tell, my lord. I am what you see before you, nothing more nor less."

"What I see before me, fellow, is a scoundrel with a glib tongue. What do you expect to gain from this invasion into my household?"

"I *had* hoped to gain employment. Temporary, menial employment, for just long enough to earn myself a pair of boots."

"Boots?" Lord Pattinger glared at him. "What sort of sham is *that*?"

"It's no sham, but it *is* a long story. Suffice it to say that my condition was so weak when your daughter found me that employment was not possible for me. Your daughter kindly offered me this hospitality—hospitality, I admit, much more luxurious than I deserve or had any right to expect—until such time as I am pronounced fit."

"Hmmm." His lordship lifted his pince-nez again and studied Oliver intently for a seemingly endless moment, cocking his head in such a way that Oliver was reminded of Moira. Then his lordship dropped his glasses and took a step closer to the bed. "What would you say, fellow, if I offered you a sum of money large enough to buy yourself boots and a great deal more?"

"I would ask, my lord, what I was expected to do in return."

"What you would be expected to do would be to *leave this house*."

"But I don't understand," Oliver said. "You needn't offer me money for that. This is your house, after all. All you need do is order me from the premises."

"Ah, but you see, the matter is not so simple. My daughter seems to be taking a great deal of enjoyment in playing the role of Lady Bountiful. If I were to order you from the house, she might very well become angry with me. She has a hot temper, while I, as you see, am a calm, contemplative man. I do not enjoy quarreling, especially with her. So if you were to take the money I offered and leave quietly on your own, she would not know I had a hand in your departure and would vent her anger in *your* direction rather than in mine."

"I see." Oliver's body stiffened, and his senses alerted themselves for an attack. This was Lord Pattinger's opening salvo, the first volley in the battle that Moira had warned him was going to come, the battle that had already felled three other suitors. His instincts warned him to move carefully. "But this has all been in the nature of a supposition, hasn't it, my lord? From the way you expressed yourself, I don't believe you are actually making this proposition to me, are you?"

Lord Pattinger continued to feel his way carefully. "But if I were—?" he pressed, still not committing himself.

Oliver decided to skip the skirmishing and move to direct confrontation. "But even if you *were* actually offering me money, my lord, I'm afraid I would have to decline."

"Would you indeed?" his lordship asked in an ominously quiet voice. The only outward sign of his inner anger was a flush of redness that showed itself on the tips of his ears and the back of his neck. "Why would you wish to decline? I thought your goal in all this was merely to earn yourself a pair of boots."

"It was. But the situation has changed in the fortnight or so since I first came here. I have since given a promise to your daughter that I would remain here until *she* dismisses me. I do not break my promises, my lord. If you want me out of this house, I'm afraid you'll have to order me to leave . . . and take the consequences with your daughter."

His lordship's flush deepened. "Considering your precarious position in this household, that response was a bit rash, wasn't it?"

"I don't think so. What have I to lose, after all?"

One look at Lord Pattinger's angry face, and Oliver felt a decided flush of victory. His firmness in facing the question head-on and turning the offer down without roundaboutation had made him the winner. Of the first round, anyway.

His lordship fixed an icy glare on the young man's face. "You have a cheeky manner, fellow, and an impudent tongue!"

"So I've been told," Oliver responded mildly.

Lord Pattinger lifted his spectacles one last time and stared at Oliver coldly. Then he dropped the glasses and turned on his heel. "Well, I shan't bother to make you that proposition. I'll leave it to my daughter to dismiss you. I don't suppose she'll permit a vagabond with a brazen tongue to remain here very much longer." He walked sedately to the door. But he turned back before leaving. "They found you in the stable, is that right?"

"Yes, my lord."

"A vagabond, without employ or any means of support?"

"That's right."

His lordship shook his head in disbelief. "Shocking. Utterly shocking. There's no telling what sort of riffraff one might find on one's doorstep these days. The whole country is going to the dogs." And with those flattering last words, his lordship took himself out the door and slammed it behind him.

CHAPTER
❧❧ ❧❧
FOURTEEN

OLIVER DID NOT REPORT TO ANYONE, EVEN MOIRA, ABOUT HIS interview with Lord Pattinger. He even parried Henry's persistent queries. His lordship was evidently not going to take any action to curtail Oliver's presence in the household, so Oliver saw no reason to reveal anything to anyone about the conversation. To report on it would have had no purpose than gossip, and Oliver did not like gossip.

Meanwhile, the rest of the family had arisen and, alone or in pairs, had drifted down to breakfast, until everyone was gathered round the table. Barbara, with her ball only three days away, could speak of nothing but the festivities. As she babbled on excitedly about the potted plants that had been delivered to bedeck the ballroom and the cases of champagne that were expected to arrive this very day, it occurred to Moira that, in her absorption in the myriad details of the ball, she'd forgotten that Thomas Oliver had no evening clothes to wear—no clothes of any kind, for that matter. "Why did I not think of this before?" she moaned to Alberta and Horatio, who had lingered with her at the breakfast table after all the others had departed. "There are just a few days left to make preparations! How am I to have an evening coat and breeches made for him in time?"

It was Horatio who came up with a plan. "You must take a coat of mine, and a pair of my silk breeches, too, and hire a tailor to adjust them to his size."

"But what about shoes?" Alberta asked. "If I remember, the fellow came to us without so much as a pair of shoes on his feet."

"Good God! *Shoes!*" Moira gasped.

Horatio could not think of a solution for *that* problem. "I'd gladly give him a pair of mine," he said, "but I have unusually small feet, and shoes can't be altered as easily as breeches."

"But he must have dancing shoes for the ball," Moira said worriedly. "And boots for the rest of the time. If anything, I *owe* the man a pair of boots. Oh, dear, what shall I do?"

"Good heavens, Moira," Alberta said in disgust, "you make it sound as if the man is Cinderella, and you need a fairy godmother to wave a wand and provide him with glass slippers! Shoes for the ball, indeed! If the fellow has no shoes, he won't go, that's all. I don't see why you want him at the ball, anyway."

"You don't understand, Bertie. He *must* go!" Moira insisted. "I have my reasons."

"If your reasons have anything to do with your ridiculous declaration that you're going to wed him, I don't want to hear them," Alberta cried in a burst of impatience.

"Now, now, my dear," her husband cautioned, rising and going to her, "you mustn't excite yourself. Besides, I thought you *liked* Thomas."

"I *do* like him," Alberta said, pulling a handkerchief from her bosom and sniffing into it, "but that doesn't mean I want a deuced *groom* as a br-br-brother-in-law! And it doesn't mean I think he ought to be p-present at the b-ball, either!"

Horatio threw Moira an apologetic look as he helped his wife to her feet. "Come now, dearest, don't cry. You must try to keep yourself calm, for the sake of the little life you are carrying. Come along to the sitting room and stretch out on the sofa. You'll feel better after a little rest."

He helped his wife out of the breakfast room and soon established her on the sitting room sofa. Then, excusing himself, he ran back to the breakfast room. "Don't fret, Moira," he said to his sister-in-law who still sat at the table sunk in depression. "We'll manage to get shoes for Thomas somehow. Perhaps his feet are not too different from mine. I'll run upstairs and measure them."

Moira, encouraged by Horatio's optimism, immediately set about the business of putting things in motion. She sent for a tailor and a haberdasher, and while waiting for them to arrive, she consulted with Horatio's valet about which of Horatio's evening coats might possibly be suitable for Oliver's broader shoulders. It was the valet who suggested that one or two of the local bootmakers might have some shoes in readiness that could be made to fit Mr. Oliver. On the basis of that suggestion, Moira quickly sent notes to the best bootmakers in both Maidstone and Chatham, asking them to come to the manor house as soon as possible and bring with them whatever boots and dancing slippers they had on hand that might fit a foot which (by Horatio's measurement) was eleven inches long.

That done, she turned her attention to Thomas himself. The man had probably never attended a ball before, and therefore there was a great deal he needed to learn about deportment in a ballroom. But she could do nothing to prepare him until he was on his feet. She had to see the doctor this very morning!

She waited impatiently for the doctor to arrive, but it was almost noon when Henry informed her that Dr. Dunning was with Mr. Oliver at that moment. Moira ran down the hall and waited impatiently outside Oliver's door for Dr. Dunning to emerge. When he finally came out, she took his arm and walked down the hall with him. "Unless there's real danger to Mr. Oliver's health, Dr. Dunning," she said to him urgently, "please permit him to get out of bed today."

The doctor glanced at her curiously. "What's the hurry?"

Moira bit her lip nervously. "Well, you did say, didn't you, that he would need only eight or ten more days of bedrest? It was on the basis of that prediction that I arranged the date of our ball. I don't wish to seem heedless of Mr. Oliver's health requirements, but the ball is to be held in just three days. If he's to attend—and it means a great deal to me that he does—he has to be measured for a suit of clothes, and for shoes, and for all sorts of things . . ."

The doctor nodded. "Well, no need t' worry yer pretty

head," he said understandingly. "The boy seems t' be quite recovered. There's no pain when I press on his skull where the lump was, an' that's a fact!" He gave her a triumphant grin. "I've already told him he can get up and dressed t'day."

He expected her to express her delight at his news with at least a smile, but he didn't get even that. Instead, she bit her lip worriedly. She had another, more difficult, request. "There's something else I must ask you," she mumbled, lowering her eyes in shamefaced embarrassment. "It will sound as if I have no concern for the fellow's health, but I really do. That's why you must be honest with me. He really needs to have a couple of dancing lessons. Will that do him harm?"

"*Dancing* lessons?" The physician stopped where he was and frowned in disapproval.

"I know it sounds utterly frivolous, Doctor," Moira explained, "but you see, he and I are going to announce our betrothal at the ball, at which time it will be appropriate for him to dance with me."

"Betrothal?" The doctor looked at her, shocked. "You and Mr. *Oliver*? *Betrothed*?"

"I don't see why you're so surprised, Dr. Dunning," she said, putting her chin up defensively. "Mr. Oliver is perfectly respectable."

"Yes, o' course he is. Leastways, he seems so t' me." He peered at Moira, his brow furrowed. "I myself have taken a real likin' t' the lad, an' that's a fact. If I had a daughter, I'd approve o' him fer her in a trice."

"But not for me?"

"Well, m' dear, y're different. Y're a lady, now, ain't ye? I admit 'tis no business o' mine, but ye can't be tellin' me that yer father approves."

"I don't need his approval," Moira said stiffly. "I'm of age."

"But . . . the man has no title. In fact, I been told he's naught but an ordinary laborer."

"But an extraordinary *man*, don't you think so?" Moira retorted proudly.

The doctor gave her a measuring look. Then one corner of his mouth turned up in a crooked smile. "He might be, at that. He has character, I b'lieve, an' that's worth more 'n titles.

Nevertheless, girl, y're showin' the world a fine bit o' courage, I'll say that fer ye."

Moira felt a stab of shame. The doctor admired her now, but what would he think a few days from now, when the gossips reported to him that she'd jilted the fellow? "It doesn't take much courage . . ." she murmured lamely.

The doctor patted her hand affectionately. "Don't worry, lass. Yer father'll come round when he knows the man better. I tell ye, if I were yer father, I'd be *proud* of your choice, an' that's a fact."

Moira sighed. "Thank you, Doctor. That was good to hear. Now, as to the dancing lessons . . ."

The physician shook his head. "I can't say I'm pleased t' allow it, but very well, ma'am, he can do a bit o' prancin' about. But only fer short periods durin' the day, mind, 'til he's certain sure that the strain doesn't leave him with headaches and nausea."

"I won't let him do too much," she promised. "If he should show the slightest sign of weariness or discomfort, I'll send him off to bed."

By this time they had reached the bottom of the stairs. "Be sure ye do, m'dear," the doctor said, waving his black bag in farewell. "Y're a brave little lass, an' that's a fact. Best o' luck to ye!"

Moira watched him go, her expression troubled. His admiration for what he thought was a courageous act filled her with shame. She wasn't acting courageously at all. She was using trickery and making Thomas Oliver a tool in her machinations. *I'm a selfish, calculating, manipulative sham who doesn't deserve an iota of admiration*, she told herself. *And that's a fact!*

CHAPTER
❦ ❦
FIFTEEN

So Oliver was permitted to leave his bed at last. But his joy in his freedom was short-lived. No sooner was he up and dressed, wearing an elegant blue silk dressing gown and houseslippers provided by Horatio, than he was suddenly besieged with what seemed to him an army of tailors, haberdashers, and bootmakers. One after the other they measured and poked and pinned him unmercifully. First the haberdashers measured him for three shirts—one for evening wear, two for daytime—all of which were to be made especially for him and to be ready on the following day. Next, a tailor and two assistants spent the better part of an hour chalking up a riding coat and an evening coat belonging to Horatio, which had to be broadened in the shoulders, let out across the back, and shortened at the sleeves. Then the tailors pulled and pinned a pair of silk breeches over his thighs and round his waist until they fitted like a second skin. That done, he was immediately called to the upstairs sitting room to select a pair of boots and another of dancing shoes from a huge pile that two bootmakers had brought for him. And, finally, the haberdashers returned, bringing him several sets of "unmentionables" and insisting that he try them on and approve their quality and fit.

By the time the tradesmen were finished with him and had taken their departure, it was teatime. Henry the footman, entering Oliver's room with a message from Moira, found him collapsed on his bed. "Done in, are ye?" he asked sympathetically. "Well, ye'd better get back on yer feet in a 'urry. Miss Moira says that since the doctor 'as given ye leave to quit yer bed, the family requests yer presence in the downstairs sitting room fer tea."

Oliver groaned. "Damnation, I can't. Give my apologies."

"Too tired, are ye?"

"No, of course not. There's nothing I'd like better than to get out of this room. But it's impossible. In spite of all the pinnings and fittings, I have no clothes at the moment but the robe and slippers that Horatio provided me. Even the boots I chose have been carted away for altcrations!"

But Henry strutted over to the wardrobe, and withdrew Oliver's own chamois breeches and broadcloth shirt that had been cleaned and put away in the wardrobe for him. "Will these do?"

"Henry, what would I do without you?" Oliver chortled, and he eagerly jumped up to dress. He put on his old clothes over a new singlet and smalls, and, not wishing to appear before the ladies in his shirt-sleeves, wore Horatio's frogged robe in place of a coat. Thus attired, he went out of his room and down the stairs for the first time since they'd carried him up ten days before.

At the sitting room door, Oliver hesitated. Already uneasy at the prospect of facing the entire family in a formal setting, he was not made more confident by his slapdash appearance, for an outfit consisting of casual breeches, dressing gown, and houseslippers was definitely not proper for an afternoon social gathering. He peered inside the room nervously. The whole family was gathered within, except Lord Pattinger himself. Moira was perched on a chair near the tea table serving tea to her two sisters and their menfolk. Horatio was assisting by carrying the tray of biscuits and cucumber sandwiches round to each of the others. It was a pleasant scene, the atmosphere cheerful and unthreatening, so Oliver took a step inside. Barbara was the first to notice him. "Thomas! You came!" she greeted in eager welcome.

"Of course he came," Moira said, smiling at him warmly and patting the chair beside her for him to take. "Why shouldn't he?"

"I almost didn't," Oliver admitted, crossing the room, making his bows to the ladies and taking the chair she indicated. "I felt real terror at the prospect of facing Lord Pattinger and all you ladies attired like this. But I see his lordship has not joined you yet."

"Father does not often join us for tea," Barbara explained. "He says he despises tea-cake talk, which is how he describes our conversation."

"As for your attire, Thomas," Horatio said, beaming at him fondly, "I think you look magnificent."

"It's your dressing gown, old chap, that looks magnificent," Oliver retorted, "but you'll have to admit it's scarcely suitable garb for taking tea with the ladies."

"Invalids can be excused their informal attire," Alberta assured him pleasantly, having forgotten completely her fit of pique over the breakfast table. "You look very fine, Thomas. Do you know that I chose that robe for Horatio myself? It was last year, for his birthday, wasn't it, Horatio, my love?"

"Yes, dear," Horatio said, offering Oliver a sandwich, "but it suits Thomas so very well that I think he should keep it."

"It doesn't suit me at all," Oliver demurred, looking down at the enormous frogs and the satin lapels with exaggerated awe. "It's suitable for no one lower than a duke, with the possible exception of so noble a personage as yourself. But I thank you very much for lending it to me, and also for letting the tailors ruin two of your coats in my behalf."

"What is he talking about?" Godfrey asked his betrothed in bewilderment.

"He has no clothes," Barbara explained in a whisper. "He was set upon and robbed on the road, you see. So Horatio let him have one of his evening coats so that he can attend our ball."

"Robbed, was he?" Godfrey gave Oliver a look of sympathy. "Even of his hunting coats?"

"Of everything, I'm afraid," Barbara said.

"That is a shame. I say, Thomas, I can let you have one of *my* hunting coats. I daresay it would fit across the shoulders."

"That is very good of you, Sir Godfrey," Oliver said. "If the occasion should arise when I'd need one, I'd be happy and grateful to avail myself of your generosity, but I doubt that I shall be doing any riding to hounds in the near future."

Horatio choked back a laugh. "As you yourself pointed out, Godfrey, old fellow, this is not hunt country."

"No, it's not, much to my regret," Godfrey agreed glumly.

Moira put down her teacup. "Since we've managed to fit Thomas up well enough to attend the ball," she said, "I think it behooves us to make sure he enjoys it."

"What do you mean?" Alberta asked suspiciously.

"We ought to teach him to dance."

"Dance?" Barbara's eyes lit up. Of all of her sisters, she was the one who most enjoyed dancing. "Of course we should. Oh, what fun!"

"But doesn't he know—?" Godfrey began.

"That's right, we haven't bothered to ask Thomas if he already *knows* how to dance," Horatio cut in, looking at Oliver over his spectacles challengingly.

Oliver understood exactly what Horatio was trying to do. The fellow was encouraging him to admit that he was perfectly capable of making his way in a ballroom. But he also knew that an admission of such knowledge would raise suspicions about his identity. And in spite of Horatio's urging, he still wished to keep his identity secret. Nevertheless, he *was* uncomfortable about having to lie again. "Well, I . . . I . . ." he stammered.

"Goodness, Horatio, you can't expect Thomas to know such things!" Alberta scolded.

Horatio, however, would not be stopped. Growing more certain every day that Thomas Oliver was not the simple vagabond he pretended to be, and wishing all the others could see the fine qualities in Thomas that he saw, Horatio took every opportunity to push the man into revealing himself. This was one of those opportunities. He therefore began to argue with his wife, while giving a broad wink to the man he now thought of as a friend. "Thomas knows how to *speak* like a gentleman, doesn't he?" he pointed out. "What makes you think he can't *dance* like a gentleman? *Can* you dance, Thomas?"

Oliver gave his friend a withering glance. "I can dance as well as most vagrants," he said.

"There, Lord Becclesworth, I hope you're satisfied, now that you've sufficiently embarrassed poor Thomas," Horatio's wife snapped at him. She then turned to Moira. "But, Moira, love, you can't expect to teach him to be at home on a dance floor in a mere three days."

Horatio did not give up. "Let him have a try," he insisted. "I'd wager he's a quick study."

Sir Godfrey didn't agree. "Learning dancing is not like learning to shoot or to ride," he pointed out. "I've been dragged out to the dance floor since boyhood, and I still feel awkward. I'd rather sit a horse any day."

"Oh, pooh," Barbara said, pulling her betrothed to his feet. "You do perfectly well on the dance floor. Let's all go to the music room right now and give Thomas a lesson. Bertie can play for us."

This everyone was willing to do, and before long Alberta was established at the large pianoforte in the music room, with Godfrey and Barbara making up a set with Moira and Oliver. Whenever Oliver claimed not to know a step, Horatio stood up and demonstrated it for him. In this way they went through three different country dances. Despite the fact that Oliver was wearing bedroom slippers, he acquitted himself very well. But he was careful not to "learn" too quickly.

After an hour, Moira called a halt. "This has been delightful," she said. "I thank one and all for helping Thomas to make such excellent progress. But I promised Dr. Dunning I would not let Thomas overdo. Go upstairs to rest, Thomas. We'll practice again tomorrow, if everyone's willing."

Later, Horatio poked his head into Oliver's room. "I suppose you're furious with me," he said.

"Well, I was," Oliver admitted. "Did you or did you not promise not to voice your suspicions to anyone?"

Horatio came in and closed the door. "I didn't voice my suspicions. I merely tried to give you an opportunity to open up to us."

"I don't wish for such opportunities, thank you," Oliver said bluntly. "I'd rather keep things as they are. But since no harm was done, I'm no longer angry at you. In fact, I'm rather grateful to you."

"Grateful? Good God, why?"

"Because you gave me the opportunity to dance with Moira." Oliver smiled mistily at the recollection. "Do you know how it feels to hold her, Horatio? It's positively dizzying. Twirling her about the floor was a delight. Her step is so light that she feels weightless. She was unlike any young lady I've ever danced with before."

Horatio frowned. "I know, Thomas, I know. She's a breathtaking female. But I hope you remember my warning about letting your emotions become entangled . . ."

"I remember. Don't worry about me, old chap. I've got my feet on the ground. I admit the possibility that this situation I've become involved in will end badly, and I'll have to pay a heavy price for it. But for the time being, I may as well enjoy myself. That's why I have a favor to ask of you."

"Favor?"

"Yes. Tomorrow, when they give me my next dancing lesson, will you suggest that they teach me the waltz?"

Horatio blinked at his friend worriedly. "The *waltz*? But that's so . . . so . . ."

"Exactly!" Oliver lay back against the pillows, his hands behind his head, and beamed at the ceiling dreamily. "Whatever happens later, to waltz round the room with Moira in my arms will make it all worthwhile."

CHAPTER
❧ ❧
SIXTEEN

FOLLOWING MOIRA'S SPECIFIC SUGGESTION, OLIVER MADE HIS first appearance in the breakfast room two days later. Since some of his new clothing had been delivered earlier, he was elegantly dressed in Horatio's newly altered riding coat, his own breeches, a new shirt, and a pair of new boots. Thus attired, he felt almost like his old self again. He strode into the room with the confidence befitting the Honorable Oliver Sherrard, but when he saw that his table companions were not only Moira and Barbara, but Lord Pattinger himself, he stopped short. *Why didn't I anticipate that I'd have to face old Pattinger this morning?* he berated himself. *I could have waited upstairs, come down with the late risers, and missed him altogether!* "G-Good morning," he stammered uneasily.

"Thomas! How splendid you look!" Barbara cried, clapping her hands in impulsive applause. But then, with a nervous glance at her father, she retreated, lowering her hands to her lap, and letting the glad welcome fade from her eyes.

"Good morning, Thomas," Moira greeted, beaming at her protégé. "Yes, you do look splendid."

Oliver blushed. "Clothes do make the man, don't they?" he muttered.

Moira glowed with pride. "Father, I don't believe you've met my . . . er . . . Mr. Oliver," she said. "Thomas, this is my father, Lord Pattinger."

The two men exchanged glances. "His lordship and I have already met," Oliver said.

Moira shook her head. "We can't count that dreadful morning when you fainted in our hallway. You were scarcely in condition to meet anyone."

"Mr. Oliver is referring to another meeting," Lord Pattinger corrected, looking Oliver over from head to toe through his pince-nez.

Moira stiffened. "*Another* meeting?"

"One morning earlier this week, when I called on him," his lordship said indifferently.

"You *called* on him?" Moira asked her father in a choked voice.

"Yes, I did. I trust you have no objection. This *is* my house, I believe."

The startled girl turned to Oliver. "Why did you not mention it, Thomas?"

"Yes, fellow," Lord Pattinger echoed with a touch of malice, "why *didn't* you mention it?"

Oliver looked at him pointedly. "I thought that your lordship would prefer that I didn't, considering the subject of our conversation."

"Oh?" Moira glared at her father in suspicion. "And what was the subject, may I ask?"

"No, you may not," her father snapped. He then turned on Oliver a look of fierce authority. "And you are not to say another word on the subject, fellow!"

But Moira would not be denied. "What was it, Thomas?" she insisted.

Barbara, seeing poor Thomas caught between two strong antagonists, tried to help. "Don't you think we should l-let Thomas take some breakfast?" she intervened timidly.

Pearce, the butler, also hoping to ease the tension, stepped forward. "Some eggs, Mr. Oliver?" he said quickly.

Moira put up a restraining hand. "In a moment, Pearce," she said firmly. "I believe Mr. Oliver was about to answer my question."

Oliver, however, did not feel caught. He realized for the second time that he could parry Lord Pattinger's attacks by

simply facing them, so he calmly took the plate the butler held
out to him and sat down, his self-assurance restored. "The
subject, ma'am, was the date of my departure. His lordship
wished to know how long I intended to presume upon your
generous hospitality."

"I see," Moira said carefully. "And what did you answer
him?"

"I told him that the time of my departure was entirely up to
you."

"Thank you, Thomas," Moira smiled, relieved. "Was that
all?"

"That was the gist of it, ma'am," Oliver said.

"Good. Then, please, Thomas, do go on and eat your eggs
before they get cold."

Lord Pattinger threw down his spoon angrily and rose
magisterially to his feet. "How far do you intend this farce to
go?" he asked his daughter icily. "You've given this . . . this
person a room in the house for an indefinite period. And a new
suit of clothes, I see. Do you mean to invite him to join us at
all our family meals as well?"

"That is my intention, yes," Moira answered flatly. "I hope
you have no objections."

"Of course I have objections," her father snapped. He put a
hand to his forehead for a moment and shook his head
hopelessly. "I kept those objections to myself when I believed
you were merely showing an excess of hospitality to a man
who was ill," he said, stalking to the door. "What I did *not*
expect was that you intended to *adopt* him!"

Moira stared after him open-mouthed until he disappeared
down the hall. Then she burst into a spasm of uncontrollable
laughter. "*Adopt* him!" she gasped. "*Adopt* him!"

Barbara blinked at her. "I don't see why you find that
laughable."

"Don't you?" Moira managed between peals of laughter.
"It's really so funny . . . when one thinks of . . . how
father will feel after . . . after tomorrow night. He'll be sorry
that I *didn't* adopt him!" And she burst into another gale of
laughter.

"Tomorrow night?" Barbara asked worriedly. "What about

tomorrow night? What are you thinking of, Moira? Is something going to happen at the ball?"

Moira, realizing that she'd said too much, caught her breath and gained control of herself. "There's nothing for you to worry about, Babs. It will be a lovely ball, I promise."

"But you said—"

"Never mind what I said," Moira said in her most reassuring manner. "I was just being silly."

But Barbara was not reassured. Instead, her eyes widened in horror. She rose slowly from her chair, her cheeks whitening. "Of course you're not going to adopt him," she gasped in sudden comprehension. "I know perfectly well that was just father's little joke. I know what you're planning. You're going to go ahead with your threat, aren't you? That silly threat we've all almost forgotten about!" Bursting into tears, she stumbled to the door. "And you're going to use m-my b-ball for the announcement! Do you know what *I* think, Moira P-Pattinger?" she cried as she ran from the room. "I think you're h-*horrid*!"

Moira shut her eyes in despair. "Oh, dear! I *am* horrid," she moaned.

Oliver studied her with sympathy. "If you truly mean that, ma'am, it's not too late to change your plans."

Moira blinked at him. "Change them? Do *you* think . . . ?" But she suddenly became aware that Pearce and one of the housemaids were still in the room (and too busily rattling teapots and chafing dish covers to be entirely innocent), and she clamped her mouth shut.

"Do I think what?" Oliver prodded.

She shook her head. "I'll go after Babs and have a talk with her. Please finish your breakfast, Thomas. I'll see you later."

It was not until late afternoon, however, that Oliver saw her again. In the meantime, the house began to fill with guests. Susan and Jeffrey arrived at midmorning, several other family members arrived during the afternoon, and Moira's favorite Aunt Joanna arrived from London just before tea. Oliver, summoned to take tea with the family, found the sitting room filled with people. Horatio took him by the arm and dragged him about, introducing him to all the new arrivals. Oliver took particular note of Moira's aunt, looking her over carefully to see if he could discern why Moira wanted to go to live with her. The impression he received was of a female of rare unconventionality. Joanna, Lady Upsall, was a woman in her fifties who'd been widowed so long she seemed spinsterish. It seemed to Oliver that she rather relished being thought of as eccentric. Dressed in the mannish style of a bluestocking, she expressed herself with loud authority, laughed gustily at her own or anyone else's wit, and in general had the air of a woman of strong-minded independence. Oliver liked her, even though he caught her staring at him from time to time with a disconcerting keenness.

Horatio also introduced him to Susan and Jeffrey, Lord and Lady Presswood. Susan, with auburn hair and doe-shaped eyes like Barbara's, was quite plump and matronly but seemed very good-natured. She, like Lady Upsall, seemed to take particular interest in Oliver. Although he found Susan perfectly agreeable, her matronly manner and appearance made it hard for him to believe that she was younger than Moira. She invited him to sit down beside her, and she made sure his plate was loaded with sandwiches and cakes. She asked him all sorts of questions in a motherly style, which he tried his best to answer without giving himself away. He suspected that her interest in him had been aroused by either Alberta or Barbara; one or the other must have told her how he came to be among them. He was certain of it when he noticed that Lady Upsall had seated herself right behind them and was listening to everything they said. It seemed that both Susan and Lady Upsall had been informed of Moira's interest in him.

After he excused himself from Susan's company and went off into a corner to observe, he noticed that Susan and Lady Upsall began to whisper together and throw him occasional glances. From their pleased expressions, he surmised that they approved of him. It would have been a satisfying feeling, except that he knew that Moira herself did not.

But it was Susan's husband Jeffrey, Lord Presswood, in whom Oliver was most intensely interested. He did not like to admit to himself that he viewed Jeffrey as a rival, but the defensive dislike he felt for the man, even before they met, was surely an emotion generated by jealousy. Of all Moira's suitors, Jeffrey was the only one she was thought to have loved, and that was enough to make Oliver green with envy. Jeffrey was standing near the tea table when Horatio pointed him out, and Oliver noted at once that the infamous Lord Presswood was already surrounded by three giggling and obviously enraptured young ladies—Moira's cousins, Horatio said—who had come all the way from Yorkshire for this occasion. Oliver felt his whole body grow tense and his fingers curl into fists.

Jeffrey turned out to be almost exactly the sort of man Oliver expected. He was darkly good-looking—his features not as perfect as Godfrey's, but more strongly shaped—with a high forehead beautifully accented by dark waves of hair streaked dramatically with silver. He was dressed in so fashionable a style as to reveal an inordinate interest in his appearance. What made him even more attractive to the ladies was his repartee; he seemed to know a great deal about the personages in society, and he spoke of everyone from the Prince to the doyens of Almack's with intimate mockery. Women seemed to flock around him, and Oliver could see that the man was conceitedly aware of their admiration. That self-satisfied air was enough to increase Oliver's already active dislike, but the feature that earned Oliver's strongest repugnance was Jeffrey's full-lipped, lascivious mouth. It was the mouth, Oliver decided, of a vain, self-indulgent lecher. It was no longer jealousy that made Oliver dislike him; now it was the man himself.

Oliver, standing out of the way and stirring his tea absently round and round in his cup, watched Moira dispensing tea and exchanging pleasantries with the guests. Although he'd not noticed her giving Jeffrey any particular attention, he couldn't help wondering what feelings she still harbored for him in her heart. The thought that she'd ever fallen in love with that peacock was irksome enough; that she might still care for him was more than he could bear.

At that moment, Jeffrey turned away from his circle of admirers and approached her. Oliver saw Moira turn and smile up at her erstwhile suitor and present brother-in-law. That smile was enough to make Oliver's stomach clench in disgust. Unable to endure seeing any more, he turned quickly away, muttered to Horatio that he was too tired to remain any longer, and left the room.

He prowled his bedroom like a caged tiger, MacDamon excitedly yapping at his heels. What had he done to himself? he wondered. After promising himself to keep his emotions in check, had he nevertheless fallen in love with the lady? He was, he told himself, ten ways a fool! Horatio had warned him; his own instincts had warned him. And yet here he was, torn apart by feelings over which he seemed to have no control, jealousy and rage and a misery so overwhelming that it seemed more like grief than love. How had he let it happen? And, more important, how could he make it pass?

The answer came immediately to mind and shone like crystal in its beautiful clarity: *I should leave this place at once!* How perfectly obvious! "That's the answer, isn't it, Mac?" he asked, bending down and rubbing the animal's shaggy ears. It was a solution that would make everyone happy but Moira. Alberta would be happy, for she'd no longer have to worry about having a vagabond gardener for a brother-in-law. Barbara would be happy, for there would be no embarrassing announcement to mar her ball. Lord Pattinger would be ecstatic: he'd be rid of the vagrant without incurring the anger of his daughter. And Oliver himself would be happy—or at least begin to recover from this misery—because he would have left the source of that misery behind. Horatio might be disappointed, but he could write to Horatio later, explaining everything. The only one who'd suffer from his defection would be Moira herself. He would have let her down. But her scheme was a foolish one from the start; he'd not been consulted on the planning of it, she'd cozzened him into the execution of it, and he'd be damned if he'd blame himself for the failure of it.

He could leave right now! He had his breeches, Horatio's coat, and a pair of boots. The boots, of course, were of her providing, but he'd send her the money for them as soon as he got back home. To take his departure, he didn't have to do anything, prepare anything, wait for anything. There was no need even to write a note. None of them would expect a vagrant to write a good-bye note. They'd be grateful he didn't steal the family silver before he made off! All he had to do was tuck MacDamon under his arm and go.

Without allowing himself another moment of hesitation, he lifted up the dog and started for the door. He would take the back stairs. Unless someone came to call him down for another dancing lesson, his absence wouldn't be noticed until dinner time. By that time he'd be halfway to Surrey, and this peculiar adventure would be only a memory. He had only one regret—that he'd not had the chance to waltz with her. It would have been wonderful to have waltzed with her just once.

He took a last look round the room, threw open the door, and stopped short, startled at finding someone right outside the door, someone standing there frozen in place just as he was, her hand lifted as if just about to knock.

It was, of course, Moira.

CHAPTER
❧ ❧
SEVENTEEN

"OH!" MOIRA SAID IN SURPRISE. "I WAS JUST ABOUT TO KNOCK."

"Were you?" Oliver asked, feeling as guilty as a child caught with his hand in the cookie jar.

"Yes." She looked at him questioningly. "Were you taking MacDamon for a walk at this hour?"

"I . . . er . . . didn't think you'd need me," he muttered lamely.

"But I do." She crossed the threshold with her purposeful stride and beckoned him to follow. "There are a great many things we must talk about."

He followed her into the room, feeling trapped. "Have you decided to abandon your plan?" he asked hopefully, letting MacDamon loose to cavort about her skirts. "After seeing how distressed Barbara was this morning, I can't help feeling it might be best to—"

"No, Babs and I had a long talk, you see." She sat down on the edge of the bed. "Come and sit here beside me, Thomas. And as for you, MacDamon, be still! I want to talk to your master without any disturbance from you!"

Both dog and man sat down obediently, the animal at her feet and the man at her side. Oliver tried not to look at her, but, as if she had purposely intended to undermine his resolve, she was particularly lovely at this moment, and he couldn't keep his eyes from her face. Her hair was charmingly tousled, her eyes still sparkled from the stimulation of the tea party, and her cheeks were deliciously flushed. *Damnation!* he thought. *Why didn't I make my escape two minutes earlier?*

"Babs and I talked all morning," Moira began. "She'd been fearful from the first that I intended to marry you, and she guessed that we were to announce it at the ball. She was dreadfully upset at the prospect. I finally had to tell her my real intent—"

"That you aren't really going to marry me?"

"Yes. It was only by that admission that I was able to calm her down."

"Naturally," Oliver muttered sarcastically. "It must have been a relief to her to know that she would not have to recognize me as a relation."

"Heavens, Thomas," Moira said, cocking her head at him in surprise, "you sound offended. Babs has nothing against you personally."

"No, of course she hasn't. No one has anything against me 'personally' unless you become so witless as to wed me."

"Thomas! How bitter you sound!" She looked at him worriedly. "What's changed you? What's gone wrong?"

He clenched his fists, trying to get his emotions under control. "Nothing, ma'am. Nothing at all. I'm only . . . tired."

Her expression of alarm altered at once to one of guilt. "Yes, of course you are. So much excitement . . . all this company . . . all this tumult. And the doctor warned me that you may not be fully recovered. I'm a thoughtless wretch. I shall go at once and let you rest. We can talk later."

"No, there's no need to go," he said. "There may not be time later. I'm fine, really. I *want* to hear what you have to say."

She studied his face for a moment and then nodded. "Very well, then, I'll be brief. The most important thing I have to tell you is that I made one concession to Babs."

"A concession? Don't tell me you agreed to let her give Sir Godfrey back to you!"

"Thomas! What a distasteful thought!"

"Why distasteful? You considered wedding him at one time, didn't you? What makes him distasteful now?"

"It's not Godfrey who's distasteful!" she said angrily. "It's

you! You know perfectly well that Babs loves him. How can
you think so little of me that you would believe I would
willingly make her unhappy? And besides, how can you think
I'd ever take him back? Didn't we agree that Godfrey is a bit
of a fool?"

"I thought we did," Oliver admitted, "but if you could be so
foolish as to fall in love with someone like Lord Presswood—
that court card Jeffrey!—I suppose you might be foolish in
other ways."

She stiffened in enraged offense. "How *dare* you speak to
me in this way, Thomas Oliver! You forget yourself!"

"No, ma'am, I don't. I am never permitted to forget who I
am . . . or my place in this house."

She jumped to her feet and wheeled on him furiously. "If
you are implying, by that retort, that this has anything to do
with your lack of rank, you are insulting! I would take offense
at the Prince himself if he dared to disparage my private
feelings!"

He heard only one thing in all those words. "You *are* in love
with Lord Presswood, then?" he asked warily.

"It is none of your business whether I am or not."

In despair, he ran his fingers through his rebellious hair. "I
can scarcely believe it of you," he muttered miserably.

She was too furious to notice his pain. "You are a dastard to
believe it of me! Jeffrey is my own sister's husband!"

"But he was your suitor first."

"Yes, he was. That doesn't mean that I—" She caught
herself up, struck by the realization that she was about to
explain herself. She didn't understand why, but she had a
sudden, rather humiliating need to justify herself to him.
Almost against her will, she sank down beside him again. "If
you must be told," she said quietly, her eyes lowered, "he
made a most attractive suitor. It's easy, at first, for a girl to fall
in love with his sort, you know. It's only later that the charm
wears thin."

Oliver's heart swelled with sudden joy. She did not love
Jeffrey after all! He wanted to sweep her up in his arms and
dance her round the room. He wondered what she would say if
he did it. Slap his face, no doubt. The surge of joy retreated as

quickly as it had come, as his logical mind pointed out to him that although she didn't love Jeffrey, it did not follow that she therefore loved *him*.

"But all that is neither here nor there," Moira said with a sigh. "Tomorrow night is all that should concern us. Do you want to hear about my concession to Babs or not?"

"Of course I do, ma'am," Oliver said with a noticeable lack of enthusiasm.

Moira chose to ignore his glumness for the moment. "I agreed to make our announcement to the family at dinner *before* the ball, instead of causing a furor at the ball itself. The ball is for Babs, after all. It would not be fair to turn attention to myself. And there will be twenty or more at dinner, so the announcement of our betrothal will be public enough to impress my father as to the seriousness of my intent. Do you think I'm right?"

"I have no opinion, ma'am. This is your scheme, not mine."

Her brow furrowed in bewilderment. "What *is* the matter with you this afternoon, Thomas? You've been belligerent about everything I've said."

"I'm sorry," he said. "I didn't mean to be." He was aware that he was not making the conversation easy for her, but he couldn't seem to help himself. "Please go on."

"There isn't much more." All she had left to discuss with him was how he was to comport himself at the dinner, but she felt reluctant to say these things. His mood was strange this afternoon, and he might interpret her remarks as belittling him. She dropped her eyes to the hands folded in her lap. "I only want to tell you a few things about the dinner," she said hesitantly, glancing briefly at his face before going on. "You are probably not familiar with large formal dinners like this, so I thought that . . . that you should be prepared."

"Yes. Go on."

"Well, you see, after the dinner has been consumed and the covers removed, the hostess generally invites the ladies to leave, thus permitting the gentlemen to enjoy their brandies."

"I've heard of that custom, ma'am."

She threw him another troubled glance. "I don't mean to disparage you by these explanations, Thomas. How can I tell what you know and don't know about my sort of life? I only want to make things easy for you."

"Yes, I understand. I didn't take offense."

But something in his tone made it impossible for her to believe him. Her eyes, clouded with confusion, searched his face. "Dash it all, Thomas," she burst out, "stop looking at me that way! I am not a haughty, condescending prig!"

"I never said you were, ma'am."

She blinked at him for a moment, biting her lip unhappily. Then, with a shrug of frustration, she proceeded. "I thought that the best time for the announcement would be right before the ladies take their leave. Since you and Horatio seem to have become friendly, I think he'd be the appropriate person to make the announcement." She paused, waiting for a reaction from him.

"If it's my approbation you want, ma'am, you have it. Horatio will do very well. Have you told him yet?"

"No, I still don't want anyone to know. If our news gets out ahead of time, who knows what someone might do to circumvent us. That's why I think it best to keep our secret until the formal announcement is made. Babs has sworn she will not breathe a word."

"Then how will Horatio know—?"

"I shall hand him a note just beforehand. After he reads it, I'll give him a signal and he'll stand up and make a toast to us. Then, Thomas, you must get up from your place, come round to me, help me up, and . . . and take my hand while they drink to us." Here she blushed a bright pink. "It also might be appropriate for you to . . . to look at me a bit fondly."

He was undone by her blush. The bitterness and resentment that had clogged his chest seemed to melt away. "I think I can manage to do that," he said, a small smile turning up the corners of his mouth and breaking through the tightness of his expression.

His little smile warmed her. "Can you, Thomas?" she asked in a grateful whisper.

"I can even kiss you, if you like," he offered.

She gasped. "Kiss—?"

"Yes. Like this." And before he even knew what he was

about, he pulled her into his arms and kissed her hard and long. She was so startled by the abruptness and unexpectedness of the act that she did not resist. She lay so limp and unresponsive in his arms that, when he realized it, he let her go. For a long moment they stared at one another. In that moment, he thought his chest would explode from the wild hammering of his heart. His eyes took in her wide-eyed gaze, the color that rose and faded in her cheeks, and her full mouth, slightly open and trembling. He groaned from the joy and pain of it, and pulled her to him again. Slowly, deliberately, he pressed his mouth to hers, urgent with pent-up passion. One of his hands slipped round her waist and pulled her tight against him, and the other cupped her cheek, then crept round her throat and up to her hair where it clenched a handful of red-gold curls. He felt her stiffen against him for a moment and then suddenly yield, her body bending to him, a slim reed yielding to the wind, and a sound came from deep in her throat like a stifled cry. He felt a surge of triumph. *She loves me*, he thought, *I can feel it!* But no sooner had the feeling swept over him than she stiffened again, and with a force astounding in a girl so slim and feminine, pushed back and broke from his embrace. "No!" she cried, lifting her hand and rubbing the back of it against her mouth as if to wipe away the kiss and all memory of it. *"No!"*

His heart sank. "Moira—?"

"No!" she said again. Her breast heaved in what he now realized was more fury than passion. "Thomas, how could you?"

"I don't know," he muttered. "I thought . . ."

"That was despicable!" she accused. "Utterly vulgar!"

His bitter anger returned in full force. "Vulgar? Yes, of course. That's *just* what it was. Well, ma'am, you should have expected it. How else does a vagrant behave?"

She stared at him, trying to bring her vision of him back to what it had been before. Thomas Oliver was never vulgar. What had gotten into him today? His behavior had been strange all afternoon. "It must be my fault," she murmured after a moment, her voice choked with emotion.

This change in her from angry accusation to self-blame startled him. *"Your* fault?"

"I have misled you. This situation . . . this bedroom . . . this intimacy. I shouldn't have allowed matters to . . . to . . . get out of hand. It was wrong of me. Especially since this is not your way of life. How could you be expected to know ours? Our ways . . . our standards are different from yours."

He shut his eyes to blot out the tearful look of her. What she'd just said had been the deathblow of his hopes. To her he was and always would be a vagrant she'd found bruised and bloody in her stable, nothing more. A low, despicable creature she'd befriended out of pity and her own temporary need. She could not—would never—see him as the man he was.

He got up and turned away from her. "My standards are not so different," he said quietly. "In *any* society it's considered vulgar for a man to embrace a woman against her will. I do apologize."

"And so do I. I've treated you with the intimacy of a brother. The younger brother I never had."

"I am not much younger than you, ma'am. If there's a difference in our ages, it is too slight to matter."

"Everything matters, I'm afraid. Backgrounds, ages, everything. I thought, mistakenly, that treating you as a younger brother was the most comfortable way to offer you friendship. The results show how wrong I was. I shall keep a more proper distance in future, I promise." She came up behind him and touched his arm. "But can you . . . will you remain my friend, Thomas?"

He sighed in defeat. "Yes, of course," he said, turning and taking the hand she offered. "As long as you need me."

"Thank you, Thomas." She slipped her hand from his hold and turned to go. "I think we can forget what happened just now. We won't speak of it anymore. But you must promise, Thomas, never to do it again."

"Yes, ma'am," he said, playing the humble vagabond to the hilt.

She went to the door. "Thomas?" she asked over her shoulder.

He noticed that her lips looked bruised. He took perverse pleasure in the sight. "Yes, ma'am?"

The bruised lips curved in a shy smile. "Tomorrow, when they are toasting us," she said, "you may kiss my hand."

He smiled back. "Yes, ma'am," he said. "Since all else is forbidden, a kiss on the hand will be better than nothing."

When she was gone, he stared at the closed door ruefully until MacDamon's barking shook him from his brooding. "Yes, yes, Mac, I hear you. You want to know why we don't run off as I planned? Well, I'll tell you, old man." He lifted the dog in his arms and sat down with him on the edge of the bed. "She needs me to play out her little scheme. I'll give her that. It will all be over soon. You and I can stand it for a little while longer, can't we?"

MacDamon barked an undecipherable answer.

"You say I'll be sorry?" Oliver, more miserable than ever, swept the dog up in a tight embrace, burying his face in the shaggy fur. "I know it, old boy. I'm sorry already."

CHAPTER
❧ ❧
EIGHTEEN

HENRY HAD BEEN MOST HELPFUL IN ASSISTING OLIVER TO DRESS for the ball, but when it came to tying neckcloths, he was all thumbs. "Cain't do it, Mr. Oliver," he admitted after crushing three of them into a state of uselessness. "Per'aps we should send fer Alfred."

"Alfred?" Oliver asked.

"Lord Pattinger's man. Though Alfred's so 'igh in the instep, 'e won't like dressin' a . . . a . . . ." Here, realizing he might be offensive, he stopped himself.

"A vagrant?" Oliver suggested.

"Anyone without a title."

"Then let's not bother to ask him," Oliver said, calmly taking a fresh neckcloth and tossing it round his neck, "I'll do it myself." He stepped up to the mirror and quickly folded the neckcloth into a perfect Oriental. "There. How's that, Henry? I'd say it was tolerable."

Henry gaped admiringly. "More 'n tolerable, I'd say. Very posh indeed! Where'd ye learn t' do it? Were ye per'aps a gentleman's gentleman, an' not a gardener at all, like everyone believes?"

Before he could answer, there was a knock at the door. "Are you dressed, Thomas?" came Moira's voice. "I'm bursting to see how you look!"

Oliver hesitated. He had not seen Moira since the emotional outburst of the previous afternoon, for he'd not gone down to take a meal with the family and their guests. He'd excused himself by claiming to be weary and needing rest before today's important festivities. She'd been avoiding him, too, for she'd not come near his room in more than twenty-four hours. Yet here she was now, right outside his door, sounding as warm and friendly as if nothing had passed between them.

Henry misinterpreted the reason for his hesitation. " 'Ang it, 'ere y' are in yer shirt-sleeves. Quick, lemme 'elp ye on wi' yer coat, an' then ye'll be all ready. 'Ere we go!" With the coat on and buttoned, Henry took one last, approving look at his charge and then hurried to the door. "Come in, miss. Mr. Oliver's all dressed."

"Yes, I see!" She stepped over the threshold in a rustle of silk and studied him from top to toe. "Thomas! You're perfect!"

But it was *she* who was perfect. Oliver hadn't ever seen her look quite so breathtaking. She was wearing a slim, pale peach gown cut delectably low across the bosom and partially covered by a billowing overdress of silver tiffany silk. The shiny fabric was so sheer that it seemed to him she was surrounded by a cloud. Glints of silver sparkled all over her, from the tiny silver shoes that peeped out from below the gown, to the silver bracelet clasped on her wrist over her long white glove, to the narrow band of silver filigree that was set among her red curls. He found the vision so dazzling he was unable to speak.

Moira, reading his admiration in his eyes, blushed. "Henry," she said, turning to the footman to cover her embarrassment, "you are to be complimented. However did you learn to tie an Oriental?"

"Is that whut it's called, ma'am? An Oriental?" the footman asked. "Well, ma'am, I thank ye fer yer kind words, but it wasn't me who—"

Oliver found his voice in time to cut the fellow off. "Henry may not know the *name* of the fold, but he certainly knows how to tie it," he said hastily. "Thank you, Henry, for all your assistance."

"Yes, sir, Mr. Oliver," Henry muttered, throwing Oliver a

puzzled look. "If you 'ave no more use fer me, I'll be goin' downstairs. Mr. Pearce'll be needin' all 'ands tonight."

After he'd closed the door behind him, Oliver continued to gape at the vision before him. "It's fortunate I don't have a headache, or I'd believe I was dreaming again," he murmured.

"If that's a compliment on my appearance, sir," she said with a shy smile, "it's the strangest one I've ever received."

"It's a compliment, sure as check," he assured her. "I would have phrased it more conventionally if I weren't certain you'd have heard those conventional compliments so often before."

"That depends. What sort of conventional phrase did you have in mind?"

He shrugged: "Oh, something like 'you are too beautiful to be real.'"

She felt her throat tighten. "No one has ever said anything like that to me," she admitted, finding herself suddenly breathless.

"Well, I've thought from the first that the suitors you seem to have chosen are a most inadequate lot."

"I can't argue with you on that score," she laughed. "Isn't it remarkable that a man I discovered in my stable should be better at phrasing a compliment than any of my chosen suitors? Even better than I can myself, it seems, for I can't think of a proper phrase to compliment *your* appearance."

"That's only because I have an inspiring subject, and you don't."

"That's not true. Look at yourself in the mirror, Thomas. You look to the manner born in those evening clothes. You have wonderful shoulders and a really fine leg." She pulled him to the mirror and turned him toward it, touching his face lightly with a gloved finger as she spoke. "And see, the swelling is gone from your chin, and even the skin round your eye is no longer discolored. Godfrey may be Grecianly perfect in features, and Jeffrey may ooze silver-haired distinction, but your face, I think, has more manly charm."

"Has it indeed?" Foolishly carried away by her words, he captured her hand and pulled her to him. "For someone who can't phrase a compliment, I'd say you are doing very well."

Her green eyes turned as frightened as a rabbit's. "Thomas! You're . . . you're not going to k-kiss me again, are you?"

"Well, I'd very much like to. But not if you object. I'm not so vulgar as all that."

"I do object. Please let me go."

"My manly charm is not enough to win you, then?"

"*Please,* Thomas . . ."

He dropped his hold on her and turned away. "I'm sorry, ma'am. It seems I'm unused to compliments. They go to my head."

"Perhaps it's only because you're dressed and ready for your role as my betrothed," she suggested gently. "Like a good actor, you're getting in the spirit of the part."

"How kind of you to explain my 'gaffe' away like that. Yes, I think the role *is* affecting me."

"Then let's go down and perform," she said, turning to the door, her overdress billowing behind her. There she paused and turned back to him. "If you are ready, sir, I would be happy for your escort."

"Yes, ma'am," he sighed, crossing the room and offering his arm. "I'm as ready as I'll ever be."

CHAPTER
❦ ❦
NINETEEN

THE DINING HALL GLEAMED IN THE LIGHT OF TWO CHANDELIERS and three branched candelabra set at even intervals on the long dining table. Twenty-four diners, clad in festive splendor, sat round the table eating, drinking, and filling the air with the cheerful noise of self-satisfied people enjoying themselves. An army of footmen, all in full livery, ladled creamed soup into the diners' ornate, gold-rimmed bowls; loaded their Minton china dinner plates with sliced roast meats, lobster patties, poultry fillets, and an astounding variety of vegetables; filled their cut-glass goblets with imported Burgundy; and offered them a choice of pastries from huge trays of tarts, nougats, iced cakes, soufflés, and all sorts of jellies and creams.

The diners were either members of the family or guests who had come some distance and were staying at the house for the weekend. They were all so well known to one another that conversation flowed easily. Despite the formality of their dress, the table settings, and the service, an air of comfortable intimacy permeated the room.

At the head of the table, Lord Pattinger observed the activity coolly through the lenses of his pince-nez, occasionally offering a word or a thin smile to his sister Joanna, seated at his right, or to his son-in-law Jeffrey at his left, but otherwise confining his attention to the various dishes put before him, which he nibbled at gingerly and which elicited from him either mild approbation (expressed by a twitch of his nose) or such decided disapproval that a mere flick of his hand would bring a footman running over to remove the offending dish at once.

At the other end of the table, Moira, with practiced efficiency, saw to the management of the repast by means of unobtrusive signals to the butler, while at the same time keeping up a lively conversation with all those seated near her. Oliver, seated not very far away from the hostess, watched her performance with admiration. Susan, Lady Presswood, was on his right and made a very pleasant dinner companion, chattering away cheerfully and requiring no more than an occasional nod from him as encouragement to go on. On his other side, near the center of the table, sat the blushing bride-to-be, just opposite her betrothed. Barbara, in a white lustring gown trimmed with pink roses, looked becomingly flushed and happy. Nearby, Alberta and Horatio, also opposite each other, were proudly accepting good wishes from the guests on the imminent birth of what everyone hoped would be a son and heir.

While the footmen were passing out the pastries, Horatio was handed a folded note. Though he was puzzled, he nevertheless was wise enough to open it on his lap, below the tabletop. He read it twice, adjusted his spectacles, and read it once more. Then he flicked a questioning look at Moira, who was watching him. Moira gave him a firm nod. But Horatio didn't move until he'd thrown Oliver a similar look and received a similar response. Then, with a worried glance in the direction of the host, he took a deep breath and tapped on his wineglass with his spoon for silence.

The diners looked up at him as he rose, anticipating a toast to the betrothed couple. Horatio cleared his throat. "I'm not gifted at speechmaking," he began modestly, "but—"

"Speak up, Horatio!" Lord Pattinger barked. "We can't drink to a toast we can't hear."

Horatio colored in embarrassment. "It seems my esteemed father-in-law agrees as to my lack of gifts," he muttered ruefully. Then, raising his voice with an effort, he went on. "But, unworthy though I am, I am honored to have been chosen, not to offer a toast to our newly betrothed Barbara and her Godfrey, for that will come later, but to make a surprise announcement to you. Our own beloved Moira has asked me to tell you that she has, this day, accepted an offer of marriage from a gentleman who, in the short time we've known him, we in the family have grown very fond of and have come to admire and respect, Mr. Thomas Oliver."

The diners gasped, and a murmur of puzzled voices rose in the air. Jeffrey was heard to mutter, "Who the devil is Thomas Oliver?" Aunt Joanna's eyebrows rose in astonishment. Lord Pattinger dropped his wine goblet, which fell upon his dinner plate and shattered with a resounding crash. Ignoring all this, Oliver got up and went round the table to Moira's side.

Horatio raised his glass. "To Moira and Thomas!" he intoned.

The guests, though surprised and confused, got to their feet. "To Moira and Thomas," they echoed. Oliver smiled at Moira as "fondly" as he'd been directed and lifted her hand to his lips.

But Moira's eyes were fixed on her father far down at the other end of the table. He had not risen but was glaring at her in fury. It was not until the guests had reseated themselves that he rose slowly, a storm cloud gathering strength, and pointed a shaking finger at her. "Your sense of humor leaves much to be desired, my girl!" he said, his tone quiet but ominous. "Now tell everyone the truth . . . that this is nothing but a silly joke."

Moira took Oliver's hand in hers and squeezed it reassuringly, but her eyes remained on her father's face. "It is no joke, Father," she said, forcing a bright smile. "Please sit down. Pearce, have all the glasses refilled. We must now drink to Barbara and Godfrey."

"You heard me, Moira Pattinger! Apologize to all of us *at once*!" Lord Pattinger's last words were emphasized by a swing of his arm. It was a wide, angry gesture; it knocked over all the goblets in the vicinity and swept several dinner plates to the floor with a dismaying crash. Women screamed. Gentlemen gasped. Jeffrey, who'd been splattered with wine, jumped to his feet uttering a curse. Barbara burst into tears. Godfrey dropped his head in his hands in embarrassment. Susan turned to Moira, demanding to know what this was all about. Lord

Pattinger, in impatience, swung his arm in the other direction, causing the breakage of more china and crystal with another resounding crash. The servants, perplexed by the unexpected disorder, ran about haphazardly hither and yon in a pointless flurry. The once cheerful atmosphere of the room was abruptly transformed to one of alarming noise and confusion.

Horatio bravely started from his chair with the intent of trying to restrain his father-in-law from further violence. Suddenly a sharp cry from Alberta pierced the air. "Horatio!" she screamed, reaching out a hand to him, her arm stiff with agony.

"Dearest, I'm only going to try to calm your father," he explained. "No need to upset your—"

"No!" she gasped, shaking her head. "No! I—"

Something in Alberta's cry alarmed Moira. "Bertie, please," she said soothingly, dropping Oliver's hand and going round the table to her sister, "don't concern yourself about this. It's all going to turn out well, I promise."

But Alberta continued to wave her arm frantically. "No, not . . . you," she gasped, shutting her eyes and wincing. "You don't . . . understand." She pushed her chair back from the table with one hand, holding the other one against her stomach. "Quick! Get . . . Horatio! I'm afraid I . . ."

Moira, unable to understand what her sister was saying, stared at her aghast. "Bertie, what on earth—?"

"The midwife!" Alberta muttered, rising clumsily from her chair and grasping Moira's arm in a viselike grip. "Get . . . the midwife!"

"Oh, my God!" Moira clasped the swooning Alberta in her arms, slowly sinking with her to the floor. "Horatio, help me! I think the baby's coming!"

CHAPTER
❧ ❧
TWENTY

A MERE TWO HOURS LATER, THE BALL WAS IN FULL SWING. THE music was so lively and the ballroom atmosphere so festive that the thirty-odd guests who arrived after dinner were not aware that a family drama had been enacted earlier. In Moira's absence, Susan had taken over the duties of hostess, and she'd kept things running so smoothly that Barbara and Godfrey were able to recover their good humor and enjoy to the fullest the congratulations and good wishes of all the company.

Those guests who'd witnessed the scene in the dining room were able to put it out of their minds because of the absence from the ballroom of the key players in the earlier drama. They knew that Alberta was engaged in the act of birthing, and they hoped there would be news before the ball was over, but nothing else that had happened seemed particularly significant. The knowledge that Miss Moira's betrothal was somewhat strange—and that Lord Pattinger was upset by it—made an interesting bit of gossip, but it was not something to trouble the minds of distant relations and weekend guests or to interfere with the pleasure they took in the dancing. Even Alberta's labor, though its onset had been dramatic in the extreme, was in itself not a particularly remarkable activity; babies were born every day. It was certainly not a sufficient reason to cancel the ball. And so the ball proceeded, with only five people absenting themselves from the festivities: Alberta, who was otherwise occupied; Moira, who was with her; Horatio, who was pacing about distractedly in the upstairs sitting room waiting for the baby to arrive; Oliver, who stayed at his friend's side; and Lord Pattinger, who had stalked out of the dining room right after Alberta was carried off and had shut himself in his study for the remainder of the evening.

The midwife, two housemaids, and Moira were upstairs in Alberta's bedroom, attending the mother-to-be. Dr. Dunning had been summoned, too. When he arrived, he looked over the situation and then went down the hall to the sitting room to reassure Horatio that matters were proceeding normally. "But the wee one is slow in coming," he explained. "I'm afraid yer wife's labor will be a long, difficult one, an' that's a fact. Perhaps ye should try to get some sleep."

But Horatio shook his head. Sinking down on the sofa with a groan, he dropped his head in his hands and braced himself for a long vigil. The doctor promised to make further reports from time to time, and returned to the care of the mother. Horatio looked up at Oliver. "You don't have to stay, Thomas," he said. "I don't mind if you go to bed for a few hours."

"Not on your life," Oliver declared. "I'm here for the full stretch."

But the words were barely out of his mouth when Henry appeared in the doorway. "Lord Pattinger's lookin' fer ye, Mr. Oliver," the footman informed him uneasily. "Says 'e's awaitin' ye in 'is study."

Horatio and Oliver exchanged glances. "Dash it, Henry," Oliver muttered, "can't he wait until the baby comes?"

"He says now, Mr. Oliver. I don't think 'e'd like it if I said ye wuz waitin' fer the baby."

"No, he wouldn't," Horatio agreed. "He'd probably ask if you were passing yourself off as a midwife now."

Oliver gave a short, mirthless laugh. "Oh, very well, Henry, tell him I'll be right along." He said nothing else until Henry had gone. Then he sank down beside Horatio on the sofa. "What do you suppose he wants?"

"To chop you up in little pieces and feed you to the hounds," Horatio said glumly, "but I suspect he'll settle for having you thrown out into the night."

"You're probably right. Oh, well, I've sponged on his

hospitality for longer than I ever expected. It's time I was on my way."

"On your way?" Horatio looked at his friend with a troubled frown. "But what about Moira? You're as good as betrothed, you know, now that it's been announced."

"Once his lordship has dispensed with me," Oliver sighed, getting to his feet, "I suspect he won't have much difficulty convincing Moira to send me packing."

"You don't know Moira. If she's serious, he'll have the *greatest* difficulty."

"*If* she's serious."

"Are you saying she isn't?" Horatio prodded. "Was that announcement tonight nothing but a joke, as Lord Pattinger claimed?"

"Time will tell," Oliver responded cryptically, strolling to the door. "If I win this round, I'll be back with you in a trice. If I don't, I'll write to you and explain it all. Meanwhile, Horatio, you know I wish you and Alberta all the best. I suppose I'm expected to say that I hope it's a boy, but in truth I've always thought that, if *I* became a father, there's nothing I'd like better than a pretty little girl to dandle on my knee."

He waved jauntily to his troubled friend and went quickly down the long corridor and round the bend to the west wing. He tapped on the door of Lord Pattinger's study with admirable firmness and was immediately told to enter. His lordship was not seated at his desk but standing before the fire, leaning on the mantel and staring down into the flames. "Sit down," he ordered, not bothering to look up.

Oliver sat. "The news from the doctor, my lord, is that your grandchild will make an appearance sometime before dawn," he offered, his tone warm and conciliatory.

"So I've heard. I don't need you, fellow, to bring me information about my own family."

"Sorry," Oliver muttered. "I didn't mean to encroach."

"You've done nothing *but* encroach," his lordship snapped, turning to face his visitor. "What will it take to get rid of you, eh? One thousand pounds? Two?"

"I've already told your lordship that I want nothing from you."

"Don't take me for a fool, or play the fool yourself! If you think you can do better by standing fast until wedding my daughter, you are more of an idiot than I take you for. Whatever Moira says now, in the end she will *not* marry you. You will find yourself with nothing. I could simply wait until this farce has played itself out, and let you learn the lesson for yourself, but I want you gone and my household returned to peace and order *now*. Therefore, I will go as high as three thousand. It is many times more than you could earn in your lifetime. Take it and go."

"I don't think you understand me, my lord. Money means little to me. My word, on the other hand, means much. I am promised to your daughter. Only she has the right to release me from that promise."

Lord Pattinger threw up his hands. "*Five* thousand, then." He came up to Oliver's chair and looked down at him through his spectacles. "Five. It is my final offer."

Oliver made a move to rise. "Good," he said, "for that means we needn't prolong this conversation. I beg to be excused, my lord."

Lord Pattinger pushed him back into the chair. "You are not excused. I'm not through with you yet, fellow."

"May I remind you, my lord, that I have a name? I hope you will not think me oversensitive in finding the epithet 'fellow' to be somewhat demeaning, but would *you* not find it an affront to be always called 'fellow'?"

"*I* would, certainly. I would find it the height of disrespect. But *I* am not a vagrant without even a pair of boots to call my own."

"I see. Then am I to understand that only men of property are entitled to respect? And that those of us who are not propertied are not even worthy of the respect of being addressed by our own names?"

"Exactly so. But then, 'fellow,' I am offering you a chance to change all that for yourself. With five thousand pounds you will be a man of property and have all the respect you desire."

"Thank you, but I don't desire that sort of respect."

Lord Pattinger gritted his teeth. "Do you know what you're saying, you idiot? You are refusing *five thousand pounds*!"

"Yes, my lord, I am."

"Do you really expect me to believe that the slim chance that Moira might marry you is worth five thousand pounds to you?"

"The chance that Moira might marry me is worth more to me than all the money in the kingdom."

"You, fellow, are *insane*!" He wheeled about, strode to his desk, and leaned heavily on it, his head down. "My daughter is threatening to wed a man who, in all probability, has escaped from Bedlam!"

"If you set your daughter's worth at five thousand pounds, my lord, I think *you* are more fit for Bedlam than I am."

Lord Pattinger glared at him over his shoulder. "Mind your brazen tongue, fellow, or I shall have you taken out and thrown into the duck pond."

"That, my lord, is what I expected you to do."

"No, I won't be goaded into that," his lordship muttered. "Moira would probably run after you and wed you dripping wet, just to spite me! I'll have to think of something else. But believe me, fellow, I shall think of something. And when I do, you'll be sorry you ever set foot in this house!"

"Yes, my lord. And now may I be excused?"

"Yes, yes, get out of my sight!"

Oliver went quickly to the door. "Then I'll bid you good night, my lord."

"You may save yourself the trouble. I will have a dreadful night, what with babies being born, and betrothals being celebrated, and young idiots spurning gifts of a veritable fortune! A *dreadful* night. What I wish *you*, fellow, is as bad a night as mine!"

CHAPTER
TWENTY-ONE

IT WAS MORE THAN AN HOUR PAST DAWN WHEN DR. DUNNING, rolling down his shirt-sleeves, came into the sitting room where Horatio and Oliver, unshaven and red-eyed, waited impatiently for news. "It's a girl," he announced cheerfully. "She's tiny but a healthy specimen, an' that's a fact. The mother is exhausted but well."

Horatio leaped to his feet, overjoyed. "May I see—?"

But Moira appeared in the doorway, holding the swaddled infant in her arms. "Here, Horatio," she whispered, smiling. "Come and see your baby. Bertie thinks you should call her Grace."

Horatio took the bundle in his arms and beamed down at the tiny, red-faced infant, now fast asleep. Overwhelmed by this first taste of fatherhood, he could not take his eyes from the diminutive, shriveled face. "Oh, my!" he breathed. "Isn't she beautiful?"

But Oliver had eyes only for Moira. She was vastly altered from the vision that had floated on a silver cloud into his bedroom only twelve hours before. Her silver hairband, as well as the gloves and bracelets, were gone, her silk dress was crushed beneath a huge, blood-smeared apron, her hair was damp and matted against her head, and her face was lined with weariness and covered with droplets of sweat. Yet he, like the besotted new father, wanted only to breathe, *Isn't she beautiful?* He had an almost uncontrollable urge to gather her in his arms and kiss the weariness from her forehead. At that moment he understood the depth of his feeling for her. It was a feeling deeper than any he'd experienced in his life. He was a lost man.

Moira, her eyes moist with tenderness for the new father in his happiness, took Horatio's arm and led him out of the room to his waiting wife. The doctor and Oliver watched them go. Then Dr. Dunning sighed with satisfaction and put on his coat. "Well, I'm off to home. And you, ye young scapegrace, ye're lookin' worse 'n me, an' that's a fact. Get yerself t' bed at once! Doctor's orders!"

Oliver nodded obediently and went off down the hall. But his step had neither the jaunty satisfaction of the doctor's nor the stumbling joy of Horatio's, for he could anticipate only the dubious pleasure of a wild greeting from MacDamon and a very lonely bed.

He slept so deeply that when he finally woke, he didn't remember at first where he was or why he was so abominably depressed. It was not until MacDamon barked an excited greeting that the events of the night before slowly came back into memory, and he understood the cause of his depression: the pain of a deep, unrequited, incurable, and probably permanent passion. *Why didn't anyone ever warn me that love is synonymous with misery?* he asked himself as he threw off the covers and climbed out of bed.

The clock on the mantel informed him that it was almost teatime. Wondering if he, in his role as Moira's new betrothed, was expected to make an appearance at tea, he dressed himself as quickly as his frisking dog permitted in his old breeches, the last of his new shirts, and his precious boots. He was just putting his arm into Horatio's remodeled riding coat when there was a tapping at the door. MacDamon raced round his legs as he crossed the room to open it. "Moira!" he exclaimed to the vision in the hallway. "Did you come to collect me for tea? I was just coming down."

"No, there's plenty of time for that. But I have news for you. May I come in?"

He stepped aside to let her pass. She was indeed a vision in a high-necked muslin walking dress of Lincoln green, with a starched white collar and a bewitching little satin bow at the neck. Her face had lost all tinge of weariness and now glowed with excitement. "I take it that mother and baby are doing well?" he asked as he followed her in.

"Yes, very well," Moira said, picking up MacDamon and stroking him absently. "Little Grace is taking her feedings like a hungry little kitten, and Bertie is convinced that there's never been a baby in all of time more beautiful, more good-natured, or more brilliant." She perched on the bench of the dressing table and sat MacDamon on her lap. "But I haven't come to bring you the news from the nursery. I have something of more immediate concern to tell you. I had a talk with my father today."

"Oh?" Oliver sat down on the edge of the bed facing her. "Did your father tell you of our interview?"

"Yes, he did. He said I'd attached myself to a crazy man." Oliver smiled ruefully. "He may very well be right."

"I don't know how to thank you, Thomas," she said, keeping her eyes fixed on MacDamon and her hand busily smoothing his neck. "You gave up a fortune for my sake."

"There's no need to thank me. If it weren't for you, I might very well have died in that stable."

"Nevertheless, most men would have taken Father's offer. It is ten times what I can give you."

"Then I'm not like most men."

"I knew that from the first." She looked over at him with an expression he couldn't fathom. "We've won, Thomas. Because of your steadfastness, Father has surrendered."

"Surrendered?" he echoed stupidly, his mind seeming to resist accepting what he was hearing.

"Yes, completely. He's agreed, at last, to let me go to London to my aunt."

"Oh, he has, has he?" An icy hand seemed to grip his chest. "On condition that you get rid of your latest suitor, of course. Me."

"Well . . . yes, I told him I'd cry off." She looked at him questioningly. "Isn't that what we'd planned to do?"

The grip on his chest was so tight that he was surprised he

was able to breathe. "Yes, it is," he said. "It's exactly what we planned. When do you intend to announce your 'change of heart'?"

"Today at tea. I think I'll simply say that we were not serious. That it was all a joke, just as Father said it was."

"I see. My role is finished, then."

"Yes. Now there's nothing left of our little plot but for me to fulfill my final obligation to you." She set MacDamon on the floor and stood up, pulling a folded paper from her sleeve. "Here, Thomas," she said, her cheeks becoming tinged with color as she held the paper out to him. "It's a letter to a Mr. Jennings, my man of business in London. As soon as he receives it, he will provide you with five hundred pounds. You may claim it in person if you wish; or you can have him send it to wherever you are."

Oliver got to his feet, but he was stiff with fury. "You once called me vulgar, ma'am. Don't you think that you're the one being vulgar now?"

The color washed from her cheeks. "Vulgar? What do you mean? I'm fulfilling our agreement. I don't see why that's vulgar."

"Don't you? If it were money I wanted, wouldn't I have taken your *father's* offer?"

"No, you wouldn't. You are not the sort to break your word. I know that I can never adequately repay you for what you've done, Thomas. God knows, no other man of my acquaintance ever withstood Father's bribes." She took a step toward him and held out the paper. "For that alone you deserve a reward, don't you? Please take it."

His fists clenched in anger and frustration. "Damnation, ma'am, try to think! Imagine yourself in my place this once. Think of what I've been doing for you these past days. Do you imagine that five hundred pounds—or even five thousand—can be compensation enough for having to act the humiliating role of your unacceptable suitor, the suitor *so repellent* that the mere threat of wedding him brings your proud, hitherto unyielding father to his *knees*?"

"Thomas!" she gasped, white-lipped. "I never meant—! No one ever found you repellent! How can you even think it?"

"How can you not think it, when everything happened exactly as I just described it?"

"It is not at all a fair description! Please, Thomas, don't be overly proud. I offer you this reward in sincere gratitude."

"Thank you, Miss Pattinger," he said between clenched teeth, "but I think as little of your gratitude as I do of your reward." And, pulling the letter from her hand, he ripped it twice, crumpled the pieces, and tossed them to the floor, where MacDamon came and sniffed them interestedly.

Moira stared at Oliver's angry face, aghast. "If the role was so distasteful to you, Thomas, and the money, too, then why—"

"Why?" He gave a bitter, self-mocking laugh. "Why did I agree to do it? For the only reason a man ever undertakes to humiliate himself. For love, ma'am."

"Oh, Thomas, no—!"

"Oh, Moira, *yes*! I love you. One would think you'd have guessed it before this. But not being susceptible to the emotion yourself, you may not be able to recognize it in others."

"Not susceptible—?"

"I suppose I have no right to blame you. I was warned. Her father's daughter, they told me. An ice maiden. I should have known better."

"I'm not an ice maiden!" Her eyes filled with tears. "Oh, Thomas, I never meant to hurt you. I'm so sorry . . ."

He held up a hand and turned away. "No, don't be sorry. I didn't reject your 'reward' to make you sorry. I only want you to understand why I won't take it. Your offer of money belittles what I feel."

"But . . ." She wrung her hands in helpless anguish, unable to understand her own turmoil or to ease his. "Please, Thomas, you must let me do *something* for you."

He wheeled around and grasped her shoulders. "Then let me take my own reward. My own vulgar reward." And, pulling her roughly into his arms, he kissed her mouth. It was a kiss meant to make her feel what he felt, to melt the ice in her, to burn into her memory so that, when he was gone, she would always feel him on her mouth. With that one kiss, he tried to express his anger and his passion and the terrible longing that he knew he would never lose. But after a moment, when he felt her resistance weaken and her body become soft and pliable in his arms, a wave of tenderness swept over him. He wanted to cradle her, rock her gently, hold her safe and protected in his arms against all the storms of life. It was *this* feeling he wanted her to remember most of all . . . the sweet, close, tender part of loving. He lifted his head, the tenderness still glowing in his eyes, and with one hand still tight on her waist, he lifted the other and smoothed her cheek. Her eyes were wide and startled, and her lips slightly open, as if poised and ready for more. But Oliver would not kiss her again. "Good-bye, Moira Pattinger," he said softly, drinking in the sight of her. "When you are the rage of London, I hope you'll remember this vulgar kiss I stole."

Then he let her go, scooped MacDamon up in his arms, and strode to the door. "Come on, Mac," he said. "We've used up our welcome. Let's get out of here."

CHAPTER
❧ ❧
TWENTY-TWO

HE WAS BACK WHERE HE STARTED FROM, WALKING THE ROADS OF England, heading for the south coast. *More or less* where he started from, he reminded himself. The *more* was MacDamon, a most welcome companion. The *less* was a longer list: a beaver hat (which was lost), a rucksack (which had been stolen), completely empty pockets, a battered head, and a very bruised heart.

Some of those losses he intended to retrieve, and to that end, his first stop was the Twin Elms Inn. It was just after dark when he reached it. Tucking MacDamon under his arm, he entered the taproom and looked round. Maggs, the innkeeper's wife, was already busily serving platters of mutton chops and tankards of home-brew to the half-dozen patrons already on the premises, but Louch and the boxer, Ironfist, were not among them. Oliver tapped the rotund woman's shoulder. "Good evening, Maggs."

She turned and peered at him closely, shifting her heavy tray to her left shoulder. "Know me name, do ye?" she asked, puzzled.

"Don't you remember me?" Oliver prodded. "I've put up here before."

Her brow cleared. "Fer certain, sir! I 'member ye clear as day. Ye spent the night, less 'n a fortnight ago, ain't that right? An' ye paid yer shot wi' a gold guinea."

"Right as rain," Oliver said with a smile. "I'll take a room for tonight, if you have one."

"For you, sir, anytime." She smiled back, showing a missing tooth. "We don't git many round 'ere 'oo pay wi' gold."

Oliver hoped she would not ask to see the color of his money now. "And a basket for my friend, here," he said, patting his dog.

She shook her head. "Not in yer bedroom. I can find a place fer yer animal in the stable," she offered.

"No, I want him with me."

The woman eyed the dog with distaste. "Seems a strange sort of dog fer a gennleman to carry about, if ye wuz t' ask me. Bit if 'e won't bark all night, I s'pose ye can keep 'im wi' ye."

"And I'd like you to rent me the private parlor, too," Oliver said, easing his conscience with the old adage, *In for a penny, in for a pound*. If his plan was successful, he'd manage to pay. If not, well, he'd worry about it later.

"Oh, yes, sir! Our private parlor'll suit ye just fine. Right 'cross the passage there. Make yerself comfy-like, an' I'll be right along t' take yer order."

"Very good. And bring along a bit of rope when you come, will you?"

"Rope, sir?"

"Yes. A few feet will do. I need to . . . to tie up a box."

"Yes, sir, but I'll 'ave t' charge ye fer it. We don't give away rope fer nothin'."

Oliver made a gesture with his hand to indicate that he was completely indifferent to the charge. To his relief, she continued to accept on faith that he still had gold in his pockets. "There's one thing more, Maggs," he added. "I have a bit of business with one of your patrons, a gentleman called Mr. Louch. Do you know him?"

"Yes, sir, 'e comes 'ere regular."

"Every evening?"

She looked at him suspiciously. "Mos' every evenin', yes. What does a gennleman such as yersel' want wi' the likes of 'im?"

"I . . . er . . . have something for him. Will you send him in to me when he arrives?"

"Yes, sir, if that's yer wish. But ye'd best 'ide yer purse when 'e sets hisself down. A smoky cove, ol' Louch."

"He's always in the company of another fellow, a Mr. Finley, is that right?" Oliver asked.

"Yes, that's right. Ironfist Finley. Best boxer in the county."

"Well, I'd like you to ask Mr. Finley to wait a few minutes *outside* the parlor door until he's invited in. I need a few words with Mr. Louch in private."

"I'll tell 'im," the woman agreed, but after Oliver started toward the private parlor, she added a warning. "If yer up t' some 'avey-cavey doin's, me young sir, ye'd better not do 'em on *these* premises, gold or no gold!"

Later, when she came to the parlor with his length of rope, Maggs was startled at the dimness of the room. She lit the candle in the center of the table and offered to light a few more. "Lemme light the sconces, too, sir," she suggested with unwonted generosity. "Ye don' want t' take yer dinner in the dark, do ye?"

"The firelight is quite sufficient, thank you," he answered. "And Maggs, don't bother to bring my dinner until after I've seen Mr. Louch."

Oliver closed the door after her and began to make his preparations. First he cut off a length of rope and tied MacDamon to the leg of the heaviest piece of furniture in the room, a shabby, chintz-covered sofa that stood against the wall opposite the fireplace. "It's only for a little while," he explained to the animal who, if one could judge by the hurt expression in his eyes, was direly offended. "You've got to be kept from dashing about underfoot. Come now, Mac, don't look at me like that! It's for your own safety. And please, old chap, don't bark if you can possibly restrain yourself."

With MacDamon taken care of, he turned his attention to some other details. He cut the remaining piece of rope in two and stowed the pieces in his coat pocket. He untied his neckcloth, pulled it off, rolled it up and slipped it into another pocket. He blew out the candle on the table. He moved a chair to the fireplace, placing it with its back to the flames. Then he sat down facing the door, the fire behind him, and waited.

He did not wait long. Within fifteen minutes, Louch poked his head in the door. " 'Oo is that?" he asked, squinting in at the shadowy figure silhouetted by the fire. "Is it me ye wuz wantin' to see?"

"Yes, please come in, Mr. Louch," Oliver said silkily, noting with satisfaction that Louch was wearing a very familiar hat. "Come in and see what I have for you."

MacDamon growled, but Louch did not seem to hear. However, the little braggart did hesitate. Torn between curiosity and suspicion, he could neither bring himself to step over the threshold or withdraw. "Kin me chum come in wi' me?" he asked.

"In a moment. But first I have something for you alone. You alone, Mr. Louch."

Louch strained for a moment more to try to make out the identity of the shadowy figure before the fire, but, not succeeding, he withdrew his head. Oliver heard him muttering instructions to Ironfist. "If ye 'ear me shout, come in like a shot, eh, Jim? Like a bloomin' shot!"

When Louch opened the door again and stepped over the threshold, Oliver was ready for him. He sprang to his feet, crossed the room in two strides, and captured Louch from the rear by throwing an arm tightly round his throat. The familiar beaver rolled from the miscreant's head as he choked and gagged from the pressure of Oliver's arm. MacDamon began to bark wildly. Before Louch could recover from the shock of the sudden attack, Oliver stuffed a handkerchief in his mouth with his free hand. "Quiet, Mac!" he ordered as he whipped out his neckcloth. He let Louch flail about while he bound the cloth over the braggart's mouth and round his head.

Calmly and efficiently, while Louch kicked and struggled, Oliver pulled the little fellow's two arms to his back and tied his wrists tightly with a piece of rope. Then he lifted him bodily and dumped him on the sofa, causing MacDamon to leap up and down to see for himself what his master was doing. What Oliver was doing was catching Louch's flailing legs in a tight hold and tying them at the ankles.

With the fellow thus secured, Oliver went to the table and lit the candle. Holding it up, he turned to the sofa. "Well, Mr. Louch, take a look at your assailant. Do you recognize me? You should, you know. You were wearing my hat."

The little man's eyes widened as if seeing a ghost. His body twitched and a groan of agony issued from his throat.

"Yes, I see you do," Oliver said, smiling. "Surprised you, eh? Did you think I was dead? That you'd done for me?"

Another twitch and groan issued from the trussed-up body on the sofa.

"No need to twitch like that, Mr. Louch," Oliver said pleasantly. "I don't intend to cudgel you and split *your* skull, though it's no less than you deserve. I have other plans for you. So if you'll just lie there quietly—and you, too, Mac!—we'll call in your friend and get on with this."

He placed the candle back on the table and went to the door. "Mr. Finley, please come in," he said, pushing open the door but keeping himself back in the shadows.

Ironfist, so huge that he had to stoop as he stepped over the threshold, pulled off his cap and looked round with innocent curiosity. A growl from MacDamon and a groan from Louch drew his eyes to the sofa. "*Blimey*!" he exclaimed. "Whut—?"

Oliver closed the door quietly behind the boxer. "Good evening, Mr. Finley," he said.

Finley wheeled round. "Whut's the lay 'ere?" he asked, frightened. "Whut do ye mean by trussin' up me chum?"

Oliver walked over to the table, into the light. "Do you recognize me, Mr. Finley?"

Ironfist blinked at him for a moment. Then his eyes widened and his jaw dropped. "No!" he gasped. "It cain't be!"

"What is it, Finley? Don't you trust your eyes?"

"Be ye a . . . a *ghost*?" the large man whispered, awe-struck.

"No. I'm no ghost, as you'll soon discover. We have some unfinished business, you and I. As I recall, we were in the midst of a mill when your 'chum' over there saw fit to interfere. Well, I've fixed it so that he can't interfere now. Take off your coat, Ironfist Finley. We can move the table and set to it right here, or we can fight out in back of the stables. The choice is yours."

Ironfist's slack-jawed expression did not change through all of Oliver's speech. "You *ain't* a ghost?" he asked again.

"Would a ghost want to engage in fisticuffs? Of course I'm no ghost."

"Be ye alive, then?"

"Yes, no thanks to you."

"Oh, bless me soul, *alive!*" the huge man muttered, and to Oliver's astonishment, he sank to his knees and burst into tears. "Oh, thank the Good Lord 'e ain't dead!" he wept, rocking himself back and forth. "I didn't kill 'im!"

Oliver stared at him in bafflement. "Why are you taking on like this, man? It wasn't you who cudgeled me. It was your friend there."

But Ironfist didn't seem to hear him. He just kept rocking himself back and forth, weeping with joy. His emotion was so loud and so genuine that even MacDamon began to whimper in sympathy.

Oliver, flabbergasted, strode over to the trussed-up Louch. "What's gotten into him?" he demanded.

Louch twitched in his bonds and made incoherent sounds in his throat. Oliver pulled him to a sitting position, undid the knots in the neckcloth, and pulled it off. "Well, speak up, fellow! What's the matter with him?"

Louch spat the handkerchief from his mouth and coughed. "Whut're ye gonna do t' me?" he asked nervously.

"Never mind that now. Tell me what's wrong with Finley."

Louch shrugged. "Poor Jim's been tetched in 'is upper works since the day we crowned ye," he explained. "We took ye fer dead, see?" He wet his lips with his tongue and glanced at Oliver's face uneasily. "We never meant fer t' kill ye. I didn' expec' the blow t' be so . . . so weighty."

"It was weighty, all right," Oliver said ruefully, rubbing the back of his head in recollection.

"Aye. We 'ad a real fright seein' ye layin' there, all white an' limp. Made me sick t' my breadbasket, I kin tell ye."

Oliver raised an eyebrow. "Very sensitive of you, I'm sure."

"But, see, it was worser fer Jim, some'ow. Seein' ye

dead-like, well, it made 'im loony. 'E ain't slept, 'e won't eat, 'e won't even fight. 'E says we're gonna rot in 'ell fer whut we done."

"And so you may. But, dash it all, I've been counting on a mill with him. I almost had him that day. If you hadn't split my skull, I would have had him. I've been dreaming of knocking him down. I can't think of a more satisfying revenge. Can't you talk to him? Make him stop that deuced weeping!"

"Jim, quit yer snivelin'," Louch called out obligingly. "The gennleman on'y wants a bit of a mill. Very sportin' of 'im, if ye wuz t' ask me."

Finley sniffed, wiped his nose with the back of his hand, and got clumsily to his feet. "I won't mill wiv 'im," he said. "Not ever."

"Why not?" Oliver asked, crossing to him. "There's nothing wrong with a fair fight. I'll not go to the magistrates even if I lose."

"Ye'll lose fer sure," Louch put in. "It's Ironfist there, y'know, not some damn trifler. Ye'll lose."

"That remains to be seen," Oliver retorted. "I was the boxing champion of my form at school. What will you put up to back your boast?"

"Put up?" Louch asked, blinking.

"Yes. What's left of my twenty-nine guineas, eh? You can't have spent all of it in less than three weeks."

"I 'ave a guinea or two left," Louch said carefully.

"I 'ave *all* of me share," Finley said, eagerly emptying his pockets. "I never spent a penny. 'Ere, take 'em back! I never want t' look at a yellowboy agin." And he threw fourteen gold guineas upon the table.

"No, confound it, Mr. Ironfist Finley, I want to finish that fight!" Oliver insisted. "Come on, man, we're wasting time. Shall it be here or outside?"

"No, sir," the huge man said. "Never again, long as I live. These 'ere fists . . . they're a curse. If ye wish t' swing at me, go on. But I'll not swing back. I'm givin' up boxin' ferever."

"But hang it, man, *you* didn't kill me! The only thing you

did that was reprehensible was taking that scoundrel there to be
your friend."

Ironfist Finley shook his head. "No, ye don't understand. I
never thought about whut my fists could do 'til I felt me fist
break yer nose. It wuz the mos' dreadfulest sound. It made me
sick y'see. Real sick. Then I seen ye layin' on the ground, wi'
yer face so white, an' the blood leakin' over yer mouth, an' yer
chin swellin' up like a biscuit in the soup, an' I thought, may
the Good Lord fergive me but I done somethin' real sinful!
Then—Oh, God!—it began t' rain on ye, big cold drops
runnin' down yer face." Here poor Finley became so deeply
affected by his story that he began to weep again, his shoulders
shaking with emotion. It took a few moments before he could
get himself under control. Then, with a shuddering sigh, he
wiped his eyes with his sleeve and went on. "So we laid ye
under the 'edge, but it wasn't whut anyone would call a proper
burial. Well, it was then that somethin' went strange in me. I
couldn' bear it, y'see. Seein' ye dead like that. I *couldn'*! I
couldn' move 'r take me eyes from ye. Louch, 'e 'ad t' drag me
off! 'E kep' sayin' not t' worry, that I'd get over it, that the
gold in me pocket would 'elp me to ferget. But I didn't ferget.
I kep' seein' yer poor, bleedin' face every time I closed me
eyes!" He sank down at the table and dropped his head in his
arms.

"But, Finley, old chap, I'm *not dead*. Here I am, hale and
hearty as I've ever been," Oliver said consolingly.

Finley lifted his head, a beatific smile transforming his face.
"Yes, it's a miracle fer certain!" he exclaimed in a hushed
voice. "The Good Lord felt me misery an' is givin' me a
chance t' redeem meself!"

Oliver, nonplussed, threw a helpless look at Louch on the
sofa. "Does he mean it? Has he really given up boxing for
good?"

Louch shrugged. "When a man gets religion, no one kin talk
'im out of it." He licked his lips again, his shrewd eyes
carefully watching every change of expression on Oliver's
face. "Whut'll ye do now?" he asked.

"About you, you mean? I'm thinking, man, I'm thinking."

"Ye said ye'd not go to the magistrates," Louch reminded him.

"No, not the magistrates. If I did, they might sentence you to the gibbet, and poor Finley with you. Though hanging is just what *you* deserve, your friend does not."

"Ye mean ye'll let me go?" the miscreant asked hopefully.

"Not quite," Oliver said, striding across the room to him. He untied his hands. "Empty your pockets, Louch."

The little man hurriedly did so, tossing two gold guineas and some shillings and coppers on the table.

"Is that all?" Oliver asked suspiciously.

"Yes, sir. That's all. I swear!"

"Don' swear to a lie, chum," Finley said reproachfully. "Ain't ye 'ad enough o' gammon an' sham?"

Louch glared at him and threw two more guineas on the table.

"*Now* is that all?" Oliver demanded.

"Aye," Louch said glumly. "That cleans me."

Oliver pocketed a dozen guineas and pushed the rest toward Finley. "There," he said. "That's for you. The new you."

"Thank you, sir," the ex-pugilist said, "but I don' want it."

"Put it in the poorbox, then," Oliver said, bending down to untie MacDamon, "when you go to church to give thanks for your 'miracle.'" He stood up, tucked the dog under his arm, and came round the table to Finley. "I ask only one thing in return."

"What is that, sir?"

"That you keep a sharp eye on your friend, here. If ever he tries again to rob anyone or to cheat in any way, you must let him feel your fists."

"But I swore I'd never—"

"The Good Lord would not disapprove of your using your fists to keep a sinner on the straight and narrow."

"Aye, that may be so!" The boxer lifted his fists and studied them with a slowly dawning smile. "Usin' me fists to keep a sinner straight! Whut an idea!"

"As for me, I think I'll be on my way," Oliver said, half to himself. "It will remove temptation from Mr. Louch's vicinity. Besides, this place depresses me. Good-bye, gentlemen. You can be sure I shan't forget any of our meetings." He strolled to the door, but then came back and picked up the beaver hat that had rolled into the far corner. "I hope you don't mind, Mr. Louch, if I take back my hat. You've had the use of it long enough."

He went out the door but stuck his head back in a moment later. "One thing more, Finley," he said. "When Maggs comes in to collect what I owe her, make *him* pay it. With one of the guineas the liar still has in his pocket."

CHAPTER
❧ ❧
TWENTY-THREE

MOIRA STOOD WHERE OLIVER LEFT HER, STARING WIDE-EYED AT the door through which he'd just disappeared. She was shaken to her core. Her lips still burned with the pressure of his kiss, and her emotions seethed with anger, humiliation, and all sorts of other feelings she could not name. The man she knew as Thomas Oliver, vagabond and trespasser, had just had the temerity to accuse her of thoughtlessness, selfishness, and condescension. On top of that, he'd dared to kiss her! *Again!* And then he'd turned on his heel and left her, without giving her the opportunity to defend herself against his slanderous attacks on her character or to slap him for the liberty he'd taken with her person! He would be made to pay, the very next time she saw him!

But would there *be* a next time? He'd taken his little mongrel dog and gone out the door with something like finality. From what he'd said, and the tone in which he'd said it, she had the impression that he was leaving the house for good. Had he really meant it? Could he really be gone? No, he wouldn't have left so abruptly. He'd said good-bye to *her,* of course, in his vulgar way, but he hadn't said it to anyone else. He would surely have wished to say good-bye to Barbara, to Godfrey, to Susan who'd so quickly taken to him, and especially to Horatio. He certainly would not leave without saying good-bye to Horatio. Perhaps, if she hurried, she could catch him with

Horatio. There still might be time to give him a piece of her mind.

She ran down the hall to Alberta's bedroom, where she was sure Horatio would be found. He'd spent every possible minute there since the baby had come. She was not mistaken. She found Horatio sitting on the edge of his wife's bed, gazing fondly at the child in Alberta's arm. But Thomas was nowhere in evidence.

The new parents both looked up at her entrance. "Come take another look at little Grace, Moira," Alberta said. "Don't you think her eyes are hazel? Horatio insists they are brown."

Moira looked. "I think they are hazel, too," she said, valiantly trying to force thoughts of Thomas from her mind, "but Dr. Dunning says that a baby's eye color often changes after a year or so. I would withhold judgment if I were you."

Horatio adjusted his spectacles and peered at her. "Is something amiss, Moira? You seem distraught."

"No, nothing's amiss. Everything is going particularly well, in fact. Except . . . tell me, Horatio, have you seen Thomas this afternoon?"

"Thomas? No. Why do you ask?"

"Because I think he may be leaving us. I wondered if he'd come to say good-bye to you."

"Thomas? Leaving *now*?" Alberta frowned in annoyance. "He wouldn't leave now. He hasn't seen the baby yet."

Horatio studied his sister-in-law's face intently. "Has something passed between you and Thomas, Moira? Have you quarreled?"

"No. Yes. That is, I suppose one could call it a quarrel." She took a nervous turn about the room. "Our betrothal is over. I've cried off."

"Cried off?" Alberta echoed, shocked.

"I'd say that crying off one's betrothal can be called a quarrel, yes," Horatio muttered dryly.

"Why in heaven's name did you cry off?" Alberta demanded.

"That's a strange question coming from you, Bertie. You objected to my wedding him from the first!"

"I *never* did!"

"Come now, Bertie," her husband interposed. "Be honest. We all hounded Moira—you and I and Babs, too—trying to convince her to send Thomas packing."

"We might have, just at first," Alberta admitted, "but *now* I find Thomas a very charming fellow, and so does Horatio, and if you want to wed him, Moira, we haven't the slightest objection."

"But I don't wish to wed him. I never did. I only pretended I did, to force Father to agree to let me go to London."

"Good God, Moira, was *that* your game?" Horatio asked in shocked disapproval. "How can you have used poor Thomas in that way?"

"I didn't 'use' him," Moira said defensively, knowing in her heart she had. "He was in on my scheme from the first."

"*In* on it? You mean he *agreed* to let you use him so?"

"Yes, he did. We had a bargain. He had as much to gain as I. I gave him a comfortable place in which to recuperate, didn't I? I put food in his mouth and clothes on his back. He himself admits he might have died but for me!"

"Yes, Horatio, dearest," his wife put in. "No one could have been kinder than Moira. After all, the man was a stranger."

"No one denies that she was kind. More than kind. But kindness, like virtue, is supposed to be its own reward, is it not? One isn't supposed to demand payment for it."

Moira faced him with a troubled frown. "How can you say I demanded payment?"

"Didn't you?" Horatio accused. "In return for that show of human kindness, you used him for your own purposes, did you not?"

Moira twisted her hands together in anguish. "I don't see why you call it *using* him. What was the harm?"

"To announce to the world one day that he is your betrothed and to jilt him the next is using him, if you ask me. Doesn't it seem so to you? You made him play the fool for you!"

"But we had an *agreement,* dash it! A *business* agreement. He did it to earn five hundred pounds!"

Horatio was taken aback. "Thomas? For five hundred pounds?" He shook his head in bewilderment. "I wouldn't have believed it of him."

"Nor would I," Alberta agreed.

"Why not?" Moira pressed. "What's wrong with his doing me a service for a fee? A very good fee, I may add."

"Nothing, I suppose," Horatio said, feeling unaccountably disappointed in his friend. "He just doesn't seem the sort to sell himself, for whatever amount, to be used for a scheme that was both dishonest and humiliating."

Moira lowered her head. "No, he isn't the sort to sell himself," she admitted, her voice low and choked with shame. "He refused the money."

"Yes, of course he did!" Horatio exclaimed, expelling a breath in relief. "That's more like what I would have expected of him."

"Thomas is a very admirable man," Alberta said thoughtfully.

Moira nodded, her throat burning with unshed tears. Somewhere, somehow, she'd misjudged Thomas, her own feelings, everything. She'd made a huge mistake, but she wasn't sure how or why. "It seems that you both are more in sympathy with him than I," she muttered in confusion. "He didn't take a penny from me, and you're proud of him for it. Whereas I . . ."

"You what?" her sister asked.

"I keep wishing he *had* taken the money. He deserves it, doesn't he? After being used and humiliated, all he got for his trouble was a"—she turned away so they wouldn't see her cry—"a paltry p-pair of boots!"

She left the room and ran down the hall to the staircase, wiping away her tears. She had tea to serve, guests to entertain (for most of the guests were still on the premises), and another company dinner to arrange. She had no time for self-indulgent emotions. Thomas had helped her accomplish her goal, and now he was gone; there was nothing more she could do about him. She would simply announce to the assembled company at tea that her betrothal had been a joke, and then she would put him out of her mind.

But when at last she fell wearily into her bed that night, she realized that he had not been out of her mind for a single moment. Instead of feeling triumphant about having won her victory, instead of having a head full of exciting plans for her newly won freedom, she was experiencing a terrible sense of loss. The cause of this unwonted depression could be summed up in four words: *Thomas Oliver was gone.*

She lay awake, trying to fathom the meaning of her emotions. From the first moment she'd laid eyes on Thomas, she'd thought of him as a means to an end. She'd never thought of him as a man she could seriously consider marrying. She'd made a threat to her father, and he was the means of carrying it out. A tool. Something to *use.*

But he wasn't a tool. He was a man. In Alberta's words, an *admirable* man. So admirable, in fact, that in a little more than a fortnight he'd won Horatio's friendship and had been able to convert Alberta from antagonist to supporter. Alberta had said in so many words that she would have "not the slightest objection" if Moira wed him! Susan had liked him from first glance. Babs, too, had taken to him early. The only reason Babs had ever objected to him was her inability to believe that Moira could possibly have stopped loving the "beautiful" Godfrey. Even Aunt Joanna had remarked today at tea that she was rather sorry Thomas Oliver was not Moira's betrothed after all, that he'd seemed a manly, clever fellow with the blunt honesty she liked in a man. The only one in the family who'd not been won over was her father, but no man who'd ever crossed their threshold had been able to win *his* approval.

No one could claim that Moira herself hadn't liked Thomas from the first. After all, she'd seen his worth before any of them. It was *she* who'd taken him in when he'd appeared to be nothing more than a battered, impoverished vagabond. She'd been taken with his smile, she'd noticed his ready wit, she'd liked his face even when it had been bruised and swollen. She'd been the first of the family to appreciate his virtues. But now all the others seemed to have forgotten where he came from, and *she hadn't.* She'd never been able to dismiss from her mind the fact that he was a penniless vagrant without background or family connections. He could not be considered an equal . . . not to Miss Moira Pattinger, eldest daughter of a man of wealth, property, and title. She had not been able to envision herself wed to a nobody. *Oh, dear God,* she admitted to herself at last, *I have been a haughty, condescending prig!*

But if she could make herself see beyond her toplofty prejudices, she might finally be able to understand her confusing feelings. And the truth was, except for his lack of social standing, Thomas Oliver was everything she'd ever wanted in a man. And what was the importance of social standing anyway? What was its value when compared to the joy that comes from loving and being loved? Thomas's presence in the household had brought an exhilarating vitality to every moment of every day. She loved being with him, laughing with him, talking to him, or just looking at him. There was a bubbling intimacy in every look they exchanged, even before he'd ever taken her into his arms and kissed her.

And then, of course, there were the kisses. Not in all her twenty-six years had she been so stirred by an embrace. She could shut her eyes and relive each of those kisses in explicit, exquisite detail. She could feel the tingle of her skin where he'd stroked her cheek, the agitation of the blood in her veins when he held her close, the electrified shock of the pressure of his lips. And, if those memories were not agony enough, there was one even more exquisitely painful: the clench of her heart when he'd said he loved her. The sound of his voice saying these words, angry and resentful though he was when he'd said them, had thrilled her through and through. Somehow she knew that no matter who said words of love to her in the future, no one would affect her in the same way again.

She turned on the bed and hid her face in her pillow. The truth was that she loved him. She, the toplofty Moira Pattinger, wanted nothing more in life than to wed a penniless vagabond she'd discovered in her stable. If he by some miracle were suddenly to appear in this room at this very moment, she would throw herself into his arms and declare without reservation that she loved him more than life. That was the fact she had to face. But having faced it, she also had to acknowledge the possibility that it was too late to do anything about it.

The next morning, after a fitful night's sleep, she awoke to an appropriately gloomy morning. A heavy rain fell from an oppressively dark sky, its steady rhythm occasionally upset by gusts of wind that sent loud spatterings against the windows.

As she dressed, every thought depressed her: the thought of the number of guests she still had to entertain, of her plans for the future that now no longer excited her, of the long dreary day ahead of her in which there would be no sight of Thomas to chase away the doldrums. In a kind of desperation, she sought out Henry. "Have you seen anything of Mr. Oliver since yesterday?" she asked bluntly.

The footman shook his head. " 'E's gone, miss. Lock, stock, and doggie."

"How do you know that, Henry? Did he say good-bye to you, then?"

"Yes, miss, 'e did. 'E stopped off below stairs on 'is way out, t' thank me fer what I done fer 'im. Almos' like a real gennleman, Mr. Oliver was."

"Yes, he was. He didn't, by some chance, mention where he was going, did he?"

"No, miss, he didn't, but . . ."

"But what?"

The footman's lips curled in amusement. "But I kin guess where 'e made 'is first stop."

"Really?" She felt a sudden leap of hope in her chest. "Where is that?"

"The Twin Elms Inn, miss, 'bout four miles down the High Road," he told her, adding importantly, "I 'appen to know that Mr. Oliver 'ad some unfinished business there."

It took Moira less than half an hour to throw on a bonnet and shawl, order a carriage, and drive it herself through the downpour to the Twin Elms Inn. All through the ride, her heart sang with hope. He would be there! He couldn't possibly have left the shelter of the inn in such weather. As soon as she caught up with him, she promised herself, she would tell him honestly and without roundaboutation that she'd changed her mind . . . that she wanted them to be betrothed after all. *Really* betrothed. Her father would just have to learn to accept it.

But there was no Thomas Oliver to be found at the inn. Yes, he'd been there, all right. The innkeeper's wife didn't know his name but she recognized Moira's description at once. "Dark-'aired gennleman in a tweed coat? Yes, ma'am, 'e wuz 'ere las' night. Took the private parlor. But he didn't stay even long enough to eat 'is dinner. By th' time I brung in the tray 'e wuz gone, 'im an' that li'l mongrel dog of 'is."

Moira walked sadly out the door and, ignoring the effect of the downpour on her bonnet and her thinly clad shoulders, stood looking down the road that stretched to the horizon in forlorn desolation. There was no sign of human life on the entire length, only muddy puddles of water pockmarked with raindrops and littered with dead leaves. In its gray, wet bleakness, the view was the most melancholy she'd ever beheld. But she knew that her sense of desolation was not the fault of the rain. The sight of that empty, empty road would have broken her heart even in the brightest sunshine.

CHAPTER
❧ ❧
TWENTY-FOUR

MOIRA DIDN'T BECOME THE RAGE OF LONDON. IT WAS TRUE THAT when she first arrived at Upsall House, her aunt's London residence, in early March of 1817 (a full month before the official start of the social season), her outstanding beauty set tongues wagging and stimulated fervent excitement among the eligible gentlemen, but by the time the Season was in full swing the report that she was an ice maiden had been widely circulated, and the rumors killed her chances. It was her own fault. Every man who'd tried to penetrate her cool reserve had received a firm rebuff.

"It *is* your own fault, Moira," her aunt Joanna said at the breakfast table after her niece had been on the town for more than a month. "You deserve your ice-maiden reputation."

Moira looked over at her aunt from the window seat where she sat, her legs tucked under her, sipping a cup of morning coffee. "Do I, Aunt? I don't know why. What have I done to deserve it?"

"It's not what you've done, my dear. It's what you've failed to do." Joanna examined the small pile of invitations that had been delivered that morning, noting with a sigh that their number was dwindling every day. "You've given not one of the several gentlemen who showed an interest in you the least encouragement."

"But, my dearest aunt, how could I? I didn't wish to encourage them."

Lady Joanna Upsall peered at her niece in concern. The girl was breathtakingly lovely, even now, so early in the morning, before she'd dressed. There she sat, with a pale April sunshine lighting her tousled red curls, her lithe form wrapped in a softly shapeless blue morning robe, looking like one of Botticelli's Graces, voluptuous and vivid and exquisitely sad. One would think the gentlemen would be hammering down the door for her, but instead she was being painfully ignored. The only reason the aunt could think of was that the girl was untutored in the techniques of dalliance. At the advanced age of twenty-seven, and after having three near betrothals, she was still not skilled at the art of courtship. "I wish I understood the ways of the social world myself, my love," she said worriedly, "but all I can conclude is that you must be doing something wrong. Anyone with your spectacular appearance should have become the belle of the ton by this time."

"But what am I doing wrong, Aunt?"

Joanna shrugged. "I don't know. I am the last person qualified to give advice on the subject. With this horsey face of mine, I never was, even in my dreams, a belle. I never had a suitor in my life. I was always too boyish by half, a clumsy, awkward clod."

"But you married Upsall. And it was the happiest of unions, they say."

"Yes, but he couldn't be called, by any stretch of the imagination, a suitor."

"Then how did he manage to win you?"

Lady Joanna's overlong face brightened as a glow of recollection lit her eyes. "Well, my beloved Upsall was a scholar, you see, who rarely lifted his eyes from his Greek texts. We met on a spring day when we both happened to be strolling down a path in Hyde Park from opposite directions, each of us with nose in book. He charged into me, of course. I dropped my book and stumbled—I was a dreadful gawk!— and in his effort to support me, he stepped on my book. 'Damnation,' I said vulgarly, 'you've squashed my *Nicomachea*!' He picked it up, looked at it, and gaped at me. 'Good God,' he asked, 'are you reading Aristotle in *Greek*?' He'd never before met a female who could read Greek, you see.

Especially a beautiful one, he said. The idiot thought me beautiful, can you imagine? And since I'd never before met a man who found me beautiful—or one who could or *would* talk to me about philosophy—it was love at first sight. He didn't have to court me. From that moment, there was never any question that we would wed."

"Oh, how lovely!" Moira murmured, eyes moist. "I wish that love could have come to me like that!"

"What do you mean, 'could have'? There is still time."

Moira shook her head. "No, not for that match-made-in-heaven sort of love. I think I've missed my chance." She lowered her eyes to her coffee cup. "There was a man once . . . who thought, when he first saw me, that I was a fantasy created by his 'overwrought imagination.' It was a rather lovely, significant sort of encounter, but I . . . I failed to recognize it."

"Oh, my poor Moira," her aunt exclaimed with a pang, "is *that* what's been keeping you from accepting the attentions of the eligibles you've encountered here? A wounded heart?"

"Yes, I'm afraid so." She turned to stare out the bow window upon the little walled garden in which jonquils were just beginning to bloom. "I hoped I might get over it once I came to town and lost myself in the social whirl, but I haven't yet managed to recover."

"Who was it, my love?" her aunt asked quietly. "Not Jeffrey, I hope. He isn't worth a single tear. The man's not capable of loving anyone but himself."

"No, it wasn't Jeffrey. But to be fair, Aunt Joanna, he's managed to keep Susan happy all these years."

"Only because Susan is perfectly content to run the estate and have everyone address her as Lady Presswood. She never yearned to find a 'mate of the soul.' But if it wasn't Jeffrey, then who—?" She stopped and gave a little gasp. "That attractive Mr. Oliver, *that's* who it was!"

"Yes," Moira admitted with a little catch in her voice.

"But what happened? The fellow adored you. I saw it in his eyes."

The young woman put a hand to her forehead, the mere

memory of the past bringing a spasm of pain. "I was a fool. As I said, I failed to recognize the truth of my feelings."

Joanna, having been shaped only by her own romantic experience and utterly naïve about others, couldn't understand Moira's explanation. "How *could* you not have recognized it?"

Moira bit her lip. "Tell me the truth, Aunt. Would you have recognized true love if Upsall had been a mere commoner and not the Earl of Penhaven?"

"My dear girl," Joanna exclaimed in surprise, "how can you ask anything so silly? I didn't know Upsall's title until the day I married him. And it wouldn't have mattered a jot if I did. He was Upsall! Whatever else he was was entirely irrelevant."

"Yes, of course," Moira murmured, choked with shame. "I shouldn't have asked."

"Did you cast off Mr. Oliver because he had no title?" her aunt asked, shocked.

"I don't have your . . . your p-purity of character, Aunt," Moira said, crestfallen. "I *told* you I was a fool! Please, let's not speak of it anymore."

"Very well, my love," Joanna said gently, "after one more question. Are you sure it is quite finished? That there is no chance—?"

"None at all. He's gone. I shall never see him again."

Joanna expelled a long breath. Then, stiffening her back, she said firmly, "Then, my dear, you must set your mind on finding some other love. You can, you know, if you try. If you don't frighten off the candidates by making them believe you to be an ice maiden."

"What can I do to change my reputation, Aunt Joanna, if I don't understand how I earned it in the first place?"

"You earned it by coldly rejecting all the advances made to you," her aunt explained. "You should have encouraged at least a few of them."

"Why should I have encouraged someone whom I could never love? That wouldn't have been honest, would it?"

"No, I suppose not. But these girls who become the toasts of the town . . . don't they have hordes of admirers hanging about them? The more swains they have hanging about, the more the world admires them. Those girls certainly don't care for *all* of their hangers-on, yet they must encourage their advances."

"Is that what I must do? Encourage hordes of young men to follow me about?"

"It does sound vain and frivolous," Aunt Joanna sighed. "Dear me, I'm quite out of my depth. I wish I could advise you, Moira, my love. I wish I knew something about the art of flirtation. I'm a poor specimen of an aunt."

Moira jumped up and knelt beside her aunt's chair. "You are the most decent, honest, wonderful of aunts!" she declared, embracing her. "Much too fine to know anything about vanity and much too profound to trouble your head about flirtation."

Joanna looked fondly down at her niece and smoothed back the tousled curls from her forehead. "How can those fools think you cold?" she murmured. "You have the warmest, most affectionate nature!"

"Oh, who cares what they think of me? Perhaps I'm not the sort to make a success in London society. At twenty-seven, it's much too late for me to learn to be a simpering, coy little flirt. I shall probably never marry. What you should teach me, Aunt Joanna, is how to live independently alone, like you." She smiled up at her aunt, her eyes suddenly taking on a twinkle. "Do you think you might teach me to read Greek?"

CHAPTER
❧ ❧
TWENTY-FIVE

LATE THAT NIGHT, NOT MORE THAN A HALF-DOZEN STREETS FROM Upsall House, John Sherrard, the Earl of Lydbury, was sitting on the chaise in his wife's dressing room watching her plait her hair in preparation for bed. He was still in evening clothes, having removed only his coat and substituted a smoking jacket of red Florentine silk. "I'm worried, too, Emma," he was saying. "Nothing we've done for Oliver's entertainment seems to have shaken him from his lethargy. I warned you that it would be of no avail to come up from Lydbury and open the London house."

"I know you'd prefer to be in Surrey," Emma said, her fingers expertly kneading the strands of long black hair into a smooth braid, "but I shall enjoy dashing about in society for a change. It isn't only for Oliver's sake that I wanted to come."

"Balderdash! Don't pretend to me that you really wanted to leave little Edward, even if only for a month. Besides, you know you dislike town life as much as I."

Emma, Lady Lydbury, a sturdy, sensible woman with a sweet, perfectly oval face that was kept from beauty only by a slightly ruddy complexion, turned from the mirror and faced her husband with a sigh. "But, dearest, we couldn't go on watching your brother mope about like a brood mare who's lost a foal. We had to do *something*. I was sure a few weeks on the town would cheer him."

"It hasn't so far," her husband muttered, obviously discouraged.

"Well, it's only been a few days. Tonight's was only the second fete we've dragged him to. Didn't he ask any of those pretty young ladies to dance?"

"Not one. I tell you, Emma, that beating he took on his walking tour did more than break his nose. It did some damage to his psyche. He's a different man since his return. I sometimes think the only thing he cares about is that deuced mongrel dog of his. I'm surprised he didn't insist on taking MacDamon here to town with him!"

Emma curled the end of her braid round a finger thoughtfully. "I don't think Oliver is fundamentally changed, my love. It's only his mood that's altered. And I don't think it was the beating that altered it."

"No?" His lordship eyed his wife curiously. "What was it, then?"

"A woman. I'm sure of it."

"A *woman*? Impossible. He's only a boy!"

"He's almost twenty-four, John, and very much a man. And if you ask me, twenty-four is an age when a young man is particularly vulnerable to women's wiles."

"You think he fell victim to some female, then? That he fell in love and was rejected?"

"I wouldn't be at all surprised if that were the case. Although why any woman would wish to reject our Oliver is quite beyond me."

"Well, to be truthful, my love, he hasn't much to offer a woman," the Earl said thoughtfully, "other than his family connections and a great deal of charm."

"He has enough. When you settle his affairs, he'll be sufficiently well-to-do, won't he? And he's already found a place in civil service. Didn't he say he was going to begin his career in the fall?"

"All that is true, but many of you ladies seem to prefer a man with property and a title," his lordship pointed out ruefully.

His wife threw him a withering look. "If that's the sort of lady Oliver became enamored of, then perhaps it's just as well she rejected him. This family can do without a social-climbing hussy!"

"That may be, Emma, my love, but it doesn't help solve the problem. If it *is* an affair of the heart that has made him so depressed, what can we do about it?"

"We can find him another girl. The best cure for heartache is another love. And what better place for our purpose than right here in London?"

"It doesn't matter if we found him a girl here in London or in Timbuktu if he won't look at her. He didn't look at any of the ladies tonight. He just sat all evening with that friend of his from Oxford and some other young bucks and listened to them talk about pugilism. The only time he showed any animation at all was when he regaled them with a tale about some boxer named Ironfist who turned religionist."

"Well, dearest," his wife said cheerfully, turning back to her mirror and placing a lace-trimmed nightcap on her head, "tomorrow is another day."

The Earl got up and, muttering something derogatory under his breath about unwarranted optimism, crossed the hall toward his own dressing room. But before he opened the door, he heard the clink of a glass from the floor below. Curious, he went down the stairs and found his brother sunk deep in a wing chair in the drawing room, his feet up on the hearth and a glass of brandy in his hand. "I say, Oliver, it isn't like you to drink alone," he scolded.

"Come join me, then," Oliver said, waving his glass toward the bottle of brandy on the sideboard.

His lordship poured himself a drink and sank into a chair facing his brother. "You didn't seem pleased by the festivities tonight," he remarked.

"I enjoyed myself well enough," Oliver said without enthusiasm.

"'Well enough' is poor praise. What's wrong with you, Oliver? You've been in the dismals ever since you cut short your walking tour and came home to Lydbury."

"I was in the dismals on the tour," Oliver said. "That's why I cut it short. But I'm fine, John, truly. No need to trouble yourself about me."

"But I *am* troubled. I sometimes think that blow to your head has done you damage."

"You're off in your reckoning, old man," Oliver assured him, taking a hearty swig of his drink. "My head is good as new."

"How's your heart, then?" the brother persisted.

Oliver looked at him curiously. "My heart?"

"Emma thinks you've been wounded in love."

"Oh, she does, does she?" Oliver, refraining from further comment, simply frowned at the fire.

"Women like to believe they can sense these things," John ventured.

"Yes, they do."

"She's right, isn't she? Confound it, Oliver, tell me! Has some foolish chit floored you?"

Oliver sighed. "If she was a foolish chit, she couldn't have done it," he said in surrender. "She was a full-fledged champion."

"Was she?" John studied his brother with true sympathy. "I'm sorry to hear it. It's hard for a novice at the game to stand up to a champion."

"So I've discovered."

"Bruised you pretty badly, did she?"

Oliver stared into the flames. "Left me reeling a bit. But I'll get over it."

"Yes, of course you will. Emma says that all it takes is another go into the ring."

"Not I. Once was enough."

"Don't be a clunch. The world is full of lovely girls, any number of whom would be capable of mending your wounds. All you have to do is make yourself available. You don't enjoy wallowing in your misery, do you?"

Oliver's eyebrows rose in surprise. "Is that what I've been doing? Wallowing?"

"I'm afraid so."

"Good God! How revolting! It's this blasted lethargy. I can't seem to shake it off. What must I do to cure myself, John?"

"Stop resisting our efforts to push you into society, that's all."

"But, dash it all," Oliver objected, running his fingers through his hair, "I have some good reasons for my resistance. For one thing, I'm not suited for ballrooms. For another, I'm deathly afraid I'll run into her."

"Who? The very girl we're speaking of?" He blinked at Oliver in astonishment. "Here in London?"

"Yes, I think so. When I last saw her, she gave me to understand that London was her express destination."

John rubbed his chin thoughtfully. "Then you're *bound* to run into her sooner or later, that is, if she's a lady of quality."

"She's that, all right. Very high in the instep, in fact."

"I see. And you're fearful of your feelings should you see her again?"

"Half of me is. The other half . . ."

"Yes?"

Oliver smiled bitterly into his brandy glass. "The other half would take great satisfaction in giving her the cut direct."

"That's more like the brother I know," John said with a grin, getting to his feet and raising his glass. "Onward and upward! Bloody but unbowed! No little chit, no matter how high in the instep, can get the better of a Sherrard!"

"Hear, hear!" Oliver cheered, pulling himself up and clinking his glass against his brother's. "No Sherrard worthy of the name will henceforth be known to wallow."

They drained their glasses, threw them cavalierly into the fireplace and, arms about each other's shoulders, headed for the stairs. It was not until they reached the landing that the bravado faded. "You won't back down, will you, Oliver?" John asked, his face clouding. "You'll go to all the fetes that Emma wishes you to attend, and you'll dance with all the pretty girls?"

"Yes, John, yes," his brother said with a surrendering sigh. "Word of a Sherrard."

"One thing more, Oliver. What if you meet that chit again—the one who floored you? You said you're somewhat fearful of such an occurrence. As I said before, if she's here, you may very well run into her. London society does not encompass a very large circle."

"Let's forget I ever mentioned her," Oliver said, waving

away the problem with a flip of his hand. "Let's put her out of our minds completely. She's probably betrothed by this time anyway."

"Betrothed?"

"Yes. She becomes betrothed very easily." He proceeded up the stairs with a determinedly lively step. "I wouldn't be surprised to learn," he tossed back over his shoulder, "that she's betrothed herself to the very first title she encountered."

CHAPTER
❧ ❧
TWENTY-SIX

LADY DEWITT, ONE OF SOCIETY'S MOST ACTIVE HOSTESSES, WAS giving a party at which, it was rumored, the Prince would put in an appearance. Since Prinny was known to enjoy a crowd but not a crush, only forty invitation cards had been sent out, which would keep the attendance down to a manageable eighty. With the number of guests thus limited, all the recipients considered themselves quite fortunate. The Sherrards were therefore doubly fortunate, having received *two* cards for the affair: one for Lord and Lady Sherrard (Emma being first cousin to the hostess), and another for Oliver himself (for Lady DeWitt, in need of bachelors, wanted to be sure of his attendance).

Another one of the desirable cards found its way to Upsall House, for Lord DeWitt had been a close friend of the deceased Lord Upsall and always insisted that his wife include Upsall's eccentric widow on her guest lists. And Lady DeWitt, nothing if not gracious, had appended a note on the bottom of the card specifically requesting Lady Upsall to extend the invitation to her houseguest, Miss Moira Pattinger. Thus did circumstances conspire to create a situation in which Moira and Oliver might meet again.

But although they arrived at the DeWitts' door within ten minutes of each other, and although they milled about with the rest of the guests for more than two hours, they did not see each other. Circumstances were not so favorable as to permit a face-to-face confrontation for a while yet.

The DeWitts' London residence was impressive, with high-ceilinged hallways and enormous rooms, but their drawing room, even with the doors thrown open to encompass the circular entry hall, was not quite enormous enough to hold eighty guests without crowding. Especially tonight, when everyone was milling round the entryway watching for the Prince. Lady DeWitt had let it be known early that Prinny had given his word that he would certainly arrive before midnight. But when the clock struck eleven-thirty, and there was still no sign of him, Lady DeWitt's smile became forced.

Excitement mounted as the clock ticked on. Liveried footmen made their way through the press, carrying large trays of champagne and smaller ones of canapés. The hostess began to fear that the supply would run out before the Prince made his appearance. But at ten minutes to midnight, the front doors were thrown open and, to her intense relief and the crowd's delight, the royal entourage made its entrance.

The Prince was impressively attired in the most ornate of evening wear. His protuberant stomach was compressed into a tightly buttoned, striped satin waistcoat (from which a number of fobs and trinkets hung down), and above it he wore a velvet-collared evening coat bearing a number of royal decorations. The assembled guests, most of whom had met him personally, applauded his arrival with enthusiasm. Though his popularity was waning among his less-affluent subjects, the Regent was very much adored in these circles. The assembled guests opened a path for him through the entry hall to the drawing room but pressed closely together on either side of the "aisle" in hopes of catching his eye and winning a personal greeting.

The Prince, who very much enjoyed this sort of social engagement, paraded in peacocky importance down the aisle, calling out greetings and waving his hand at those friends he recognized. Sometimes he even stopped his progress and exchanged pleasantries with some lucky guest. One of the lucky ones was Lord Lydbury. "Good heavens, Lydbury," the

Prince exclaimed, "what are you doing in town? I thought you were in love with rustication."

"Good evening, Your Highness," Lydbury said, bowing. "I came up for my wife's sake. A woman needs a bit of society once in a while."

"Of course she does, and so does a man," the Prince said, poking his finger into Lydbury's chest to emphasize his point before turning to Emma with a smile. "How do you do, my dear? Rustication agrees with you." And he kissed her hand.

"I don't think you've met my brother, Your Highness," Lydbury added. "May I present Oliver Sherrard?"

"Oliver Sherrard?" The Prince turned to Oliver with brows raised. "I know that name. Let me think! Ah, yes! Didn't you box at school with my nephew, Harry FitzClarence?"

"Yes, Your Highness," Oliver said, making his leg. "I still remember his punishing right."

"Well, *I* remember that he told me you bested him consistently. I must have you both to Carlton House one day soon. Perhaps we can arrange another match. Nothing I'd like better than seeing you two fellows box."

"Ah, but Your Highness would have to cheer for Harry, wouldn't you?" Oliver asked with a bold grin. "Family loyalty and all that? Knowing that Your Highness was against me would surely put me off my game."

The Prince threw back his head and guffawed. Then he slapped Oliver on the back. "You have my word, my boy, that I'll practice strict impartiality. The very strictest impartiality." With another clap on Oliver's shoulder, he turned back to John. "I like your brother, Lydbury. You must bring him to me at Carlton House." With that he proceeded on his way down the aisle.

Back among the press of guests who'd been ignored by the royal visitor, Miss Moira Pattinger had watched the scene in white-faced astonishment. As soon as it was over, Lady Upsall turned to her. "I say, Moira, wasn't that your Thomas?"

Moira turned a pair of blind eyes on her aunt's face. "Yes! Yes, it was," she murmured in stupefaction, "but how—?" Her heart was beating much too loudly, and her blood seemed to drum in her ears. Then the floor began to heave under her feet.

Good God, she thought in panic, *I'm going to swoon like a green girl and cause a dreadful scene*. "Please, Aunt, help me out of here," she murmured, clenching her hands tightly to keep herself from succumbing to the frightening dizziness. "I must sit down."

Joanna, seeing how white her niece's face had become, immediately put a supporting arm round her waist and led her from the room. They should have made an eye-catching pair, the older woman looking thin as a rail in black lace and the younger spectacularly beautiful in green satin, but with everyone else's attention riveted on the Prince, their exit was not noted. Joanna, who knew the house well, led the trembling girl a few steps down the hall to a small sitting room. There Moira dropped down upon a loveseat near the fire and sank back against the cushions. "Thomas!" she breathed in stunned disbelief. "Thomas! *Here!*"

Her aunt looked down at her in concern. "We could have been mistaken, couldn't we?" she asked. "It could have been merely an uncanny resemblance."

Moira shook her head. "He even had the little bump on his nose. I am not mistaken."

"But you said Thomas Oliver was a vagrant, looking for work as a gardener. How can such a man be a crony of the Regent? Besides, *this* fellow seems to be related to the Earl of Lydbury."

Moira put a trembling hand to her forehead. "I don't understand how it can be so, dearest, but it *was* Thomas."

"Then I'm going out to find him and bring him here to you. Let him explain—"

"No, Aunt Joanna, you mustn't!" Moira cried, looking up at her aunt in terror-stricken confusion. "I *couldn't* . . . ! I can't face him now. I don't understand what this is all about, but I must have time to . . . to *think*."

Joanna peered down at her, her brows knit. "You are dreadfully pale, my love," she said after a moment. "Let me get you some brandy."

"No, no," Moira said, shutting her eyes. "Not brandy. Just a glass of water, if you would, please."

"Water will do no good. At least let it be champagne."

Not waiting for an answer, Joanna walked quickly from the room. She went directly down the hall to the drawing room, where music was now playing and people were milling about in chattering groups, sipping champagne, waiting for the buffet dinner to be served downstairs, and, in the meantime, keeping watchful eyes on the Prince to see who would next win the royal attention. Joanna beckoned to one of the footmen and took a glass of champagne from his tray. With this in hand, she crossed the room to where Oliver stood chatting with Lady Lydbury and a young woman to whom he'd just been introduced. Joanna tapped him firmly on his shoulder. "How do you do, Thomas?" she said loudly.

Oliver turned, stared at her, and paled. "Lady Upsall!" he gasped.

"I'm glad you remember me," she said bluntly. "It will save explanations."

"Of course I remember you," Oliver said, his eyes looking right and left for some sign of her niece. Then, recalling his manners, he drew her into the circle. "I'd like you to meet my sister-in-law, Lady Lydbury. And this is Miss Anthea Drew. Emma, Miss Drew, this is Lady Upsall."

Emma looked at the lady in black lace curiously. "Did I hear you call my brother-in-law *Thomas*, Lady Upsall?"

"Yes, you did," Joanna replied flatly. "I was led to believe that was his name."

"Really? How curious!" Emma looked at Oliver in amusement. "Is there a fascinating tale involved here, Oliver? Something you can tell us to explain this mystery?"

"No one would like to hear the tale more than I, Lady Lydbury," Joanna interrupted with brisk implacability, "but there is someone whose curiosity is even greater than ours. She is waiting for you in the sitting room, Thomas. I suggest you go at once. And bring her this drink, will you? She needs it." And she thrust the glass in his hand, turned him bodily in the direction of the door, and gave him a little shove to start him off.

Oliver threw his sister-in-law a look of helpless apology over his shoulder and with a quick "Please excuse me!" went off to the door. Once in the hallway, he slowed his pace and tried to think. That Moira was waiting for him was enough to set his pulse pounding and to impede his mental processes. She would, of course, demand an explanation. He supposed she deserved that much; she'd always been truthful to him, so perhaps it was time to be truthful to her. But she would get no more from him. Even if he found more favor in her eyes as Oliver Sherrard than he had as Thomas Oliver, it would make no difference. He was the same man he'd always been, the man she'd seen fit to reject once before. She would not get a second chance.

With that much determined, he went purposefully forward. But when he stepped over the threshold of the sitting room and saw her, sagging limply against the back of the loveseat, with an arm thrown over her eyes, his heart failed him. She had not lost the uncanny ability to turn him to mush. He had to fight against the urge to gather her in his arms and beg her forgiveness, even though he could think of nothing for which she should forgive him.

He approached the loveseat and gazed down at her, his eyes lingering helplessly on the curves of her body, on the swell of breast and hip and the long line of thigh, all the hills and valleys subtly accented by the combined shadows and sheen of the soft green satin that clung to her in loving suggestiveness. But he didn't dare gaze at her too long. "I'm here, ma'am," he forced himself to say.

She stiffened for a moment. Then her arm fell away from her eyes, and she stared up at him. Her cheeks, already pale, turned chalky white. "Thomas!" she gasped, sitting up tensely.

"Good evening, ma'am. You seem surprised. Your aunt said you wanted to see me."

"Oh, God!" she whispered, wincing. "She *didn't*!"

He could feel the extent of her agitation. "Here, drink this," he ordered, sitting down beside her and holding the glass to her lips. "I'm afraid I really startled you."

She took a couple of sips and, slowly, the color returned to her cheeks. She pushed the glass away. "This is a change of roles," she said, her voice still breathless. "Now *I'm* the one needing care."

"Not nearly as much as I did," he said with a small, reminiscent smile.

"Perhaps not, but you seem to have made a complete and remarkable recovery." By this time she'd regained her equilibrium well enough to look him over properly. Her eyes took in his well-cut evening coat, his highly starched shirt-points, his neckcloth tied in a perfect *trône-d'amour*, the gold watch fob hanging from his white satin waistcoat, and his entire air of innate self-confidence. "You are looking very . . . er . . . very *distinguished*."

It was the wrong word. He immediately froze. "You only find me distinguished, ma'am, because you saw the Prince single me out," he said coldly. "I am quite the same fellow I was when you knew me in Kent."

"Are you, Thomas? Would the Prince single out a penniless vagabond who needed to find work to earn a pair of boots?"

"Yes, the very same. Only the appurtenances are different. When you found me, I'd been beaten and robbed of my trappings. Now I have my trappings on me. That's the only difference." But he knew he wasn't being completely honest, so his eyes fell. "That and my name."

"Yes, your name! What is it, Thomas? Or must I call you *my lord*?"

He regarded her icily. "It would please you, wouldn't it, ma'am, to discover that your vulgar vagrant is really a titled nobleman? What a story to be able to bring back home to Kent! But no, there is no such romantic ending to our story. My name is Sherrard. Oliver Sherrard. There is no title. I'm only an 'Honorable.' Sorry if that disappoints you. I'm a commoner, as common as Thomas Oliver."

"I never thought Thomas Oliver common," she said quietly. "But it *was* common of him to lie about his identity."

"Yes, it was. I owe you an apology for that, ma'am."

"Why did you do it, Thomas? Why weren't you open with me?"

He turned away from her, attempting to speak honestly but without emotion. "It was an impulsive decision, made when my thinking was impaired by concussion. Since I wanted only to earn a pair of boots, I thought it best to avoid using a noble family name that might be familiar to someone. I was embarrassed by my condition and didn't wish my brother to learn of it."

"Yes, but that was at first," she persisted. "Later, when we had become more . . . more intimate, why didn't you tell me then?"

"What for, ma'am?" he asked angrily, wheeling round to face her again. "By that time it was clear that I would serve your purposes more effectively as a penniless vagrant than as the brother of an earl. Not that your father would have welcomed a mere Honorable as a suitor for the hand of his favorite daughter, but he might have been less revolted. If I'd let it be known that I was a Sherrard of Lydbury, he might not have been as quick to agree to your terms."

"What are you saying, then, Thom—Mr. Sherrard? That you did it for me? That *your* lie is *my* fault?"

Oliver shrugged. "If the shoe fits, Miss Pattinger . . ."

"The shoe does *not* fit!" Moira exclaimed, suddenly angry. "You could have told *me* the truth without revealing it to my father, could you not?"

"Yes, I suppose I could. But I've already apologized, ma'am. What more do you want from me?"

"I don't want anything from you, confound it," she retorted, her redheaded temper rising to the surface. This conversation was not proceeding at all in a direction that she liked. He'd been cold and distant from the first moment. She had dreamed that if she ever saw him again, she would throw herself into his arms and declare undying love, but he seemed to have surrounded himself with so thick a wall of protection that any such action of hers would be not only inappropriate but downright ridiculous. The only action that could be appropriate for his coldly distant manner would be to stamp her foot in irritation and dismiss him. "It wasn't my idea to send for you," she said furiously. "It was my *aunt*—"

"Then I'll take myself out of your presence," he said, rising and giving her a sardonic bow. "Good evening, ma'am."

As she watched him go, the feeling of panic that had seized her earlier struck her again. She got to her feet and took a tottering step in his direction. "Thomas—!" One of her hands reached out to him, quite without her conscious control.

He turned, his eyebrows raised questioningly, but he said nothing.

Panic made her desperate. She could not let him leave her again without trying to breach his defenses. "My aunt lives in Portman Square," she said, pressing a hand against her breast, which was heaving as if she'd just run up the stairs. "You could call—"

"Thank you, Miss Pattinger," he cut in cruelly, "but I don't think that would be a good idea. Any further meetings between us would be pointless. Good-bye, ma'am."

He strode down the corridor without a backward look. He'd *done* it! If he hadn't quite given her the cut direct, it was the next closest thing. *I should be wildly elated,* he told himself. *I cut her down!* It was a triumph, like winning a boxing match with a champion!

So why was he feeling so damnably wretched?

CHAPTER
❧ ❧
TWENTY-SEVEN

THE MORE MOIRA THOUGHT ABOUT THE EXCHANGE WITH THOMAS—or Oliver, or Sherrard, or whatever his name was!—the more furious she became. Her formidable temper flared up like a volcanic eruption. "He *dismissed* me!" she exploded to her aunt in the carriage on their return home. "Repulsed and rebuffed me as if I were a naughty child and he my *tutor*!"

"Hush, my love," whispered the bemused aunt, "or the coachman will hear you. Besides, it will do no good for you to fly into alt. Try to come down from the high ropes and think matters over calmly."

But Moira's temper continued to seethe. All night long she tossed in her bed, reliving every moment of the encounter. She analyzed every sentence, coming to the infuriating conclusion that all his remarks pointed to the fact that he thought her a toplofty prig who was impressed only with titles. He wouldn't believe her denials, either, yet *he* was the one who'd lied! He'd attempted to apologize for the lies, but his feeble apologies were not nearly humble enough. One would think, from his cavalier attempt at self-justification, that pretending to be a homeless vagrant—when all the while he was the son of an earl with an estate, if the report she'd heard from her aunt was true, *twice* as extensive as Pattinger Downs—was only a minor infraction! How dared he belittle his transgression! With his lies—masquerading as a penniless vagabond, the *fraud*—he'd taken heinous advantage of her generous sympathy! How could he now make so little of so reprehensible an act?

And then, after all that, he'd ended the exchange with the final insult: the cut direct. She'd lowered herself by entreating him to come to her, and he'd refused! He'd treated her invitation with utter contempt! Never in her life had anyone treated her that way. She should have scratched his eyes out!

What made it worse was that she didn't deserve it. Oh, perhaps she'd used him, as Horatio had said, but she hadn't meant any harm by it. And she certainly had never treated *him* with contempt! She'd picked him up, half unclothed and bruised in body and spirit, and she'd given him bed, board, and medical care. She'd restored him to health practically single-handedly, and this—this *contempt*—was her reward! The only blessing in this whole sordid affair was that he didn't know she'd run after him to the Twin Elms Inn in the pouring rain (ruining a perfectly good bonnet in the process and giving herself a chill that took *days* to recover from) and had wept her eyes out when she'd discovered he was gone. She was humiliated enough without his having to know *that*!

By morning she was pacing her bedroom like a caged tigress. By afternoon the raging turmoil inside her was unbearable; she had to do something about it or she would burst. Her first act was to inquire of her aunt's butler the direction to the Earl of Lydbury's town house. Then she ran upstairs, threw on a dark red jaconet walking dress, the color suiting her bloodred mood, crushed a high-poke straw bonnet over her disheveled curls, stomped back down the stairs again, and ran out of the house. Her aunt, who heard the commotion on the stairs, followed after her as far as the gate, calling out, "Moira, where *are* you going in such a pet?" But the girl was too far down the street to hear.

She arrived at the Earl's residence just as the family had assembled in the downstairs sitting room for afternoon tea. The butler heard the knocker while placing a tray of sandwiches at Lady Lydbury's elbow. He completed the task, made his bow, and exited, not hurrying his stately tread even though the sounds from the knocker were growing louder and more frequent by the second. He opened the door and fixed a glacial eye on the interesting young lady who stood on the doorstep tapping an impatient foot. She was quite the prettiest chit imaginable, but her bonnet was askew, her dress was a dreadful color, and she positively glowered at him. "Yes?" he asked with chilling formality.

"Tell Mr. Oli—Mr. *Sherrard* that Miss Pattinger wishes to see him *at once*," the young woman snapped.

"Are you expected, miss?" the butler asked.

"Wouldn't you have been told if I were?" Moira asked in disgust. "Please do as I ask!"

The butler frowned. "I regret, miss, that I am unable to oblige. The family is at tea and cannot be disturbed."

"If you don't disturb them, confound it," the furious girl declared, "then I will! Step aside, man, and let me—!"

"Who is that, Cubbins?" asked Lady Lydbury, emerging from the sitting room and approaching the doorway.

"A young lady, ma'am. Wishing to see Mr. Sherrard."

"Well, ask her in, Cubbins, ask her in. You can't keep a young lady standing on the doorstep."

Moira brushed by the butler with an I-told-you-so toss of her head. "Good afternoon, your ladyship," she said, dropping the barest of curtseys. "I am sorry to interrupt your tea, but I must see Thomas at once."

"*Thomas* again?" Emma peered at Moira with considerable interest. "I suppose you mean Oliver. I can't imagine why people are calling him Thomas."

Moira reddened. "I'm sorry. I do mean Mr. Sherrard. Mr. Oliver Sherrard. Calling him Thomas was a . . . a slip of the tongue."

"I shall get him for you, of course, if you wish me to. But why don't you join us for tea, Miss—?"

"Pattinger. Moira Pattinger. You are most kind, but I have no time for tea."

"No? I *am* sorry. You seem in a high state of perturbation, Miss Pattinger. I hope Oliver—or Thomas, if you prefer—has done nothing to upset you."

"He's done a great deal to upset me, ma'am, but I would not wish to involve you in the matter." She clenched her fists in an effort to speak with restraint. "I think I can deal with Mr. Sherrard quite adequately by myself."

"Very well then, Miss Pattinger," Emma said pleasantly, "if I can't convince you to join us, I shall send Oliver out to you. Why don't you wait in the library? You and Oliver can be quite private there. Cubbins, show Miss Pattinger to the library."

"Thank you, your ladyship," Moira said as she followed the butler down the hall.

Emma watched the young lady disappear into the shadows, and then she whisked herself into the sitting room and closed the door. "Goodness, Oliver," she asked, "what mischief have you been up to?"

Oliver, about to take a bite of his cucumber sandwich, looked up in puzzlement. "Mischief?" he asked innocently.

"There's a young lady here to see someone named Thomas. You, I take it. She's quite the most magnificent-looking female I've beheld in a long time. All spirit and fire, with Irish green eyes and a head covered with wild red curls."

"Good God!" Oliver exclaimed. "Moira!"

The Earl put down his cup and looked from his wife to his brother with intense fascination. "Green eyes and red curls, eh? Oliver, is *that* the champion who laid you low?"

Oliver threw his brother a rueful look as he got to his feet. "Did she say what it was she wanted?" he asked Emma uneasily.

"No, she didn't. But I can hazard a guess." She threw her husband a twinkling look before turning back to her brother-in-law. "Poor Oliver," she said with a barely repressed giggle. "I think she wants to hand you your head on a plate!"

CHAPTER
⚜ ⚜
TWENTY-EIGHT

THE ROOM LADY LYDBURY CALLED THE LIBRARY HAD ONLY A FEW shelves of books. Most of his lordship's collection was kept in the Surrey house. What the room did have were two comfortable sofas, two easy chairs, two tall windows facing west (from which Moira could see the setting sun), and an air of comfortable intimacy. A good place, Moira thought, for a quarrel.

She had only paced the room twice when Oliver put his head in the door. "Ma'am?" he asked timidly.

"My name is Moira, as you well know!" she snapped. "You can stop calling me ma'am as if you were my servant! And you can come in, too, instead of hanging there behind the door like a damned poltroon!"

He stepped inside, closed the door, and eyed her with a mixture of caution and admiration. "So this is an example of the famous temper," he said with a glimmer of amusement in his eyes. "It's most becoming to your complexion, ma'am, but not to your language. You swear like a man."

"Never mind my complexion! And as for the rest, I take it as a compliment!"

"I'm relieved to hear it. Will you take it as a compliment if I say that *that* is an absolutely dreadful hat?"

"I didn't come to talk about hats," she declared, but she snatched it off anyway and tossed it on a sofa.

The sight of her disheveled red curls, freed from the restraint of her bonnet and gleaming like copper in the mellow afternoon sunlight that slanted in from the windows, was utterly charming. "Now *that* is a great deal better," he said, grinning at her appreciatively. "And if you take that as a compliment to your glorious hair, you will be quite right."

The glower she'd fixed on his face from the first moment he'd entered did not soften. "If I were in the mood for compliments, that would certainly serve. But I'm not."

His grin faded. "Yes, I surmised from your expression that there is evidently something I've said or done that you do *not* take as a compliment. Am I right?"

"There is *nothing* you've said or done that is complimentary, except for some flowery trifles about my appearance. Those I do not regard. As to the rest, from the moment I had the ill fortune to discover you in my stable, you've consistently insulted me! There has not been a time when you didn't imply that I am a toplofty prig with a taste for titles!"

"Yes, there has," he said in quick denial. "I found no fault with you at first. I thought you a creature of absolute perfection. It wasn't until you unfolded your blasted scheme to me that I began to think otherwise."

"Then you admit it! You *do* find me a toplofty prig!"

"Yes, I admit it."

She gasped at his frankness. "How can you, Thomas? After all I did for you? Is this your gratitude?"

"It has nothing to do with gratitude, Moira," he said gently. "I shall always be grateful for your kindness to me. Always. If there is any way I can repay it, you have only to ask."

His soft reply took some of the wind from her sails. "I'm not asking for repayment. You more than repaid me by helping me with Father. It's your insulting evaluation of my character that has raised my ire. It's unfair and untrue."

"To me it's both fair *and* true," he said, deciding that no matter how violent her temper should become, he would be bluntly honest. "Think about it for a moment. Why were you so eager to come to London that you set up an elaborate scheme to blackmail your father into permitting it?"

"*Blackmail—?*"

"Yes, blackmail is a kind of extortion, and it *was* extortion of your father, wasn't it, with *me* as the threat? But that is not the point. The point is that you wanted to come to London because the choice of suitors is greater here, is that not right?"

"Well, yes, in a way, but—"

"A greater choice of eligibles. And for you, eligibility is synonymous with social standing."

"Dash it all, Thomas, that's not so!" she exclaimed furiously. The fact that there might possibly be a bit of truth to what he'd said only aggravated her ire. How could he dare to think so little of her! She lifted her hand to slap his insolent face!

But he caught her hand in his before it could touch him. "It's time you faced the truth about yourself, Moira Pattinger," he said, pulling her to him and pinning her hand behind her. "You'd considered wedlock three times . . ."

His voice failed him. Holding her so close was having its usual effect on him. "Damnation, but you're beautiful," he muttered in spite of himself. "How is it possible you've not become the rage of London and betrothed yourself to a duke? Or have you done it without my having heard of it?"

"No, I haven't done either! But don't change the subject. You started to say something about my facing the truth about myself."

"Yes, right. As I was saying, you considered wedlock three times before I met you. Each of the three candidates was titled, and none of them had much else—with the exception of Horatio, who is a man of character but whom you didn't love anyway, so that doesn't weaken my argument. It was their rank that made them eligible, and rank was all they needed to be acceptable to you."

"Are you saying that I considered wedding them because of their titles?" she asked in outraged disbelief.

"What other reason could you have? It was only Jeffrey you told yourself you loved, but the feeling couldn't have been very deep if you recovered from it so easily. Bitter experience has taught me that, if love is real, recovery from it is long and hard."

"Confound it, Thomas Oliver Sherrard, you go too far!" She struggled to free herself from his hold, using her free hand to push against him. "I am twenty-seven years old! I don't need a mere boy of—how old are you, fellow, twenty-two!—to tell me what love is!"

Now it was his turn to be angry. "In the first place, *ma'am*, don't call me *fellow*," he said between clenched teeth. "It reminds me of the high-handed tone your father took with me. In the second place, I'm almost twenty-four. And in the third, you *do* need me to tell you about love. I don't think you've ever experienced it yourself, not in all those *long* twenty-seven years of your life. You *are* an ice maiden, just as Horatio suspected."

"I am *not* an ice maiden!" she cried, swinging her free hand at him in a rage. It caught him on the side of his face and delivered a sharp sting.

"Damn you, Moira," he cursed, grasping her hand tightly in a cruel grip and pinioning it behind her with the other, "why did you come here? I told you yesterday that this sort of meeting would be pointless."

"Yes, so you . . . did!" she said, writhing desperately in his hold. "I can recognize a cut direct, even if it was the first time I was faced with such an offense! You owe me an apology for that, you blasted . . . make-bait!"

"Hold still, vixen! Even if I wanted to apologize—which I don't—I couldn't do it with you wriggling like an eel!"

"If you want me to stop wriggling, then *let me go!*"

"Not on your life. Do you think I want my face slapped again?" He tightened his hold until she could no longer move. Not very much taller than she, he found their faces much too close for his comfort. If he didn't make an end of this contretemps, he feared she would make mush of him again. "Come now, Moira, tell me the truth," he demanded, glaring down at her. "Did you really come here just to demand an apology for my rudeness last evening?"

"Yes, and to slap your smug face!"

"Well, you've done that. If I apologize, will you then be satisfied and go home quietly?"

She looked up into his eyes and knew, suddenly, exactly why she'd come. And it was not for any of the angry reasons she'd pretended to herself that it was. "No, I will *not* be satisfied," she muttered, lowering her head so that it rested on his shoulder. "To be truthful, those were not my real reasons for coming."

"No?" Holding her hands tightly behind her with one hand, he took her chin in his other and tilted her face up, forcing her to look at him. "What, then?"

She found it difficult to meet his eyes. "It will take more courage than I possess to tell you," she hedged.

"Nonsense. If there's anything you've no lack of, it's courage."

Her eyes searched his face, seeking some sign of tenderness or affection, but if he felt any, he was hiding it. But she did have courage, so she plunged ahead. "Very well, then, the truth is that I love you," she blurted out. Then, blushing hotly, she hid her face in his shoulder again. "I think those are the words I *really* needed to say to you."

She felt him stiffen, but he said nothing. The silence was so intense and so protracted that, after an endless moment, she peeped up at him again. "Thomas? Didn't you hear me?"

"Oh, yes, I heard you," he said, his voice toneless except for a slight tinge of bitter amusement. "I heard every word."

"Well, then, don't you have anything to say in reply?"

He hesitated, wishing he didn't have to answer. If she'd said those words to him a few months ago, he would have been the happiest man on earth. Even now, every instinct of his body urged him to believe her, to crush her to him, to declare his lifelong adoration and to kiss those full, eager lips until they were both devoid of breath. But it was now too late to surrender to those instincts. His mind, and its too-particular memory, would not permit him. "You don't love me, Moira," he said, loosening his hold on her and turning away. "You only imagine that you do."

"Do I?" she asked, her heart sinking. "It seems quite real to me."

"No, it's only the romance of my new identity. I am the poor vagrant magically transformed into a prince. Well, not quite a prince, but even an 'Honorable' can be romantic, I suppose, in this prosaic world. Somewhere in your head you've made yourself the fairy-tale princess who kissed a toad and transformed him. But that's not love, my girl. That's daydreaming."

She would have been furious at those words were it not for the choked voice with which he said them. She could not be angry at what was obviously so painful for him to say. "You're quite wrong about me, Thomas," she said softly, coming up behind him and putting a hand on his arm. "As wrong as can be. I know more about love than you give me credit for. I'm not an ice maiden, you know, despite my reputation. Nor am I in love with a daydream. Please believe me, Thomas, when I say that my love for you is real and sincere."

"You called me Thomas," he said with a snort of laughter, turning round to face her. "It's ironic that you should call me that now. My name is Oliver, but it was as Thomas that I was really myself. You see, ma'am, I'm more at home roaming the countryside than I could ever be in a London town house. I'm more content in shirt-sleeves than in an evening coat. I offered myself to you heart and soul under the name of Thomas. *That* man was the *real* Oliver."

"But that's what I've been saying! Don't you understand? I hardly know Oliver Sherrard. It *is* Thomas Oliver I love!"

"What gammon!" he sneered. "It was Thomas Oliver whom you were so impatient to be rid of that you barely waited a quarter hour after you had your way with your father before offering him five hundred pounds and waving him from the premises."

She whitened. "Is that what you think?"

"That's not what I think, ma'am. It is what happened. You don't deny it, do you?"

"No, I don't deny the facts. But facts can sometimes get in the way of truth." She stepped back from him and lifted her chin, more in pride than anger. "The truth is, Thomas or Oliver or whoever you are, that I loved you even when I handed you the five hundred pounds."

"No, ma'am, that is *not* the truth! That is your present emotion trying to adjust the past to make it fit your present illusion of it. I will not permit you to paint over the ugly facts with a brush of whitewash and call it truth!"

His words struck her like blows. He was determined to think

the worst of her. The argument he'd erected against her was like an impenetrable wall; nothing she said had breached it. "You never will believe me, will you?" she asked in defeat. "You will never think my motives anything but base."

"That's right, ma'am. That's why, last night, I told you any meeting between us would be useless."

She snatched up her bonnet from the sofa. "Very well, Oliver Sherrard, you've won," she said, dashing away the tears that insisted on falling despite her effort to keep them back. "This is the last you'll see of me. I hope that makes you h-happy."

Crushing her bonnet carelessly on her head, she ran quickly from the room and down the hall, tears streaming unchecked down her cheeks. Lady Lydbury, who was waiting in the entryway hoping for another encounter with the girl, was shocked to see her tears. "Heavens, my dear," she gasped, attempting to stop Moira's headlong flight to the door by standing in her path, "what has our Oliver done to you?"

"Nothing, ma'am, n-nothing at all," Moira said, clutching at her bonnet to keep it from toppling off as she tried to evade Lady Lydbury and the necessity of explanations.

"But he must have . . . ! I mean, you are crying!"

"I am only c-crying because your Oliver is a *fool*!" Moira muttered, scooting past her. "The greatest fool in all the world!"

CHAPTER
❧ ❧
TWENTY-NINE

THERE WAS NOTHING ABOUT LONDON THAT MOIRA LIKED AFTER that day. Every fete she attended was dull, and everyone she met was shallow. Steeped in misery, she did not know where to turn to find relief. Even Aunt Joanna, whom she loved dearly, could offer little solace. All the elderly aunt could do was to offer assurances that Moira's heart would mend in time, as her own had done. "Not that one ever forgets," she added honestly, "but the sharpness of the pain does lessen."

The words were cold comfort. The lessening of pain was a bleak goal, and the time it would take to reach it seemed dreadfully distant. "I think, Aunt Joanna, that I shall go home," Moira said after the first long, miserable week had passed.

"Back to Kent?" Joanna sighed, perplexed. "But the whole point of your coming here was to escape from your father's tyranny."

"Yes, I know. But this is not home. I miss the green hills and the smell of hay. I miss the horses. I miss Babs, who will be delighted if I'm home to help her with her wedding preparations. I even miss writing letters for Father. If one must be miserable, Aunt Joanna, I think it's better to suffer the pain in familiar surroundings. It will be better for me to be busy. I know Father can be a tyrant, but he does love me."

And so, by the end of another week, Moira was back home. By the end of that same week, Oliver, too, was gone from

London. He and his brother and sister-in-law returned to
Lydbury. It was plain to the Earl and his wife that Oliver took
no pleasure in the social whirl—even an invitation from
Carlton House failed to elevate his spirits—so they gave up
trying to rouse him from the doldrums and returned to the
country, where they all preferred to be. It was at Lydbury that
the Earl again discovered Oliver packing for a walking tour.
"You're not going off *again*?" he exclaimed in horror.

"I have only five months before I report to Whitehall,"
Oliver explained. "This is my last chance to be footloose and
fancy-free. I may as well make the most of it."

His lordship again tried to convince his brother to at least do
his touring like a gentleman, with servants and a carriage and
all the gentlemanly accouterments. But Oliver was adamant. "I
shall do better this time, John," he assured the Earl. "I know
better now how to protect myself from thieves and cutpurses.
Don't worry about me."

So, in mid-May, Oliver set out for the second time on his
journey to the south, his rucksack on his shoulder and
MacDamon at his heels. He intended to take a different route
to Ramsgate this time, to avoid passing anywhere near Pattinger Downs, but as he put one foot in front of the other, his
mind drifted where it willed, and without knowing how, he
found himself at the end of the day right in front of the Twin
Elms Inn.

He peered at it in disgust. In the fading light of a clear spring
day, the hostelry looked less appealing than ever. Its red door
seemed more gaudily vulgar, its windows dirtier, and the
thatch on the roof in greater need of replacement. The thought
of supping on one of Maggs's mutton dinners revolted his
stomach. The thought of sleeping under that steeply pitched
roof depressed his spirits. Anything, even continuing to walk
on until daylight, seemed more appetizing than spending the
night under that roof. "You don't want to spend the night here,
do you, Mac?" he asked his canine companion.

In response, MacDamon raced to the red door as if to a
haven, wagging his tail happily.

Oliver shook his head. "Stupid dog. Oh, well, if you insist."

Thus, despite his revulsion, he found himself going in the door.

Maggs recognized him at once. "Ah, it's *you*, sir, come back agin!" she cried in eager greeting, wiping her hands on her dirty apron and waddling across the taproom to shake his hand. "An' yer strange li'l doggie, too! Welcome, I'm sure. Will ye be wantin' the private parlor agin?"

"No, Maggs, thank you. Just a room for the night. No dinner for me either. Just some scraps of meat and a bowl of water for my friend. I'll just sit here and have a mug of your home-brew."

She nodded, her eyes sweeping over him from top to bottom. "Ye're lookin' very fine, sir, I mus' say. No wonder ye' 'ave all 'em pretty ladies chasin' arfter ye."

He didn't pay much heed to her chatter. He sat down at the table and placed MacDamon and his hat on the chair beside him. "You needn't worry, Maggs," he assured her. "I'm not expecting any ladies, pretty or otherwise."

"Ye wasn't expectin' any ladies las' time, either, was ye? But one of 'em came lookin' fer ye anyway."

He didn't follow her at all. "What?"

"There was a lady lookin' fer ye, las' time ye was 'ere. Didn' she ever catch up wi' ye?"

"A lady? Looking for *me*?" he asked, squinting up at the woman with sharply intensified interest.

"Oh, yes, sir. Yes, indeed," Maggs said with a salacious smirk. "A real pretty one, too. Wanted t' find ye real bad. Urgent-like."

"The last time I was here?" he asked, feeling a rising excitement in his chest. "That was months ago."

"Yes, sir. Early fall it were. I 'member it well, 'cause I gave ye a piece of rope, an' the next day me Charlie, 'e needed it, an' 'e gave me a proper tongue-lashin' fer lettin' ye 'ave it. And that was the same day the young lady came."

Oliver warned himself to stay calm. In fact, he felt foolish even pursuing the subject. No one could have come to this place looking for him. No one even knew he'd come here. "There must be some mistake," he said with forced casualness.

"Whoever she was, she must have been seeking someone else."

"Oh, no, sir. It was you, all right. No mistake. She knowed just what ye was wearin'—tweed coat, brown boots, everythin'! She even knowed yer dog!"

It was too ridiculous, too far-fetched. If he had a grain of sense, he wouldn't permit himself even to *think* the thought that was hovering about in his head. When he'd left Pattinger Downs last October, he hadn't said a word to anyone about stopping off at the Twin Elms to take his revenge on Ironfist and Louch. Henry the footman might have guessed, but he'd never have said anything.

Would he?

And would Moira have even thought of asking him?

Maggs cocked her head and grinned a gap-toothed grin at him. "I'd go bail there's a awesome number o' ladies chasin' arfter ye, ain't that right, sir?"

"Not so's I've ever noticed," Oliver muttered, his mind racing around like a starved mouse on the scent of cheese, sniffing at all the beguiling possibilities.

"The one that came," Maggs went on, delighted at the opportunity to tease a gentleman about his naughty affairs, "*she* was chasin' arfter ye all right and tight! When I tole 'er ye was gone, she stood out there in the pourin' rain lookin' down the empty road like she'd lost 'er las' chance fer 'eaven, the tears runnin' down 'er cheeks an' the rain drippin' from 'er bonnet onto those pretty red curls of 'ers . . ."

Oliver's chest clenched like a vise. "Red curls—?"

"Aye, red as flame. Felt real sorry fer the poor lass, I did." She grinned down at Oliver with mischievous glee. "Ye shouldn' be so 'ard on the lasses, ye sly devil!"

Oliver leaped to his feet. "Are you sure?" he asked, grasping Maggs's shoulders in a tense grip. "A red-haired young lady came here the day after I left, looking specifically for *me*? You mustn't make any mistakes, Maggs! It's important that the time and the cast of characters are accurate."

Maggs gaped at him fearfully. "It 'appened jus' like I tole ye, sir, I swear. I coudn' fergit it, y'see, 'cause you an' the lady, ye're gentry, an' we don' get gentry stoppin' 'ere hardly at all."

Oliver's brain was whirling dizzily. If Moira *had* come after him the day after he left, then it was *before* she'd known he was Oliver Sherrard. And if *that* was so, then perhaps she really *did* love Thomas Oliver! *But don't fly up in alt so quickly,* he warned himself. *Slow down and think!* Couldn't she have come looking for him for some other reason . . . with another letter to her man of business, perhaps, or a message from Horatio? But no, those possibilities were not likely. He'd made it clear he would accept no money. And Horatio would have delivered his own message, not sent Moira in the rain. Besides, Maggs had said that the redheaded girl had stood looking down the road *like she'd lost her last chance at heaven.* What else could that mean but that Moira loved him?

"Sir?" Maggs asked, frightened. " 'Ave I said somethin' I oughtn'?"

Oliver threw back his head and laughed loudly, a guffaw of pure elation. "Maggs, my beauty," he grinned, "you've said the most delightful words I've ever heard!" Bestowing a kiss on the stupefied woman's cheek, he released his grip on her and scooped the surprised MacDamon up in his arms. "I say, Mac, old chum, didn't I tell you that this is a wonderful inn? And that our Maggs is the most wonderful innkeeper's wife in Christendom? Come here, Maggs, you old dear. Don't look so frightened! Put out your hand, Maggs. Yes, like that. You've done me the best possible turn, so I want to do one for you. Here . . . one, two, three, five gold guineas. Buy yourself a new bonnet . . . a new apron . . . a new *roof*!" And with another joyful chortle, he clapped his hat on his head and strode jauntily out of the door into the gathering dusk.

CHAPTER
❧ ❧
THIRTY

IT WAS DARK BY THE TIME HE REACHED PATTINGER DOWNS. HE made his way unseen over the grounds to the stable, slipped inside, and glanced up to the loft where George Varney slept. He could see a light under the door. "Varney?" he called. "Varney, can you come down?"

The door opened, and the spry little fellow came out and peered down through the dimness. "Blimey! It's Mr. Oliver!" he exclaimed and scrambled down the stairs.

They shook hands and exchanged news. Varney showed him a new mare that his lordship had just bought, and Oliver told him about attending an auction at Tattersall's in London at which the Duke of York had bought a horse for more than a thousand guineas. MacDamon, meanwhile, trotted round the stable as if he were making a personal inspection. After these pleasantries were exchanged, Oliver revealed the specific reason for his visit. "I need to ask a favor of you, Varney. I'd like to talk to one of the footmen without anyone else knowing I'm here. Do you know Henry?"

" 'Course I do. 'E's the one gettin' bald."

"Do you think you can bring him here to me without spreading it about that I'm back? There's a couple of guineas in it for you if you can."

The coachman grinned at him. "Come into a bit o' brass, 'ave ye, Mr. Oliver? Aye, ye're lookin' a lot more prosp'rous than the las' time I seen ye. But ye kin keep yer money in yer pocket, ol' chum. I'll be 'appy t' fetch 'enry fer ye wi'out no reward."

Fifteen minutes later, Henry came stealing into the stable. He was almost bursting with excitement. "Mr. Oliver, is it really you?" he hissed, peering through the gloom.

Oliver came out from the shadows where he'd been hiding and gave the footman a hearty handshake. When this was done, Henry stood back and looked Oliver over carefully. "Whatever chap's dressin' ye these days, Mr. Oliver, is doin' a good job of it. Ye look top o' the trees."

"No one's dressing me, Henry. If I ever get myself a valet again, it's going to be you."

"Come on! Stop bammin' me!" the footman said, grinning, unable to take seriously the improbable prospect of such a promotion.

"I'm not bamming. When have you known me to cut a wheedle? If all goes well tonight, you may become a valet sooner than you think."

"Tonight? What's the lay tonight?"

"Before I tell you, I have a question to ask you. After I left the house last fall, did Miss Moira ask you where I'd gone?"

"Yes, she did. The next mornin'. I didn't know fer sure where ye was goin', but I reckoned ye'd 'ave made straight fer the Twin Elms, so that's what I tole 'er. Did I do ye a misdeed?"

"No, Henry, not at all. You may have done me the best service of my life. I'll find a way to thank you one day. But now, about tonight. After the family finishes dinner, will you be able to get me up to Lord Pattinger's study without anyone seeing me?"

"To his lordship's study?" Henry gave him a suspicious glance. "What do ye want there? Ye ain't up to somethin' smoky, are ye?"

"I have to talk to him, that's all. Without anyone else in the house learning about it. You know how hard it is to keep anything secret in that house. That's why it's important that no one, not maids or footmen or even Mr. Pearce, get a glimpse of me."

"Leave it t' me," Henry said confidently. "I'll get ye in there."

Two hours later, Henry came back for him and led him up the back stairs to the third floor. They crept through the corridors as stealthily as thieves, keeping close to the walls and pausing at every turning to make sure the way ahead was clear. In this fashion they made their way to Lord Pattinger's study door. "I 'ope ye know what ye're doin'," the footman whispered funereally. "I don' wanna come back an' find ye layin' in a pool o' yer own blood."

Oliver grinned. "I'm only going to talk, not fight a duel," he whispered back. Then he straightened his neckerchief, dusted off his breeches, and smoothed back his hair. "How do I look? Properly respectable?"

"Neat as a drawin' pin," Henry assured him.

Oliver took a deep breath, motioned for Henry to get himself out of sight, and threw open the door. "Good evening, my lord," he said firmly, stepping over the threshold. "No, don't get up. You're going to need your strength."

CHAPTER
❧ ❧
THIRTY-ONE

THE NEXT MORNING MOIRA WOKE LATE. SHE KNEW IT WAS LATE by the brightness of the streaks of sunlight that crept in at the edges of the draperies. She leaped out of bed, pushed the drapes aside, and looked out upon the sunlit spring greenery. It was a lovely day, the kind that used to make her want to sing, but now she only sighed. It had been a very long time since she'd felt like singing.

Suddenly, from somewhere in the distance, she heard the sound of barking. It sounded just like MacDamon! Her heart contracted in her chest, and for a moment she couldn't breathe. But the sound died away almost at once and was not heard again. She must have been mistaken.

She looked at the clock on her mantel. It was after eight! Her father would already be at breakfast, and he'd told her last evening that he wanted to give her some instructions about a letter to Lord Liverpool at the breakfast table. If she took the time to dress, she would miss him. Then she would have to interrupt him in his study and face his sardonic comments about being a slugabed.

Dash it all, she said to herself, *I won't bother to dress*. It was no crime to take breakfast in a morning robe. The ladies of London did it all the time. Thus having rationalized her intentions, she quickly performed her ablutions, slipped on a pair of slippers, pulled a flowered voile dressing gown from her wardrobe, threw it over her nightgown, and ran downstairs.

She entered the breakfast room to find Barbara sitting alone at the table, reading a letter. "Hasn't Father come down yet?" Moira asked, surprised.

"Not yet," Barbara answered. "He's late this morning. Look, Moira, we've a letter from—" She glanced up at her sister and blinked in shock. "Heavens, my love, why aren't you dressed?"

Moira glanced down at her ruffled and flounced morning robe and slippers guiltily. "I overslept, so I just threw on a robe. Goodness, Babs, you needn't look at me as if I'd painted myself blue!"

"Well, you look as blowsy as a doxie in that flimsy wrapper," Barbara said in prim disapproval. "And you might at least have brushed your hair!"

"Hoity-toity! When did you become so puritanical?" her sister laughed, crossing to the sideboard and helping herself to eggs and toast. "And what do you know about doxies, anyway?"

"Nothing," Barbara admitted, "but I've always believed they like to parade about the house at all hours of the day in just that sort of brazen dishabille."

"Brazen dishabille, eh?" Moira set her plate down on the table and took her seat. "I think I rather like looking brazen. The only trouble is there's no one here to admire the view. Even Pearce seems to be absent."

"Moira, you are becoming quite shocking! It's fortunate I told Pearce we wouldn't be needing him. You certainly wouldn't want him to see you so . . . so wantonly garbed!"

"Wantonly garbed? Good heavens, Babs, the more time you spend with Godfrey the more foolishly prudish you become!"

"Is that so?" Barbara retorted defensively. "If you think *I'm* being prudish, just wait 'til Father sees you!"

"If Father says I'm wantonly garbed—or anything like it—I'll cut this robe in little pieces and eat it for luncheon." She reached for the teapot. "Did I hear you say something about a letter?"

"Yes, we've had a letter from Bertie. She writes that the baby is cutting a tooth."

"Already? How precocious little Grace is, to be sure! Does

Bertie say when they are coming down? I hope they don't intend to wait until the week of your wedding. If they do, I'll barely have time to become reacquainted with the baby."

Barbara consulted the letter. "She says to expect them all on June fifteenth. In plenty of time for the wedding."

"Good! That will give us more than a fortnight together. I, for one, will welcome having a few cheerful faces at the table with us." Moira threw her sister a mischievous smile. "And besides, Bertie *never* dresses for breakfast."

"True," Barbara said, tossing the letter aside, "but she doesn't look like a doxie, either."

Lord Pattinger loomed up in the doorway. "Who doesn't look like a doxie?" he wanted to know.

Barbara colored painfully. "No one, Father. Good morning."

Moira choked back a laugh. "Good morning, Father. You're late."

"I distinctly heard something about a doxie," his lordship insisted, crossing to the sideboard and helping himself to two eggs and a slice of ham.

"Father!" Moira exclaimed when he set his plate down on the table. "No porridge this morning? But you *always*—"

"I don't feel like porridge today," he said, his manner inordinately cheerful. "It's too lovely a day for porridge, don't you agree?"

The two girls exchanged puzzled glances. "Yes, Father," Barbara said, agape. "It's a . . . a *very* lovely day."

He reached for the teapot. "Now, what was all that about doxies?"

"Nothing very important," Barbara mumbled nervously.

"Babs thinks I look like one this morning," Moira said with a defiant toss of her head.

"Really, Barbara?" Lord Pattinger lifted his pince-nez and peered through it at his eldest daughter with interested curiosity. "I think your sister looks quite charming," he said after due consideration, and he dropped the spectacles and turned his attention to his breakfast.

Moira giggled and stuck her tongue out at her chagrined sister. Barbara lifted her eyes to heaven as if to say that as far as *she* was concerned, their father had something loose in his upper works this morning.

"I suppose you both will be busy with wedding preparations today," his lordship remarked, stirring his tea.

"Barbara will be hemming some undergarments for her trousseau," Moira said, "but I shall have plenty of time to do your letter to Lord Liverpool."

"Never mind about the letter," her father said pleasantly. "It's too lovely a day to be tied to your desk."

The two sisters exchanged glances again. There was something very wrong with their father today . . . that was certain.

Lord Pattinger glanced over at Moira curiously. "Do *you* have a trousseau, Moira, my dear?"

"*I*, Father?" She blinked at him in astonishment. "What a strange question, coming from you."

"Why is it strange? Don't all girls your age have them?"

"Only when they are preparing to be wed. And certainly not if they have a father who won't let them marry," Moira retorted.

"I wish you'd cease accusing me of not permitting you to marry," his lordship said almost plaintively. "I've told you time and again that I would certainly give my approval if the right sort came along."

"Indeed?" Moira said snappishly. "And have you ever seen, in all the years since I've come of age, a single man you would deem the 'right sort'?"

"One or two," his lordship said calmly. "One or two."

"One or *two*?" Moira snorted. "Name them, I dare you!"

"Please, Moira," Barbara muttered, "let's not get in a row. Don't press him."

"No, I want to hear this! Go ahead, Father, name them!"

His lordship stroked his chin, considering the question. "Well, there was Horatio, for one—"

"Horatio!" Moira squealed in outrage. "How *can* you—"

"Moira, please!" Barbara pleaded. "The morning started off so well—!"

"Yes, of course Horatio," Lord Pattinger went on. "He

would have won my approval if he hadn't decided he preferred Alberta."

Moira glared at him. "Well, of all the weasel-worded—!"

"Moira!" Barbara cried.

"And then, of course, there was that vagabond chap . . ." Lord Pattinger continued.

Moira gasped. *"What?"*

"You know whom I mean. The one you were betrothed to for one night."

Barbara's mouth dropped open. "I think he means Thomas!" she breathed. "Thomas Oliver!"

"Is *that* whom you mean, Father?" Moira demanded. "The man I found in the stable . . . the one you called a penniless vagrant?"

"That's the chap. Very fine fellow, that. Mind of his own, couldn't be bought . . . I liked him."

Moira felt the blood drain from her face. "I can't believe my ears! Are you forgetting that you offered him five thousand pounds to give me up? And when he wouldn't, that you relented and let me go to London on the condition that I jilt him?"

"But, my dear girl, that was only a test. I gave him a simple test, just as I did all the others. He was the only one who didn't fail. It was *you* who failed on that occasion."

"*I* failed?" Moira rasped.

"If you had refused to cry off, I would have given you my blessing."

Moira stared at him, stricken speechless. Barbara leaned forward and touched his hand. "Are you sure, Father, that you feel quite well?"

Moira rose from her chair, white-faced and furious. "Do you dare to sit there and pretend that if I had remained betrothed to Thomas Oliver, you would have been *happy* to see me wed to him?"

"I have already said so," Lord Pattinger responded magisterially, rising and glaring back at her. "I hope, Moira Pattinger, that you are not questioning my veracity."

"I most certainly am! I don't believe a word of this!"

"Then I take it you are calling me a liar! Unless I have an

immediate apology, this discussion and this breakfast are at an end!"

He waited a moment for a response, but getting none, he turned away from the table and started toward the door. When he passed the large bow window, however, he stopped and peered outside. Then he lifted up his pince-nez and leaned closer to the glass. "What's this? I see you've engaged a new gardener."

Moira, shaken and utterly confounded by her father's behavior, walked unsteadily to the window. "I haven't engaged a new gardener," she said distractedly. "Where do you see—"

She looked down in the direction in which her father was pointing. Down below, in the rose garden in which the buds were just beginning to show, a man in shirt-sleeves stood leaning on a hoe, a little mongrel dog at his heel. Man and dog were looking up at the window where they stood. The man was wearing no hat, so Moira was able to see his face clearly. At her first sight of him, she felt the ground lurch beneath her feet. "Oh, my God!" she gasped. *"Thomas!"*

"You *did* engage him then?" her father asked innocently.

Moira stared at the man below for a long moment before turning to her father in wide-eyed amazement. "You *knew* he was here, didn't you!"

"I?" his lordship exclaimed, eyebrows raised guiltlessly. *"I?"*

A trembling, unsure, long-unwatered bud of hope opened up inside her. She'd felt hopeless for so long, she was afraid to recognize it, but now there was no way for her to keep it from bursting into flower. "I don't understand any of this, Father," she said breathlessly, tears springing to her eyes, "but for whatever part you played in bringing him back, I thank you!" She flung her arms round his neck and kissed his cheek. "I'm sorry for every unkind thing I ever said to you. You are the best father *ever*!"

Barbara blinked her eyes at the scene in bewilderment. "Has everyone gone mad this morning?" she asked.

"Yes," Moira said, dashing to the door, her flounces fluttering behind her, "completely mad!"

She flew down the stairs, out the garden door, and round the side of the house. But as soon as she rounded the corner, she stopped her headlong flight. There, a mere two dozen steps away, was the rose garden . . . and Thomas. He looked very much at home in his boots and shirt-sleeves, leaning on the hoe and smiling at her with a warmth in his eyes she'd never before seen. She took two unsteady steps toward him. "Thomas—?"

MacDamon came bounding over to her, barking his welcome.

Oliver knuckled his forehead like a farmhand to his employer. "Yes, ma'am, it's Thomas Oliver."

Though her heart was hammering in her chest, she kept herself from running to him. She, too, could play this game. "Have you come back here to work in the garden, Thomas Oliver," she asked, "or did you have some other purpose in mind?"

"Another purpose? Oh, yes, ma'am, yes, indeed."

"And that is—?"

"I was hoping that I could persuade the first lady I laid eyes on this morning to marry me."

A wave of such exquisite joy swept over her that it washed away the misery that had clogged her spirit since London. But still she waited. "I see," she said carefully, lowering her eyes. "Am I that lady?"

"It seems so, ma'am. Will I be overstepping my place to ask you to come a little closer so I can make my proposal properly?"

She took another few steps in his direction. "But you once said that I'm too toplofty to want to wed a gardener," she reminded him, keeping her eyes fixed coyly on the ground.

He threw down the hoe and strode over to her. "Are you, ma'am?" he asked bluntly, lifting her chin and making her look at him. "Are you too toplofty?"

"Oh, Thomas, no!" She flung herself into his arms and threw her arms round his neck. "I've never . . . I know you won't believe me, but I think I've loved you from the very first."

As soon as he heard those words, he tightened his hold on her and kissed her, lifting her bodily off the ground and swinging her round in joyous abandon. MacDamon yipped at their heels as if he wanted to be included in their peculiar game.

But after Oliver set her down, and she'd recovered her breath, Moira looked up at him suspiciously. "I don't understand this at all, Thomas Oliver Sherrard. How is it that you're now willing to believe me, when you so steadfastly refused to in London?"

He put an arm about her. "If you let me kiss you once more," he murmured with a besotted grin, "I'll explain everything."

"No," she said, holding him off. "You'll explain first!"

"Well, you see, ma'am, I stopped at the Twin Elms Inn yesterday."

"Oh? And what has *that* to say to anything, pray?"

"The innkeeper's wife revealed to me that a certain redheaded lady came there looking for me last fall. And when she didn't find me, she wept." He pulled her to him and studied her face intently. "Do you think it's true, ma'am? Did the redheaded lady really weep?"

"Yes, she did," Moira confessed, blushing and burying her head in his shoulder. "Buckets."

He tightened his hold and pressed his lips against her hair. "I was a fool in London," he murmured. "Can you forgive me?"

"If you can forgive *me* for failing the test. Father just told me that if I had not cried off our betrothal, he would have given us his blessing."

"Yes, he told me about his 'testing system' last night."

"Last night?" She lifted her head and gaped at him. "You saw him *last night*?"

"Yes, I did. I accosted him in his study and demanded that he permit me to offer for you. I was all prepared to present him with an impressive list of my credentials—lineage, education, financial holdings, everything! But he gave in before I even began. Said he had no interest in such superficialities. That he'd made up his mind to accept me as a son-in-law long ago, during our very first interview, when I told him about my mother's pudding!"

"You mother's *pudding*?"

"Yes, but don't ask me to tell you about it now. We have more important things to do. Didn't you promise to kiss me again, once you heard the explanations?"

"Yes, I did," she said, slipping her arms round his neck. "I'm quite ready."

"Just a moment, vixen," he said, taking his turn to hold off, "there's an explanation *I* must have before permitting you to pursue your shocking advances to a gardener. Why, ma'am, if you loved me so much that you wept for me in the rain, did you offer me five hundred pounds to go away?"

"I shall never forgive myself for that, Thomas, nor for any of my actions during that whole dreadful betrothal. I didn't understand myself or my own feelings. I didn't know, until too late, how very much I loved you."

He didn't need any other words. He kissed her then and there, holding her so tightly that anyone observing them would not be able to tell where one body ended and the other began. There they stood, locked together mouth to mouth, chest to chest, and thigh to thigh, boldly exposed in the bright sunlight, not caring that they might be observed from both the stable and the house, or that MacDamon was racing round their feet, barking wildly in vociferous disapproval of this peculiar and probably decadent display.

Up in the breakfast room window, Barbara felt a similar disapproval. She was both vexed and embarrassed. And the presence of her father, the crusty and coldly critical Lord Pattinger, only increased her discomfort. Nevertheless, they both watched the scene with shameless curiosity. "Look at that!" Barbara declared at last, too shocked to keep silent. "He's holding her in a positively indecent embrace, and she isn't even *clothed*!"

"Don't be a prude, girl," her father said with bland equanimity. "Being betrothed yourself, you ought to be able to recognize true love when you see it."

"Father!" She peered at him in utter amazement. "What are you saying? Are you truly going to permit Moira to marry him?"

"Of course I am. They make a perfect pair." He turned away from the window and strolled to the door with a youthful swing to his step. "It's taken my daughters a long time to recognize it, but I have a real talent for matchmaking."

If you enjoyed this book, take advantage of this special offer.
Subscribe now and get a

FREE
Historical Romance

No Obligation (a $4.50 value)

Each month the editors of True Value select the four *very best* novels from America's leading publishers of romantic fiction. Preview them in your home *Free* for 10 days. With the first four books you receive, we'll send you a FREE book as our introductory gift. No Obligation!

If for any reason you decide not to keep them, just return them and owe nothing. If you like them as much as we think you will, you'll pay just $4.00 each and save at *least* $.50 each off the cover price. (Your savings are *guaranteed* to be at least $2.00 each month.) There is NO postage and handling – or other hidden charges. There are no minimum number of books to buy and you may cancel at any time.

Send in the Coupon Below

To get your FREE historical romance fill out the coupon below and mail it today. As soon as we receive it we'll send you your FREE Book along with your first month's selections.
